PASSION BLUE

SKYSCAPE

Text copyright © 2012 by Victoria Strauss

Amazon Publishing
Attn: Amazon Children's Publishing
P.O. Box 400818
Las Vegas, NV 89140
www.amazon.com/amazonchildrenspublishing

Library of Congress Cataloging-in-Publication Data

Strauss, Victoria.
Passion blue / by Victoria Strauss. — 1st ed.
    p. cm.
Summary: In fifteenth-century Italy, seventeen-year-old Giulia, a Count's illegitimate daughter, buys a talisman hoping it will bring her true love to save her from life in a convent, but once there she begins to learn the painter's craft, including how to make the coveted paint, Passion blue, and to question her true heart's desire. Includes historical notes and glossary.
ISBN 978-1-4778-4737-4 (paperback) — ISBN 978-0-7614-6231-6 (ebook)
[1. Self-realization—Fiction. 2. Convents—Fiction. 3. Nuns—Fiction. 4. Artists—Fiction. 5. Talismans—Fiction. 6. Magic—Fiction. 7. Italy—History—15th century—Fiction.] I. Title.

PZ7.S9125Pas 2012
[Fic]—dc23

2011040133

Editor: Melanie Kroupa

PASSION BLUE

a novel by

Victoria Strauss

SKYSCAPE

Part 1
The Talisman

❖❖❖❖❖❖

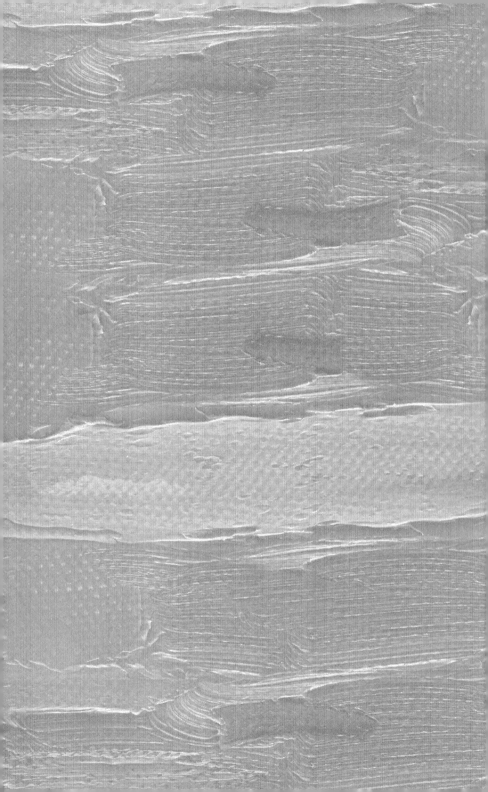

CHAPTER I

❖ The Summons ❖

Milan, Italy, Anno Domini 1487

The clouds broke apart and sunlight flooded down, burnishing the rough bark of the apple trees and tossing their shadows across the grass. Giulia caught her breath at the sudden beauty of it, her charcoal stick racing across the paper on her knee as she tried to capture the moment before it vanished.

"Giulia!" The shrill call was as sudden as a slap. Giulia jumped; the charcoal slipped, botching the line.

"Giuuuuuulia!"

Giulia pressed closer to the tree she was leaning against, hoping it would hide her, but it was already too late. She could see Clara stomping toward her between the trunks, her fat moon-face flushed with exertion and annoyance.

"What are you doing out here?" Clara planted her hands on her hips, scowling.

"What does it look as if I'm doing?" Clara was the daughter of the cooking woman who had taken Giulia in after Giulia's own mother died. She never missed a chance to try and make Giulia miserable.

"I've got better things to do than chase around trying to find you, you know," Clara said. "You're s'posed to be in the sewing room making shirts, not outside with your stupid pictures."

Giulia sighed and closed her sketchbook on the spoiled drawing. She'd finished her sewing quota early and had slipped away to the orchard, braving the chill of the mid-April day for the pleasure of some uninterrupted sketching time. At least, that had been the plan.

"What do you want, Clara?"

"*I* don't want anything." Clara looked smug. "I've been sent to fetch you. The Countess's maid is waiting in the *cortile*. She says the Countess wants to see you."

It took all Giulia's self-control not to betray what she felt. For weeks she'd been dreading this summons—ever since her father, Count Federico di Assulo Borromeo, died of a fall from his horse, plunging the whole of the household into mourning.

"Well? Don't just sit there like a lump. She's been waiting nearly half an hour, that's how long it took to find you."

The sun had gone away again and the grayness had

returned. Carefully, for she didn't want to give Clara the satisfaction of seeing her hands shake, Giulia stowed her sketchbook and her charcoal stick in the pouch at her belt, then got to her feet and shook out her skirts. She began to make her way back through the orchard, toward the great bulk of Palazzo Borromeo that rose beyond.

"Are you scared, Giulia?" Clara trotted along beside her. "I'd be, if I was you. Everyone knows the Countess hates the sight of you. Think she means to throw you out, now the master's gone?"

Giulia, who feared exactly that, did not reply.

"I hope she does. I can't wait to have the bed all to myself."

"You'll need it, as fat as you're getting."

"I'd rather be fat than a beanpole like you! A man likes something he can get hold of."

"Yes, but he also likes his hands to meet round the back."

Clara hissed. "I hate you, Giulia. Always so high and mighty, with your nose in the air and your stupid drawings, like being the Count's bastard makes you better than the rest of us. Well, you're a servant just the same as we are, and your ten drops of noble blood won't fill your stomach when you're on the street begging for pennies, or maybe doing other things to stay alive. And it will serve you right!"

Clara stopped following when they reached the *cortile*, the paved court at the heart of the palazzo, but Giulia could feel the other girl's malevolent gaze as she went to meet the Countess's maid, who was waiting by the fountain. The maid led her toward the marble stairs that rose to the palazzo's upper floors, where the Borromeo family lived in a series of magnificent suites and chambers. The stairs were for the household and its guests, not for servants or for bastards. Never before had Giulia set foot on them.

The maid left Giulia in an unfurnished anteroom with faded frescoes of hunting scenes on the walls. It seemed a very long time before the Countess entered, in a swirl of velvet and brocade.

"My lady." Giulia dropped a low curtsy. Too late, she realized that her fingers were stained with charcoal. Rising, she tried to hide them in her skirt.

"My husband made me the executor of his estate and will." The Countess's voice was as icy as the marble of the antechamber's floor. "It is my word that rules here now."

"Yes, my lady." Giulia had felt this woman's hatred many times over the years, but she could count on the fingers of both hands the number of sentences the Countess had ever addressed to her.

"You are—what, sixteen?"

"I turned seventeen in March, my lady."

"My husband made provision for you in his will. Three hundred ducats, to be used for a dowry."

Giulia gasped. She looked up before she could stop herself, into the Countess's hard dark eyes. Hastily she looked down again.

"I see you are surprised. As was I. My husband did not share this intent with me."

"My lady—I never knew—that is, I never expected—"

"No matter." The Countess waved Giulia's words away with one ring-heavy hand. "I have arranged a chaperone, as is proper. At noon tomorrow you will leave for Padua, where you will begin your novitiate at the convent of Santa Marta."

Convent? "My lady . . . I don't understand."

"It's quite simple. My husband intended that you marry. Well, I have arranged for you to become the bride of our Savior Jesus Christ. Your dowry is small, but even so the nuns have accepted it, as a favor to my family. For as you know, Padua is where I was born."

"But—" Giulia couldn't seem to get her breath. "My lady, I don't want to be a nun."

"And what possible difference could you imagine that makes to me? This is *my* house now. And *I* say: Leave my house!" The Countess's rigid self-control cracked. Rage strained her voice. "Did you think this day would not come? Did you think, when he died, you would continue as before?"

Of course Giulia hadn't been so foolish. Her mother, the most skilled of the household's seamstresses, had also been the Count's favorite mistress, and he had protected Giulia for her sake—arranging for Annalena, the cooking woman, to take Giulia in after Giulia's mother died, seeing that Giulia had her mother's place in the sewing room when she grew old enough, summoning Giulia every year to ask if she was content. Giulia knew well that his protection ended at the instant of his death. Even so, she'd hoped she would be allowed to stay. Life in Palazzo

Borromeo wasn't always easy, but it was the only home she knew.

She'd tried to prepare herself for the worst. But never, in her most awful fantasies, had she imagined this. Not the Count's bequest. Not the fate the Countess had just decreed for her.

"Now thank me, girl," the Countess said. "For I am giving you a better place in life than ever you could have gotten on your own, and an opportunity to save your miserable soul in the bargain."

Giulia raised her chin. She no longer had anything to lose. Even so, she couldn't keep her voice from shaking, as she defied this woman who had absolute power over her, body and soul. "I will not thank you," she said. "I will never thank you."

Color flooded the Countess's pale cheeks. She stepped across the space between them and slapped Giulia's face—once, twice, three times, her rings adding weight to the blows.

"You go tomorrow," she said, biting off each word. "Now get out of my sight. Never let me see you again."

Head high, face throbbing, Giulia obeyed. She didn't curtsy, a disrespect she never would have dared show before. But what difference did it make now?

She couldn't face going downstairs, where Clara would be waiting to gloat. Instead, she climbed to the storerooms in the attic. She'd often hidden there as a child, to escape the unfriendliness of the other servants or the bullying of Clara's brother, Piero, and it was still where she went when she wanted to be alone.

She found her favorite nook among the bags of grain and crates of spices and dusty furniture, and huddled there, breathing hard with horror and with rage.

I can't be a nun. I can't! She was as devout as anyone, but to be locked away from the world in a cold cloister, dressed in a heavy habit, fasting and praying and doing penance day after day. . . even to imagine it made her feel as if she were being sealed inside a coffin, or falling down a well that had no bottom.

But what could she do? Run away? She had some money, and the topaz and silver necklace that had been her mother's and was meant to be her dowry. But how far would those things take her? There was no one she could go to—her mother's parents were long dead, and her mother's brother, a soldier, had perished in an epidemic of fever. Survival would be hard enough for a grown woman with no relatives to depend on, no household to be part of, no village to take shelter in. For a girl of seventeen, it would be all but impossible.

Giulia had been brave enough, a few minutes ago, to look the Countess in the eye. But right now, this instant, she knew she was not brave enough to run away.

I wouldn't escape even if I did. She'd do everything in her power to see me caught and punished, in return for all the years my father sheltered me.

Giulia bowed her head onto her drawn-up knees, feeling the pain in her cheeks where the Countess's rings had bruised her. The Count had left her a dowry. A dowry! It was as unexpected as snow in June. She hadn't loved him; it was impossible to love a man she saw so rarely, a man she could never quite convince herself not to be afraid of. But he had been her protector, and she'd always been grateful to him—now more than ever, knowing he had tried to extend that protection beyond his death.

The Countess had cheated him. She'd cheated Giulia as well, as thoroughly as if she'd kept the dowry for herself. It wasn't just the money. It was Giulia's whole future the Countess had snatched away—the dream Giulia had cherished since childhood, of a husband, children, a house of her own. A place where she belonged. None of those were possible for a nun.

It's as if she knew the prediction of my horoscope. In the chill of the attic, Giulia felt a deeper cold. *Short of killing me, what could be a more perfect way of making it come true?*

"Oh Mama," she whispered. "What shall I do?"

She'd been only seven when her mother died. It had comforted her, then, to imagine her mother looking down from heaven, like someone leaning over a high balcony. She'd long ago left that literal image behind, but she still spoke to her mother sometimes, half-hoping, half-pretending, she was close enough to hear.

And all at once, like an answer, Giulia saw what might save her.

She caught her breath. It was not a new idea. She'd first conceived it years ago. But it was frightening and risky, and she had always held it at the back of her mind, saving it for a last resort.

Everything had changed today. Last resorts were all she had.

She wiped her eyes. With new purpose she got to her feet, and went in search of Maestro Carlo Bruni, the Count's astrologer.

CHAPTER 2

✧ Last Resorts ✧

As she descended to the palazzo's third floor, where Maestro Bruni's rooms were, Giulia found herself remembering the first time she had ever gone looking for him.

She'd been just seven years old, and her mother had been dead only a few weeks. Her mother hadn't had much to leave behind. Just a pouch of coins she'd saved, the silver and topaz necklace she had inherited from her own mother, and a cedar box holding a few small gifts from the Count, the velvet dress and linen chemise that were meant to be Giulia's trousseau, and Giulia's horoscope, rolled into a scroll case for safekeeping.

Giulia had moved in with Annalena right after the funeral, in a room just down the hall from the one she'd shared with her mother. She'd already stitched the coins into the hem of her skirt and the topaz necklace into her waistband; the cedar box she brought with her, pushing it under the bed where she now had to sleep with Annalena's two children, Clara and Piero. She left her father's trinkets and the trousseau clothes in the box, but the horoscope she concealed under the mattress, where she thought it would be safer.

She was wrong. A few days later, she returned to find the box lying open on the floor. The garments her mother had so lovingly made and embroidered were ripped and smeared with mud. The Count's trinkets were gone. So was the horoscope—all but a single torn fragment, which had fallen behind a chest.

Giulia had known Piero was responsible, just as she'd known he was the one who pulled the head off her doll and dropped it in the chamber pot and smeared the soles of her shoes with dog dung so that she tracked it about without realizing. But she was only seven, and she was afraid of Piero, who was twelve and twice her size, and she'd learned that complaining to Annalena only made things worse. So she said nothing. She packed the clothing back into the cedar box and found a hiding place in the attic. She hid the necklace and the coins there as well. For the horoscope fragment, she sewed a waxed canvas pouch that she could wear around her neck.

She'd been sad about the ruined trousseau, though she cared little about the stolen trinkets. But it was the loss of the horoscope that really hurt. The horoscope had been her mother's special gift; she'd spent all her savings to commission it from the Count's own astrologer, and it was as fine as the horoscopes of the Count's legitimate children. On one side, against a deep blue background, was a large circle divided into twelve segments, each containing clusters of spiky symbols that represented the stars and planets that had been in the sky at the exact moment of Giulia's birth. On the other side, neat columns of black-ink script described the symbols' meaning.

"This is the story of your life, my love," Giulia's mother would murmur on the nights when she allowed Giulia to take the horoscope out of its case and unroll it on the bed to admire. "Everything that will ever happen to you is written here, everything you will ever be and do. I hadn't enough to pay the astrologer to read it to me, but one day we'll go to a notary and he'll tell us what it says."

"When will we go, Mama?"

"When you're old enough to understand. This horoscope will guide your life, my love. You'll never have to be like me, stumbling blindly through the years, never knowing what choices to make, letting all your chances slip away. You'll always know what's coming, and you'll always be prepared. You don't yet know how important that is, but you will one day, I promise. Because in the end, Giulia—in the end, the only person you can rely on is yourself."

Giulia had known that Piero hadn't just torn up the horoscope, but utterly destroyed it. Even so, she hadn't been able to stop herself from looking for it—among the kitchen scraps, in the ashes of the fires, even in the foul-smelling darkness of the privies. She'd come to fear it a little, for her mother's death had taught her that the world held awful pain as well as happiness, and the star-map of a life must surely show both. Yet she wanted it back, as painfully, as hopelessly as she wanted her mother back.

Or *was* it hopeless?

A month after Piero found the cedar box, Giulia finally scraped up the courage to make her way to Maestro Bruni's rooms. He'd created the horoscope— perhaps he remembered it well enough to re-create it. "I can pay you," she told him, offering her mother's coins. But he shook his head.

"I'm sorry, child. I'm not the astrologer your mother commissioned." He was a small man, thin as a wire, with soft brown eyes and a hooked nose that reminded her of a bird's beak. She liked his gentle manner, and the serious way he listened to her. "I came into the Count's employ only two years ago."

"There's this." She held out the fragment. "Doesn't it help?"

He glanced at the symbols, then looked at the side with the writing. He frowned. "This is not a happy prediction, my dear. It says—" He seemed to catch himself. "That your stars are not favorable for marriage."

"They aren't? But why not?"

"I don't know, my dear. It's just a fragment."

"But . . . Mama wanted me to marry." Giulia's eyes filled with tears. "She said I had to find a husband to protect me. She said it was the most important thing of all. She said . . . she said I must never end up like her, living in a little room at the bottom of a big house, with a child who has no father."

"Oh, my dear." Maestro Bruni's brow creased with sympathy. "Such predictions are possibilities, not certainties. What's written on that bit of paper doesn't have to happen."

"It doesn't?"

"Our lives are written in the skies of our birth. But God gave us free will. That means we can resist the influence of our stars, and shape our lives through our own choices. Suppose . . . suppose your birth horoscope showed there was danger to you of death by drowning. You could stay away from water, from boats—anything that might cause you to drown. Or suppose, as in your case, your stars say it will be difficult for you to marry. If you do everything you can to look for a husband, rather than waiting for him, as most girls do, perhaps you will marry after all. Do you see?"

"I . . . I think so."

"There may have been predictions in the original chart to balance this one." Maestro Bruni smiled. "Would you like to find out? Shall I cast you a new horoscope?"

"Oh, sir! Would you?"

"Indeed I would. And put away your coins, my dear, I won't take even a penny. When were you born?"

"In March, sir. I'm seven."

"In Pisces, then, in . . . hmmm . . . 1470. And the day and hour?"

Giulia opened her mouth to reply. Her mother had always celebrated her name day in March. But the day and the hour . . .

"I don't know," she said in a small voice.

"Did your mother never tell you?"

Had she? Giulia couldn't remember. She shook her head.

"Then I'm sorry." He sounded genuinely regretful. "Without at least the day of your birth, there's nothing I can do."

He held out the fragment. Giulia took it, trying not to cry.

"Don't look so sad, child. Most people never know their stars. Others do, and pay no heed to the warnings written there. One can live a good life without a horoscope, and a bad life with one. Better the former than the latter, don't you think?"

"Thank you, sir." Giulia curtsied. "For your time."

"Come back and visit me if you remember more." He smiled. "Even if you don't, eh?"

Giulia never did remember more. But she had returned to Maestro's rooms whenever she could slip away. He'd been kind to her, and unlike the servants' quarters, his cluttered study held no painful memories of her mother. She was too young, then, to question why he would welcome her; it was only as she grew older that she began to understand how lonely he was, for he was unmarried, just as her horoscope predicted she would be, and his family was far away in the city of Vicenza.

He indulged her curiosity about his instruments

and books. As she proved how quickly she could learn, what had been a game became something more. He taught her to read and write, both in Italian and in the practical Latin of scholars and the Church. He let her delve into his books on history and philosophy and geography. She began showing him her drawings, which he praised as only her mother ever had before; it was he who gave her the leather-covered sketchbook that she carried always in her belt-pouch. By the time she turned twelve, he'd come to rely on her as a kind of secretary, to copy out his scribbled interpretations of the elaborate horoscopes he created for the Borromeo family: natal horoscopes for the birth of children, electional horoscopes to determine the proper times for important events, horary horoscopes to answer important questions.

The visits to Maestro fed Giulia's hunger for knowledge. But also, they were a refuge—from the tedium of the sewing room, from Piero's bullying and Clara's malice, from her uneasy position in the household, excluded from the upstairs world because of her bastardy, isolated within the downstairs world for the same reason. By long practice, she was able to ignore the other servants' coldness and occasional mockery—making fun of her charcoal-stained fingers, mincing along behind her with their noses in the air and pinched expressions on their faces, to show they thought she put on airs. But she could not always fully armor herself against the hurt and the anger. It was good to have a place where she was not only accepted, but valued. Even, perhaps, loved.

"You're as clever as a boy, my dear," Maestro sometimes told her. "I don't know what God was thinking, to give such an intellect to a girl."

Giulia knew he didn't mean the words to sting. But they did. A boy who could read and write could do so many things—even if he were a servant, even if he were a bastard. But a girl . . . no matter how clever a girl was, no matter how full of learning she stuffed her head, all a girl could do was to get married and have children.

And according to her horoscope, Giulia might not even be able to do that.

Shaking off thoughts of the past, Giulia knocked at Maestro's door, then, as always, slipped inside without waiting for a response.

Maestro's study was as familiar to her as any room in the palazzo, with its red marble floor and its smell of dust, leather-bound books, and incense. Pedestals under the windows supported an armillary sphere and a celestial globe; alcoves along the inner wall held books and astrological instruments. Another wall was almost entirely covered by a tapestry depicting the universe—Earth at the center, surrounded by the spheres of the sun, the moon, the planets, and the higher spheres of the heavens. Angels with golden wings ringed the outermost sphere, where God sat on His throne, His hand outstretched to show that it was by His will the cosmos moved.

Maestro was sitting at his cluttered desk.

He half-rose when he saw Giulia, his welcoming smile disappearing.

"Merciful saints, Giulia! What happened to your face?"

"It was an accident." Giulia raised her hand to her cheek, still throbbing from the Countess's blows. "It doesn't matter. But Maestro, the Countess is sending me to Padua to be a nun. I must leave tomorrow."

"Ah." Maestro sat down again.

"Did you . . . did you know?"

"No. But change is afoot in this house. I fear none of us will escape it."

"I don't want to be a nun." Just saying it made Giulia breathless. "I don't mind if she sends me away—just not to a convent. Could you talk to her? Please?"

"Me?" Maestro drew back. "My dear, she would not hear me. I had the Count's favor, but not hers. Between you and me, I've begun looking for a new patron."

"But if you knew someone who would give me a position—there's your cousin in Vicenza, perhaps his household needs a seamstress—"

"No, no, no. I care nothing for the Countess's displeasure, but I can't make that choice for my cousin." Maestro shook his head. "I'm sorry, Giulia. For your sake, I wish I were a man of influence, but I am not."

He is kind, Giulia thought. *But not brave.* She hadn't really expected he could help, but she'd had to ask, just to make sure all other roads were barred to her.

"Ah, Giulia, how I will miss you. A pox upon that woman and her stupid pride."

Giulia felt her throat tighten. She would miss

him too, this gentle man whom she loved almost as a father. She'd miss him terribly. But she couldn't let herself be distracted by that now.

"Maestro, do you remember telling me about your friend, the astrologer who makes talismans? Maestro Bastone, wasn't it?"

"Barbaro. Francisco Barbaro. My *former* friend, Giulia, as you know well."

"Didn't you say he lived in Porta Nuova, on Via . . . Via . . ."

"Via Sette Coltelli in Porta Orientale." Maestro caught himself. "Giulia. What are you up to?"

"I can't be a nun, Maestro. I have to do something."

"What, get Barbaro to make you a talisman to save you from the convent? Sorcery is a sin, Giulia, an invention of the devil, not just for those who practice it but for those who seek it."

"It'd just be one talisman. And I'd never want another."

"One talisman or a hundred, it's all the same. My dear, this is not the way for you."

"But I can't think of anything else! You can't help me—I can't run away—I've no one to take me in. I don't want to wind up a beggar or . . . or a whore, I don't want to be called a thief because I stole my own self and cheated the Countess of her cruelty!" She caught her breath in a sob. "If this . . . sorcerer can help me—"

"Giulia." Maestro got to his feet. He was as stern as Giulia had ever seen him. "You wouldn't even know about Barbaro had you not found his letter hidden in that book years ago. I never would have told you. I said as much as I did only to make clear to you the evil of the path he chose."

"But Maestro—"

"I would like to claim that it was he who corrupted me." Maestro raised his voice to carry over hers. "But I cannot. He and I succumbed together as apprentices, and continued as astrologers. For me, the small magics that were our first passion were enough, but he was always drawn to darker things. When he began to study the daemonic spirits, crafting incantations to summon them and rituals to bind them, I saw that we were meddling with powers God does not mean us to possess. In fear of damnation, I renounced all magic and left the house we shared. He sent me that letter, cursing me for what he called my betrayal. As corrupt as he was when I left him, I cannot imagine the depth of his depravity now. I forbid you to go to him. By the duty you owe me as your tutor, *I forbid it*."

For a moment Giulia held his gaze. Then she bowed her head, as if in defeat. "Yes, Maestro."

"Good girl."

She felt wretched to deceive him. But like the Countess, he had left her no choice. In her mind, as she often did, she heard her mother's voice: *In the end, the only person you can rely on is yourself.*

"You should have presents to go away with." Maestro left his desk and began to move around the room, reaching up to shelves, opening chests. "A supply of paper, for your drawing. A quill and an inkpot—with a cap, so you won't have to worry about spills.

Ink powder that you can mix as you need. And Ovid's *Metamorphoses*. I know how you love them."

"Oh, Maestro, thank you. But I don't know if they'll let me keep such things."

"We shall hope they will. Ah, Giulia. If you were a boy, I'd have made you my apprentice long ago."

Giulia looked at him—his clothes always a little shabby, his fingers always stained with ink, his papers always in disarray, his mind always on his books or in the stars. Normally she didn't notice, but just now she could see it clearly: *He's getting old.* A great surge of grief and affection rose up in her. She stepped forward and flung her arms around his neck.

"I'll never forget you," she whispered fiercely. "Thank you for your kindness, for everything you've taught me."

"There, there." He patted her awkwardly on the back. "God keep you safe, my dearest girl. Remember that in Milan, there is one who loves you."

"I love you too." She stepped away. "Good-bye, Maestro."

She carried his gifts up to the attic, then pried up the loose floorboard that hid her mother's topaz necklace and pouch of coins. All the while, she repeated the address Maestro had given her, so she would not forget: *Maestro Francisco Barbaro. Via Sette Coltelli. Porta Orientale.*

God, if this is a sin, forgive me. But I don't know what else to do.

CHAPTER 3

❖ The Hour of Venus ❖

The afternoon was almost gone by the time Giulia reached the sorcerer's house.

She'd known where Porta Orientale was, at least in theory—Maestro had showed her plans of Milan, with its six neighborhoods, or *portes*, arranged like pie slices around the central piazza that housed the Duomo, the city's vast cathedral. But finding her way through the streets was not the same as poring over maps. She'd quickly become lost, and the conflicting directions she had begged from passersby had taken her far out of her way. She'd begun to worry that she would still be wandering the city when night fell, at the mercy of cutpurses or worse.

But finally, like a miracle, there it was—a pillar painted with seven stilettos, marking the entrance to the Via Sette Coltelli, the Street of Seven Knives.

The sorcerer's house was protected by a stucco wall. An iron gate allowed glimpses of a garden full of overgrown yews and cypresses, through whose twisted branches Giulia could just see the house itself. Perhaps because of all the heavy vegetation, the garden seemed much darker than the avenue outside, as if night had already fallen there. A bell rope hung beside the gate.

Giulia had wondered what a sorcerer's home might look like. This gloomy place fulfilled all her expectations.

For just a moment, the fear she'd fought as she trudged the city rose up and overwhelmed her, and Maestro's words of warning sounded in her mind. She pushed them away. *I've come this far. I cannot turn back.*

She drew a deep breath. She stepped forward and rang the bell.

Clang. The sound echoed back into the shadowed garden. For a long moment nothing happened. Then she heard a creak, as of a door opening, and saw someone coming toward her—a woman, bent with age, her head wrapped in a kerchief. The woman shuffled up to the gates and peered through the bars.

"What d'you want?"

"I've come . . ." Giulia cleared her throat. "I've

come to see Maestro Francisco Barbaro, the sor—the astrologer. It's urgent."

"It always is. Can you pay?"

"Yes."

The crone lifted the bar that secured the gates. She dragged at one of them, pulling it back a little way. "Well?" Impatiently, she beckoned. "Don't be all day."

Giulia slipped through the narrow gap. The crone heaved the gate closed and reset the bar, then led the way along the wide stone path that split the tangled garden, beneath the dimness of the trees. She hurried Giulia through the house's great oaken door and down a magnificent candle-lit corridor whose elaborate frescos and polished marble were the very opposite of the garden's neglect. An enormous, high-ceilinged room lay at the corridor's end.

"Wait here," the crone instructed, pointing to a spot by the door. "I'll see if he'll receive you. He may not. He doesn't see everyone."

She hurried toward the room's other side, where a curtain hung across an opening.

"Tell him Maestro Carlo Bruni gave me his name," Giulia called after her. "They were friends once."

The old woman gave no sign that she had heard. She lifted the curtain and vanished.

The blue gray twilight admitted by the windows did little to relieve the chamber's gloom. Her back against the door, her teeth chattering with chill and fright, Giulia could almost imagine that the old woman had been a ghost, that there were no living beings in this place besides herself. For courage, she rested her hand on her mother's topaz necklace, hidden under the neck of her gown.

The curtain swept aside. A man came through, clad in a flowing robe and carrying a branch of candles.

"You say you come from Carlo Bruni, girl?"

Giulia had to try twice to find her voice. "Yes, sir."

"Who are you?" The sorcerer approached, holding up the candles. "Why has he sent you?"

"My name is Giulia, sir. I'm his pupil."

"His pupil?" He sounded skeptical.

"Yes, sir. And he didn't send me. That is, he told me your name . . . but I'm here . . . I'm here on my own."

"Ah."

Was it disappointment in his voice? He set the candles on a table and began to move around the room, lighting more candles in sconces on the walls. Giulia couldn't tell how he accomplished this—it looked as if the flame sprang directly from his fingers. The rising illumination revealed the magnificent zodiac wheel inlaid upon the marble floor, showing the twelve signs, their associated houses, and their ruling planets. As the candle flames flared up, points of light seemed to kindle on the ceiling as well. With astonishment, Giulia recognized the zodiac constellations, arranged in a ring that exactly matched the circle on the floor. Awed, she gazed upward. Scorpio glittered directly overhead; to the left was Pisces, under which she had been born.

"Carlo Bruni and I were friends, years ago."

The sorcerer stood before her. She had imagined

someone crabbed and stooped, made ugly by his outlaw pursuits, but this man was well-formed and straight, with a handsome face and large, calm eyes of crystalline blue. The silk of his robe was a deeper blue. His hair was entirely covered by a close-fitting cap that appeared, strangely, to be made of polished metal.

"The best of friends," he continued. "Did he tell you that?"

Giulia nodded. She'd assumed that Maestro and the sorcerer were of an age, but this man looked at least twenty years younger. She felt a thrill of fear. *If he can light candles with his fingers and make stars shine on his ceiling, what else can he do?*

"Did he tell you why we are friends no longer?"

"He said you quarreled, sir."

"It was the magic. It destroyed our friendship. When I heard you were here, I thought . . ." The sorcerer paused. "No matter. I was angry when we parted, but I've come to understand the choice he made. Will you tell him that for me?"

"Yes, sir," Giulia said, though she knew that if she ever saw Maestro again, she could never admit she had come here.

"What is it you want of me?"

"Sir, Maestro Bruni told me you can make talismans that influence the stars. I need a talisman so I can get married."

"I take it the young man isn't willing?"

"Oh, no, sir!" Giulia felt a blush rising in her cheeks. "It's not like that!"

"What is it like, then?"

"Sir, my natal horoscope says that my stars are . . . unfavorable for marriage. But I want to marry. I want children and a home of my own. I've always meant to find a way. But now I'm being sent to a convent against my will. I must marry soon, before it's too late."

"Our lives are written in the stars of our birth, by the very hand of God," the sorcerer said. "It is no light matter to try to change that. What you want from me is dangerous."

"But we can resist the influence of our stars." It was the first lesson Maestro had ever taught her. "With the free will God gave us. We can change our fates by our own actions."

"Perhaps. But if your actions change your fate, then that change too was written for you. A talisman is different. It will bring about the change by force. The consequences of that can be . . . unexpected."

"I'm willing to take the risk, sir."

"Marriage has its risks as well. Husbands beat their wives. Women die in childbirth."

He didn't understand. How could he? He was a man. He was his own master. Giulia hadn't understood either, when she had first learned what her horoscope fragment said—she'd been too young to know how terrible life could be for an unmarried servant woman. Her mother had known, from bitter experience—a nobleman's commoner mistress with a bastard daughter, despised by her fellow servants, dependent on her lover's favor for the roof over her head and the food in her own mouth and that of her child. The older Giulia grew, the more she learned about the world, the more clearly she saw why her mother had been so determined that Giulia must marry.

The words of the prediction returned to her, words she had long known by heart:

> . . . *major affliction by Saturn, and the Moon and Sun in barren signs, there is thus no testimony of marriage, or of children. She shall not take another's name, nor shall she bear her own at the end of life, but shall . . .*

It was a far stronger forecast than Maestro had revealed when she first visited him. Not one planet in a barren sign, but two. Not a difficult testimony of marriage—*no* testimony. Yet through Maestro, she had learned that she could fight her stars. And because she knew what was coming—because in this one thing she was prepared, as her mother had intended—she believed she could prevail. That by will and determination, she could change her fate.

From the time she began her woman's bleeding, she had been searching for a husband. She was not beautiful, as her mother had been—her features were too strong, her body too tall and straight. But her skin was smooth, her hair was thick and glossy black, and her eyes were fine, large and dark with curling lashes and arching brows. She hadn't lacked for chances. None, somehow, had gone farther than a few stolen kisses.

With each failure, she'd told herself that there

would be more opportunities. She was young. She had time. The talisman, sorcery, were possibilities she held in the back of her mind, a last resort if it became clear she could not change her future on her own. But now her time had run out. The stars, in their inexorable turning, had brought her face-to-face with her foretold fate.

She drew herself up. She met the sorcerer's gaze. She was still afraid, but no longer of him. Her fear was for herself—that she might have come so far and risked so much only to fail in the final moment.

"Sir, since I was seven years old I've known the prediction of my horoscope. Since I was ten, I've understood the life it means for me. My mother is dead. I have no family. I am a nobleman's bastard, but I was never acknowledged, so I'm a servant like my mother. An unmarried servant woman can be given away like a piece of clothing, or traded as if she were a horse. When I get too old to use my needle there will be no one to care for me. And now I'm told I must become a nun, which is only a different kind of servitude, with prayers instead of housework. I love God, sir, but that isn't how I want to honor Him! If I marry, I'll still be a servant, but at least I'll have my own life, my own place, my own family. Something of my *own*, something that belongs to me. I've been robbed of the time to find a husband for myself. This . . . this is my only chance. Will you help me?"

For a long moment the sorcerer regarded her. The candlelight lit his crystalline eyes, making their blue almost transparent. At last he nodded. "I will."

29

Giulia let out her breath. "I've got nearly fifty soldi. Will it be enough?"

"It will."

Giulia pulled her mother's coins from her belt pouch and put them in his hand. It was all the money she had, but less than she'd feared the sorcerer would demand. She'd thought she might have to pay with her mother's necklace as well.

"I will calculate when the talisman can be made, and let you know when you can return to collect it."

"You can't make it now?"

"Certainly not. Your desire is of the heart, and Venus rules the heart, so a talisman of Venus is what you need. To properly draw down Venus's influence, materials she rules on the terrestrial plane must be carefully gathered. The talisman must be made on a Friday, Venus's day, and in her hour where it falls on that day, and she must be ascendant when it is consecrated."

"But sir, I have to leave tomorrow!" Giulia tried to control her panic. "I need it now, tonight!"

"Then it will not have the proper strength. Unless . . ." He paused.

"Unless?"

"Unless I draw a spirit into the talisman. There'd be no need then to wait for the stars to be propitious."

"A . . . spirit?" Giulia had forgotten about the cold, but now she felt a chill. "What kind of spirit?"

"A planetary spirit, a spirit of Venus. The celestial realms are alive with such Intelligences. The great ones are beyond human understanding, but the lesser ones may be called and bound by those on Earth who have the skill." He smiled a little. "Many people, like your master Bruni, fear such magic, and call it daemonic. But nothing exists except by the will of God. Not magic, and not spirits either."

"And . . . the spirit . . . would make the talisman strong enough? To bring me a husband?"

"Spirits cannot be compelled to such narrow purposes. But I will bind it to your heart's desire. If your heart's desire is marriage, then that is what it will give you."

Giulia swallowed. She thought she had been prepared for anything. But a spirit . . . something *alive* inside the talisman. . . . Yet why was she surprised? Maestro had warned her.

"There's no other way?"

"Not if you must have the talisman tonight."

He waited, holding her in his crystal gaze. Giulia felt breathless, as if she were running much too fast down a too-steep flight of stairs. But this was her plan, the only one she had. Without it, there was nothing but lifelong imprisonment in the convent.

"Very well. Yes."

"It will cost more. Have you something else to pay me with?"

Not giving herself time to think, Giulia fumbled off her mother's necklace. She held it out, the honey-colored topaz gleaming, the silver links spilling from her palm.

"That should do."

She experienced an almost physical pain as he

took it from her. She closed her hands into fists and put them behind her back.

"It will take some time," the sorcerer said. "I'll sing my incantations at the hour of Venus, and it comes late this night."

"The tenth hour," Giulia said. "I know."

"Ah yes. You did say you were Bruni's pupil." He took up his candles again. "You must be hungry. I'll tell my housekeeper to bring you something."

The last Giulia saw, as he passed behind the curtain, were the links of her mother's necklace, swinging from his hand.

Giulia woke with a start. She thought she'd heard something—a clanging, as if of enormous cymbals. But the air was silent now.

She lay against the wall, where she'd finally fallen asleep, wrapped in the blanket the old woman had brought along with the food. It had been a long night. The hours had stretched like pulled sugar, and the candles hardly seemed to burn down at all. Now and then, in the distance, came a thump or a thud, the sound of a voice rising in chant or song. There were smells too—charcoal smoke, hot metal, and once, briefly, an overpowering burst of sweet perfume, as if all the flowers in the world had bloomed and died in the space of a few breaths—although Giulia was not quite sure she hadn't dreamed that.

She climbed to her feet, pushing back her disheveled hair. The windows had been blue gray with twilight when she arrived; now they were blue gray with dawn. The candles, at last, had gone out, and the starry ceiling was dark.

She heard footsteps. The sorcerer reappeared, as calm and immaculate as when she first saw him.

"It's done."

He placed a small cloth-wrapped package on a table. He pulled the cloth away, revealing an oval stone of the same lustrous blue as his robe. Inlaid upon it in some orangey metal was the image of a woman in flowing clothes, her hair falling past her knees.

"This is Venus-in-beauty, the aspect most appropriate to your need. At her feet is the symbol of Venus, which no doubt you recognize. The metal is copper, which she rules. The stone is lapis lazuli, which she also rules."

Giulia didn't know what she had expected—a spectral glow? A vibration of the air? Somehow, she had thought it would be possible to recognize the spirit's presence. But the talisman seemed completely ordinary—lovely, to be sure, but just a pendant.

"The spirit is inside?"

"It is."

"Is it . . . can it ever get out?"

"It's securely bound. It cannot escape until you set it free."

"Why would I set it free?"

"Because it is a free being. Such creatures do not feel as humans do, but it will suffer if you hold it beyond the time of your need. When you no longer require its help, break the stone into pieces. That will release it back to the heavens."

"And it won't be angry? At being imprisoned?"

"I told you, such beings don't feel as humans do." For the first time, the sorcerer showed a trace of impatience. "In any case, it is bound to your heart's desire. Your desire is its desire now." He looked at her. "Be very sure you know what that is, or you may find yourself surprised by what you receive."

"I'm sure."

"Then all will be well." He drew the wrappings over the stone again. "It's sleeping now. To wake it, and let it know it's you it serves, give it something of yourself—a drop of blood, some spittle, anything will do as long as it comes from within you—and speak its name aloud. Anasurymboriel."

"Ana—"

"—surymboriel. Thereafter, keep it on your person. Next to your skin is best."

He placed the little package in her hand. It was heavier than she expected, as if it were made of something denser than stone.

"Have you any other questions for me?"

"Sir . . ." Giulia hesitated.

"Yes?"

"Why do you wear a metal cap?"

"Ah." The sorcerer raised his hand to touch it. "According to my natal horoscope, I'm at risk of death from falling objects. I carry a talisman, but I also believe in taking practical measures." He smiled a little. Now at last the long night showed in his face—or maybe it was just the rising light of day, revealing the lines around his mouth and eyes. "We are all trying to cheat the stars, one way or another. Good-bye, Giulia. Remember me to your master."

CHAPTER 4

❖ Anasurymboriel ❖

Giulia saw no one, not even the crone who had let
her in, as she left the sorcerer's house. She ran
through the garden, where the trees held the last
of night tangled in their branches, and slipped out
the gates. All the while she repeated to herself the
strange name the sorcerer had given her, fixing it in
her mind so she would not forget: *Anasurymboriel.*
Anasurymboriel. Anasurymboriel.

She felt the weight of the talisman in her belt
pouch, and the emptiness at her throat where her
mother's necklace had been.

It was still early when she arrived at the palazzo.

The doorman grinned as he let her in.

"Out all night, eh? You won't be doing much of that where you're going."

She could hear him chortling as she ran across the *cortile*.

She went directly to the attic, where she pulled her mother's cedar box from its hiding place beneath one of the dust cloth-shrouded tables. In addition to the ruined trousseau, it held pretty stones and bright feathers she'd collected over the years, a sash she'd made out of leftover silk, a silver chain she'd found in the gutter, and the thick sheaf of her drawings.

She didn't know where it came from, her need to draw. She only knew she had always had it, even as a tiny child. No one ever taught her; it was just something she understood how to do, an instinct familiar as her own body. Any surface would serve—a smooth rock, a patch of sand, a spare bit of linen cloth—and anything that would make a mark—a piece of chalk, a sliver of charred wood.

Giulia's mother had encouraged her, bringing her scraps of paper, praising her efforts. But to her foster-mother Annalena, Giulia's scribbling was a self-indulgent waste of time, and she was scolded if Annalena caught her at it. She couldn't stop drawing, though, any more than she could stop breathing. The attic storerooms had become her sketchbook. She'd drawn in charcoal on the plaster walls, in chalk on the plank floors, in a mixture of ashes and water on the underside of dust cloths. She'd drawn things she saw and things she had never seen. She'd drawn her mother's face, over and over, pouring her grief into the pictures, her loss and pain. Sometimes she was able to reach a place where those things didn't exist, where she was not a bereft and frightened girl, where there was only the unity of hand and eye and all that mattered was the images she brought into being.

Much had changed since then. She'd learned to live with her grief, and then to live beyond it, though she could always touch it if she tried. She no longer had to draw on walls—she had Maestro's sketchbook, and the sticks of charcoal she carried in her belt pouch. She had Maestro's study, where she was always welcome—a far more friendly refuge than the chilly attic, with its fading traces of her childhood scribbles. But the drawing . . . that was the same. She was more skillful than she had been—she could draw almost anything. But it was still her favored way of escaping from her life. It still poured from her as naturally as breathing.

With Maestro's gifts, the cedar box was too full to close. But what to leave behind? There was no question of abandoning the trousseau, the only memento of her mother she had, now the necklace was gone. She sorted through her own things, setting aside all but the embroidered sash and the silver chain. Then she culled her drawings. In the end, she kept only a handful: her mother, drawn from memory, the topaz necklace encircling her throat, her heavy braid falling over her shoulder. Annalena at the kitchen fire. A portrait of Maestro. A view of his study and one of the attic. The sun and shadow in the *cortile* at noon.

The orchard, where she had loved to sit and draw or dream.

The remaining sketches she left on the table, along with the odds and ends she had discarded. Someone would find them eventually, and wonder how they had come there.

She repacked the box, putting in everything except the silver chain, then closed the lid and tied it up with cord. She removed the talisman from her pocket and threaded the chain through the copper loop at the top of the stone.

Not much light angled through the attic's tiny windows. Even so, the blue of the lapis lazuli was as brilliant as a bird's feather, and the copper inlay gleamed. Inside the stone, a spirit slept—a living thing wrenched from the heavens, imprisoned by the sorcerer's will and by her own. What had he said? *Your desire is its desire now.*

She shivered. *How do I know the spirit is truly bound? How do I know it won't get free?* She heard Maestro's words: *Sorcery is a sin, not just for those who practice it but for those who seek it.* And the sorcerer's: *What you want from me is dangerous.*

And her mother. What would she say, if she were here?

In the end, the only person you can rely on is yourself.

Giulia drew a deep breath. She licked her finger and pressed it to the talisman. "A-na-su-rym-bor-i-el," she whispered, enunciating carefully to keep from tripping over the strange syllables. Then again, for good measure: "Anasurymboriel."

She half-expected to sense the spirit as it woke: a tremor against her hand, a spark of light. Nothing happened. But when she looked up again, the attic around her seemed clearer than before, the bags and barrels and boxes more distinct, the scent of cinnamon and clove and saffron more sweet. As if the world had been veiled in gauze, which had just now been pulled away.

She clasped the talisman around her throat. It fell just below the little pouch that held her horoscope fragment; the chain showed at the neck of her dress, but the talisman itself was safely hidden. She was struck again by how heavy it was, almost as heavy as her mother's necklace.

"I'm sorry, Mama," she whispered. "I wouldn't have given him your necklace if there was any other way. You understand, don't you?"

There was, of course, no answer.

It was time to go. She raised her hand to cross herself, to say a prayer for the journey. But could she pray to God, now that she wore a celestial spirit around her neck, bound to defy God's will for her?

For a moment she hesitated. Then she lowered her hand.

"Forgive me," she murmured.

The weight of the box pulled at her arms as she descended the back stairs to the ground floor, where the kitchens and workshops and servants' quarters were.

Since her meeting with the Countess, she'd thought only about the sorcerer and the talisman. But now, for the first time, she felt the weight of what was about to happen to her. By the end of this day, she would have passed beyond the walls of Milan, beyond the only home she had ever known, beyond all that was familiar. The dim, spice-scented attic, the orchard in the spring, the serenity of the *cortile*, the way the kitchens smelled on feast days, Maestro's rooms, his books, her studies—she would never experience those things again. She would never see Maestro again, or Annalena.

And what of her mother? Palazzo Borromeo held all the memories of her mother that she had. Would the memories fade, once she was gone? Would she begin to forget her mother's face?

As long as I have my drawings, I can't forget, she reminded herself. *I'll never have to listen to Clara's taunting again. I'll never have to hide in the pantry to avoid Piero. I'll actually see some of the world I've been reading about for all these years.*

It didn't help. Fear sat in her stomach. It fluttered in her throat.

In the room she shared with Annalena and Clara— Piero had moved into the stables years ago, with the other grooms—Giulia made a bundle of her possessions: two chemises, a spare dress, her sewing kit. She left the box and bundle in the hall, and went to the kitchen to say good-bye to Annalena.

Annalena had been good to Giulia—better than she needed to be, with two children of her own. She'd cried yesterday when Giulia told her about the Countess's decree. Today they both wept, embracing amid the noise and bustle of the kitchen.

"'Tisn't right, you being sent off this way." Annalena pulled away, scrubbing at her cheeks, then using a corner of her apron to dry Giulia's eyes. "You never said nothing about wanting to be a nun."

"Don't worry." Giulia tried to sound confident. "I'll be all right."

"Maybe you can write a letter. I can get one of the clerks to read it for me."

"I will if I can, I promise. Thank you, Annalena. For all you've done for me."

"'Twasn't so much. You're a good girl." Annalena crossed herself. "I'll pray to the Blessed Virgin to keep you safe. Now go, before we both start bawling again."

There was no one else Giulia cared to say goodbye to. Though it was not yet noon, she retrieved her bundle and box and went out to the *cortile*. She set the box in the sun and sat down on it to wait.

"I'm frightened, Mama," she whispered.

To stop herself from crying again, she summoned her favorite daydream: the dream she turned to whenever she needed strength or comfort, the dream that was also a promise—her own promise, to herself, that she would never give up her fight against her stars. In the dream, the difficulties of her horoscope had been solved, and she was at home in her own house, awaiting her husband's return. Sometimes her husband was a notary or a clerk. Sometimes he was a scholar—someone who would not object to an educated wife, a wife who drew pictures. Sometimes her house was within city walls, sometimes it was outside, surrounded by orchards and fields. Sometimes children tumbled at her feet, and sometimes it was just the two of them. But always, she had a place of her own. Always, she had someone who belonged to her, and to whom she belonged.

Always, she was free.

"Anasurymboriel," she whispered. It was already easier to say.

Part 2
The Workshop of Women
❖❖❖❖❖❖

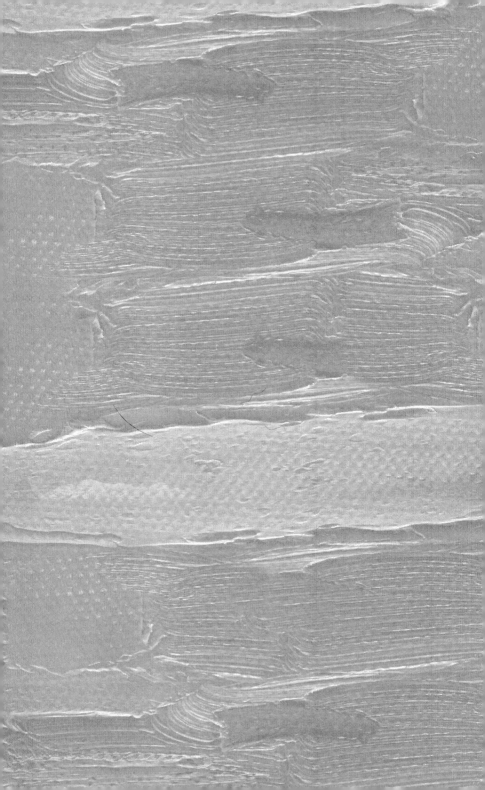

CHAPTER 5

❖ Santa Marta ❖

The carriage door sprang wide, admitting an incandescent blast of sunlight. Framed in the opening, Giulia saw an expanse of cobbled street, a slice of red brick wall.

They had arrived at Santa Marta.

In the seat opposite, Giulia's chaperone, Cristina, checked one last time to make sure the Countess's letter was safe inside its leather case. Cristina was the Countess's second cousin, and her choice as Giulia's escort was meant to reflect the Countess's high position, not to suggest that Giulia herself had any value. The same was true of the nun's trousseau the Countess had provided—a set of sheets, a pair of sandals, white woolen fabric for the habit Giulia would wear once she took final vows, lengths of linen for under-garments, and a daily prayer book, all packed into a chest of walnut wood, with a metal clasp to hold it closed.

"Come, Giulia."

Cristina gathered her skirts and let the driver assist her to the ground. With an effort of will, Giulia followed.

It was unseasonably warm for the end of April, but after the carriage's ovenlike interior the air seemed almost cool. On one side of the street, a long block of houses rose four stories high, with an arcaded walkway running along their fronts. On the other side stood an imposing red brick church, with a double-arched doorway and a huge rose window. The wall Giulia had glimpsed from the carriage began where the church ended, extending along the street as far as she could see, flat and featureless and half as high as the church itself. The wall of Santa Marta.

She tilted back her head. She could just see that shards of stone were set into its top, jutting like teeth against the cloudless sky.

I'm not really standing here. Surely this is a dream.

The journey from Milan had taken a little over two weeks. The carriage was cramped and hot; dust came through the windows, and water when it rained, and even with cushions, the seats were hard enough to make Giulia's back ache by the end of each day. But the discomforts faded beside the pleasure of watching the countryside scroll past the windows, of picnicking in olive groves, of sleeping each night in a different inn—or, if no inn were near, on bedrolls under the stars. Best of all, for the first time in her life she was able to draw to her heart's content, for there was nothing else she had to do and no one to tell her not to do it.

It had been eerie at first to wear the talisman. Giulia couldn't forget the living spirit trapped inside— a little spark of the heavens, compelled into service on the Earth. But it was so much like an ordinary necklace. As day followed day, Anasurymboriel's presence ceased to trouble her.

She'd hoped the spirit's magic would take hold before they reached Santa Marta, and she did what she could to help—dawdling in the courtyards of inns, persuading Cristina to take meals in public dining rooms rather than privately in their lodgings, braiding her hair into becoming styles and belting her dress extra tight. She was still afraid to pray to God, Whose will she had undertaken to defy; she could not pray to the spirit of the talisman, for that would be blasphemous. Sometimes, though, she couldn't help resting her hand on the place where the talisman lay beneath her clothes, and longing with all her strength for her heart's desire.

And now they were in Padua, and her heart's desire had not yet arrived. Staring up at the high, fanged wall of Santa Marta, it occurred to Giulia, for the first time, that she had never asked the sorcerer how long the talisman might need to do its work.

What if I have to spend months in this place? What . . . what if I have to spend years?

She gasped. During the journey, the talisman secure around her throat and the sorcerer's promise safe in her heart, she had never really been afraid. But now it seemed that two weeks' worth of fear fell on her all at once. The wall leaning over her, the convent waiting to swallow her—they were no longer dreamlike, but hideously, horrifyingly real. She imagined herself turning, running, not caring where she was going, so long as she escaped that wall—

Even if she would have done it, it was already too late. Cristina's arm closed firmly around her waist, urging her toward a door set into the brick. The driver followed, carrying her luggage.

Cristina pulled the bell cord. After a moment a wooden flap popped open. A woman peered through the grate that covered it, her face framed in a white wimple and a black veil.

"Yes?"

"I am the representative of Countess Marcelina Borromeo, late of Padua, now of Milan," Cristina said in her most haughty voice. "She has entrusted me with the delivery of this girl, Giulia Borromeo, to be admitted into your house. I have a letter."

"Place it in the wheel," said the nun, and banged the flap closed.

To the door's left, another grate covered an opening in the wall. Cristina slid the letter, with its big wax seal, through the bottom of the grate and into the box that waited there. A grinding sound, and the box began to rotate, delivering the letter to the nun inside. There was a pause. Giulia was aware of the noise of the street—the voices of pedestrians, the clatter of hooves, the creak and thump of the church door as it opened to let out a worshipper.

At last a bolt scraped back and a key rattled in a lock. Christina turned to Giulia.

"Good-bye, my dear."

"Don't leave me here." Giulia had not intended to say it. But her heart was pounding so hard she couldn't think.

"Oh, child." Cristina took Giulia's hands. "Try and make the best of it. None of us can know God's will. You may not see it now, but I'm sure this is His plan for you. I'll pray for you."

She pulled Giulia into her arms. Over her shoulder, Giulia saw that the worshipper, a young man with curly hair, was staring in their direction. Wildly, she imagined struggling, screaming for help. But Cristina was already releasing her, and a hand was closing around her wrist: the nun, accustomed perhaps to reluctant novices.

She felt herself pulled into the dark beyond the doorway. The driver set her luggage over the threshold and stepped back. Her last glimpse of the outside world, as the door swung closed, was Cristina, framed in sunlight, her hand lifted in farewell.

With a thump and a scrape, the nun shot home the bolt and turned the key in the door's great lock.

The floor seemed to heave under Giulia's feet. Her

heart felt as if it might split her chest. It took all the will she had to hold herself still, to swallow the frantic sobs that wanted to burst free.

She stood in a vaulted chamber with a flagstone floor and whitewashed plaster walls. It was not as dark as it had seemed from the street—a candle burned on a little table, and daylight filtered through the open grate of a door opposite the one that had just shut. A large crucifix hung on the wall.

The nun crossed the room, selecting another key from the jangling key ring at her belt.

"This is called the saint's door." She fitted the key to the lock. "Many of our sisters pass through it only once, when they come to us as novices."

But not me, Giulia told the chattering panic inside her. *I'll come out again. I will.*

On the other side of the saint's door, another nun stood waiting. She was young, and wore a white veil rather than a black one. She took the Countess's letter. Beckoning Giulia to follow, she led the way briskly along a wide loggia, its tiled floor bright with the sun that slanted between its columns. Beyond lay a formal garden, with velvety lawns and a reflecting pool flanked by dark cypresses. Giulia stared. She hadn't expected to see anything beautiful in this place.

They entered torchlit corridors. The young nun stopped at last in front of one of the many closed doors that lined the halls. She held up her hand to indicate that Giulia should wait, then knocked and slipped inside. After a few minutes she returned and gestured for Giulia to enter.

The room had the same whitewashed walls and flagstone floor as the first chamber, and was bare of furnishing except for two wooden chests pushed against one wall and a long table by the window. Behind the table sat an elderly woman, dressed in a white wimple, a black veil, and a wide-sleeved white gown. Over the gown she wore a white scapular sewn with a black cross. Another cross shone at her throat, this one of heavy gold. She was as still as an image in an illuminated manuscript, and her gaze was like the gaze of a queen: calm, commanding, unreadable.

Giulia stepped forward. Her heart was beating too fast, but the panic that had overwhelmed her in the antechamber had receded. She could still feel it, ready to rise up again if she wasn't careful—but for now, she was in control.

"My lady." She curtsied deeply.

"We don't use such earthly titles here." The old woman's voice was deep and slow. She had a proud, aristocratic face, with skin like creased linen. On her left hand she wore a broad gold wedding ring. On the first finger of her right gleamed a signet set with a dark gemstone. "I am Santa Marta's abbess. You may call me Madre Damiana."

"Yes, Madre Damiana."

"I understand there has been flooding in Vicenza. Hopefully it did not delay you too greatly."

"Only a day, Madre Damiana." Giulia was surprised. She'd imagined the nuns living in a world no bigger than their walls, unaware of what went on outside. "The waters had mostly receded by the time we passed through."

"God be thanked for that," Madre Damiana said. "We are a family at Santa Marta, Giulia. As the mother of that family, it is my duty to greet each of my daughters as she arrives, to tell her what the family expects of her, and to learn what she expects of the family. Tell me, why have you come to us?"

"I . . ." Giulia hesitated, confused. "I was sent. By Countess Marcelina Borromeo."

"Yes, child, I know it is the Countess's will that you be here." Breaking her stillness, the abbess picked up the Countess's letter, where it lay on top of the ledger she must have been reading before Giulia entered. "I do not approve of forced vocations, though it's impossible to prevent them. Illegitimate daughters, troublesome sisters, unmarriageable nieces, women who are dishonored or crippled or demented—all are pushed through the convent door by fathers and brothers and uncles who do not want the trouble of their care, and care not what trouble they may give to others. Such women bring bitterness and anguish to a community that should include only willing souls." She set the letter aside. "That is why I ask this question of every novice who enters here. Do you truly wish to give your life to God?"

Her eyes were as sharp, as unblinking, as a hawk's. For one wild second, Giulia considered telling the truth. But what good would it do? Santa Marta had already accepted her dowry. The abbess would never set her free. And what was the punishment for being an unwilling nun? Less than five minutes in Madre Damiana's presence was enough to make Giulia sure that she did not want to find out.

She looked down at the floor so her face would not betray her. "I do."

A pause. Then, unexpectedly, Madre Damiana sighed.

"So be it, child. Now, to what the family of Santa Marta expects of you. Prayer and work are our duties here, and those who work give no less honor to God than those who pray. I understand you have skill with a needle."

"I was a seamstress in Count Borromeo's household."

"You'll work in the sewing room, then. I will send word to Suor Columba. For all else, the novice mistress will have charge of you. Her name is Suor Margarita. She will see that you learn our ways."

"Yes, Madre Damiana."

"And I have scheduled your vestition ceremony for this afternoon, so you may become one of us as soon as possible."

"My . . . vestition ceremony?"

"The ceremony of your transition into the novitiate. The moment in which you abandon the profane world of men and embrace the sacred space within these walls. You will make your novice vows and exchange your secular garments for the clothing of our community."

"I have to . . . take off my clothes?"

"How else would you be able to put on your novice habit, child? The clothes you wear now will be given to the poor."

"I had a box—"

"That too."

"But—please, Madre Damiana, there were some things that were my mother's, all I have of her—if I could just keep—"

"No, no, child." The abbess shook her head. "When we enter this house we must renounce the temptations of the world. We must all become the same, rich or poor, noble or commoner. It is a rule I enforce for my novices, and . . . recommend . . . for my nuns."

Giulia stared fiercely at the edge of the table. She had known this might happen, and had taken what steps she could against it. Even so, she'd allowed herself to hope she could keep everything.

"Is there anything else you wish to ask?"

"No, Madre Damiana."

"Then I will escort you to the novice wing."

The abbess led Giulia through a maze of corridors. She walked the way she spoke, slowly and with firm dignity, her tall crook-necked staff tapping in counterpoint to her steps. The nuns they met— young and old, pretty and plain, a few with white veils, most with black—bowed and crossed themselves as she approached. Giulia thought again that she was like a queen, serenely in command of all within her realm.

The novice wing lay on the other side of another garden court, this one a simple rectangle of clipped grass with a sundial in the middle. There was a schoolroom, a chapel, and a dormitory with a double row of beds and a fireplace at one end. Several windows, their shutters drawn against the heat, faced out onto the court.

"This is yours," the abbess said, stopping before a bed beneath one of the windows. A pile of clothing and a blanket lay folded on the mattress. "There is your nun's trousseau chest that you brought with you. Make up the bed with your own sheets, then wait here for Suor Margarita." She dipped her staff toward the pile of clothes. "That is your novice habit. It is not to be put on before the ceremony."

"Yes, Madre Damiana."

"Fear not, child. What is strange to you now will soon become familiar. Our walls are high, but there's freedom to be found here, if you are willing to seek it."

Never, Giulia thought, turning her face away so Madre Damiana would not see what was in her eyes.

"You are welcome among us, Giulia Borromeo, by God's grace." Madre Damiana reached out her right hand, the one with the signet ring, and placed it briefly against Giulia's cheek. "My door is open to you always, as it is to every sister of this community."

She left the dormitory, back straight, staff tapping.

Giulia waited a few minutes, until she was sure the abbess was gone. Then she reached under her gown and pulled out a sheaf of drawings, the ones she'd brought with her from Milan. She'd removed them this morning from her mother's cedar box and secured them against her body with her belt. From her belt-pouch, she took the talisman, the little pouch with her horoscope fragment, and her sketchbook, full of the sketches she had done on the journey.

She looked around. Where could she hide everything? Inside the mattress? At the bottom of the Countess's trousseau chest? But there might be snoops among the novices, and for all she knew the nuns prodded the mattresses and searched the chests on a regular basis. Maybe a loose floor stone? She scuffed about, but the flagstones were solid. The whitewashed plaster walls were equally unhelpful—no holes, no cracks.

That left only one possibility. She crossed to the fireplace, swept clean of ashes for the summer. It was large enough for her to crouch inside. She reached up, feeling with her hands, trying to dislodge as little soot as possible. After a moment she found something, a spot where the brick had crumbled, making a kind of shelf that was large enough to hold the talisman, her horoscope fragment, and the sketchbook. She hated to be parted from the talisman, even briefly, but there was no other way.

The hiding place would be good only for as long as summer lasted. *But that doesn't matter,* she told herself firmly. *Come winter, I'll be gone.*

She ducked out of the fireplace, cleaning her sooty hands on the inside of her skirt. That left the sheaf of drawings from Milan. She undid some of the stitching at the head of her mattress, knotting the severed threads so the hole wouldn't open farther, and stuffed them inside. It wasn't ideal, but it was the best she could manage.

She took the sheets from the trousseau chest and made her bed as the abbess had ordered. She got the sandals out as well, placing them on top of the pile of novice clothing. She tried not to think of the cedar box with her mother's things inside it, given away or thrown away, gone forever, like the topaz necklace. She had nothing of her mother now, except her memories and the drawings hidden in the mattress.

"Oh Mama," she whispered.

Her throat ached with unshed tears. But she was afraid to cry, afraid that if she yielded, even a little, the awful panic would return and swallow her whole.

Since there was nothing else to do, she sat down on the bed to wait. The hateful walls pressed in. Silence sang inside her ears.

It's not for always. Soon I will be free.

CHAPTER 6

❖ False Oaths ❖

"Giulia. Giulia Borromeo."

An unfamiliar voice was calling Giulia's name. She bolted upright in sudden fear. For a moment she couldn't remember where she was. But then she saw the white-robed nun, standing at the foot of the bed, and realized that, without meaning to, she had fallen asleep.

"Come, girl. Get up, get up at once." The nun was a slender, middle-aged woman who might have been pretty if not for her tight-pursed mouth and the frown lines between her eyes. She stood pillar-straight, her black veil falling in symmetrical folds, her hands tucked into her wide sleeves. "We do not sleep during the day at Santa Marta, indeed we do not. The night is for sleeping and the day is for working, and we don't confuse the two."

"I'm sorry." Giulia stood.

"What on Earth have you done to your novice clothes? Pick them up, pick them up at once!" Somehow, the garments had fallen to the floor. Giulia bent to gather them. "No, no, no! Not like that, all wadded up! Fold them properly. When we make order with our hands, our minds follow, and an ordered mind is a door closed on the devil. I'm Suor Margarita, the novice-mistress," the nun continued. "I'll have charge of you for the next year and a half, until you take your final vows. We will get on well, you and I, if you remember that a novice's first duty is to learn, and her second is to obey."

"Yes, Suor," Giulia murmured. She had finished folding the clothes, and held them, with the sandals, clutched to her chest.

"Good, good. Now, here is what you may expect at your ceremony. Madre Damiana will ask you your name, which you will tell her. Then she will ask why you have come to Santa Marta, to which you will reply, 'For God's grace and my salvation.'"

Suor Margarita pursed her lips and waited.

"For God's grace and my salvation," Giulia repeated. She felt numb, as if she hadn't woken.

"Next she will ask you several questions, which you will answer honestly, in fear of God Who sees and hears all. Then you will be clothed and sworn. After that, you'll have time to get acquainted with the other girls. There's an hour of recreation before bedtime. Novices must keep the Little Silence during the day—that is, they may not speak unless spoken to—and all of us keep the Great Silence at night, when speech is entirely forbidden. But during the recreation hour, conversation is allowed."

"Yes, Suor. Suor, may I ask a question?"

"You may."

"Will I have to cut my hair?"

The nun's brows shot up again. "I can see you suffer from the sin of vanity, Giulia Borromeo. We shall have to do something about that, indeed we shall."

"I'm sorry, Suor, it's not that, it's just . . . I'd like to know what to expect."

"A novice who aspires to perfect obedience need not trouble herself with expectations," Suor Margarita said, but then seemed to relent. "No, at Santa Marta we do not cut our novices' hair. Not until they take final vows and receive their religious names."

Well, that's something, anyway. Giulia had thought of this while she was waiting, a horrible possibility she hadn't considered before—for what man would want a shorn-headed wife?

"Ready now? Good, good. Come along."

Suor Margarita led the way briskly out of the novice wing and along the torchlit corridors. They arrived at last in a paved courtyard with a fountain at its center. Beyond the fountain, a little chapel was tucked against the wall, its door flung open. The sun had begun to set, drowning the court in shadow; against the dimness, the chapel's candle-shimmering interior glowed gold.

Suor Margarita entered the chapel without pausing, but Giulia halted on the threshold, astonished yet again by unexpected beauty. The chapel was like a jewel box, with a glossy marble floor, walls paneled in polished wood, and a gleaming gilded ceiling. A crucifix hung above an altar draped in gold-embroidered velvet; nearby, a pedestal supported a life-sized wooden sculpture of Madonna and Child, dressed in real garments of silk and cloth-of-gold. The fat white candles burning in silver candelabra made the whole space slippery with light.

"Come, girl."

Suor Margarita gripped Giulia's arm, urging her toward the altar, where Madre Damiana stood waiting, her crooked staff in her hand.

"Welcome, postulant." The candlelight was kind to the abbess's hawkish features. "Set down what you carry."

Giulia laid the novice clothing by her feet.

"Before God, postulant, declare your name."

"Giulia Borromeo." It came out as a whisper.

"Before God, why have you come to this house of prayer and contemplation?"

Because I was forced to it. "For . . . for God's grace and my salvation."

"Before God, are you free of bond, debt, or obligation to another?"

"Yes."

"Before God, are you free of madness, melancholy, or disease?"

"Yes."

"Then today and in the sight of God, we will effect your entry into the novitiate of Santa Marta, receiving your vows and bestowing on you the habit of our community. Who stands witness to this sacred passage?"

"I do," Suor Margarita said.

"Postulant Giulia Borromeo, remove your clothes."

Giulia obeyed, unfastening her shoes, unbelting her dress, pulling her chemise over her head. She folded each garment neatly as she took it off, piling them all beside the novice clothing. She stood exposed and naked under Madre Damiana's unblinking regard. Instinctively, she crossed her arms over her breasts.

"Kneel," Madre Damiana said.

The marble was hard under Giulia's knees. Though it was not cold, she was shivering.

"O mighty God," Madre Damiana said, "accept this girl who seeks to pledge her life to You, to become the bride of Your holy Son, Jesus Christ. She has put off her secular garments and comes to You in her skin, for naked we are born into the profane world, and naked we must be when we are reborn to the sacred world. Giulia, give me your hands."

The abbess laid her staff on the floor and reached to take Giulia's icy fingers in her own.

"Giulia Borromeo, do you swear yourself to poverty, chastity, and obedience in the novitiate of Santa Marta?"

"Yes," Giulia said through chattering teeth, because

it was not possible to say anything else. But inside herself, with every ounce of will, she cried *No!*

"Do you swear yourself to work, prayer, and contemplation in the novitiate of Santa Marta?"

"Yes." *Oh, God forgive me, no, no, no!*

"It is well." The abbess released Giulia's hands and reached into her pocket, producing a small silver flask. "I mark you now with consecrated oil as a sign of your pledge." She moistened her thumb with the contents of the flask and traced a cross on Giulia's forehead. "Rise, novice Giulia, and put on your new clothes."

Giulia stumbled as she got to her feet; Suor Margarita steadied her. With shaking hands she pulled on the coarse linen chemise and the rough gray dress, kneeling again to tie on the sandals from the Countess's trousseau chest. Suor Margarita helped her with the white kerchief, wrapping it around her head and knotting the ends so that no hair showed.

"You are welcome among us." Madre Damiana drew Giulia close and set a kiss upon her cheek. "Go now to your duties."

Giulia followed Suor Margarita into the convent's kitchen, a cavernous space crammed with stoves, racks of pots and pans and crockery, and several long tables where white-veiled nuns, their sleeves tied back and their habits swathed in aprons, were preparing food. It was as hot as an oven, but the smells were delicious, and Giulia remembered that she hadn't eaten since the morning.

"Sit there." Suor Margarita pointed to a bench in

the corner. "I must go sing Vespers and then bring my novices to supper, but I'll be back to fetch you after that. I'll see you're brought something to eat."

She bustled off. One of the nuns brought over a bowl of lamb and olive stew and a hunk of fresh bread, offering it silently but with a smile. Giulia devoured it. Watching the busy scene before her, she thought miserably of the false oaths she had just sworn, in sight of God, before the Cross. Another lie to add to the many she had told since she learned she was to be sent away, another sin to increase the ones she already carried. Through the scents of the kitchen, she could still smell the oil with which the abbess had marked her, heavy-sweet and musty. She pulled the hanging sleeve of her novice habit over her hand and scrubbed at her forehead, scrubbing and scrubbing until her skin felt sore.

By the time Suor Margarita returned, cauldrons of water had been set to boil, and the kitchen workers were bringing in trays stacked with dirty dishes. Giulia followed the novice mistress through the maze of corridors. The day seemed like a long nightmare that would not end.

The sound of voices rose as they neared the dormitory. Inside, in a flicker of candlelight that made the space no more cheerful, girls sat in groups on the beds or stood at the windows, talking, laughing, playing games.

"Girls, girls!" Suor Margarita clapped her hands.

The talk ceased. They all turned to look: ten pairs of eyes in ten watchful faces, ten bodies clad in identical gray gowns, ten heads wrapped in identical white kerchiefs.

"This is Giulia Borromeo, all the way from Milan. I know you'll do everything you can to make her welcome and help her learn our ways. Give Giulia a nice greeting, please!"

"Hello, Giulia," they chorused. Giulia, uneasy under so many eyes, nodded.

"Good, good. Now go in, Giulia, and meet your new friends." Suor Margarita gave Giulia a little push. "Alessia, you are in charge."

"Yes, Suor Margarita," said one of the girls in the group by the window.

The novice mistress's brisk footsteps receded down the hall. Most of the novices were already turning back to their interrupted activities, but the girls by the window still stared, their expressions unwelcoming, as Giulia crossed to her bed.

On the neighboring mattress, two novices were playing some sort of game.

"Hello," said one of them, a pretty girl of about sixteen, with dark curls escaping from her kerchief. The other, the same age or perhaps a little younger, covered her mouth and giggled. "Watch out," she whispered, her eyes moving beyond Giulia to something at her back.

Giulia turned. The girl Suor Margarita had put in charge of the dormitory had detached herself from her friends.

"I'm Alessia," she said, her tone conveying the extreme importance of this information, and her extreme condescension in providing it. She looked older than the others, perhaps nineteen, with a prominent jaw and crooked teeth. She stood with her hands folded into her sleeves, like Suor Margarita. "I'm the senior novice here. By God's grace, I take my vows at year's end."

"And we can't wait," one of the game-players muttered.

Alessia shot her a dagger look, then returned her attention to Giulia. "Are you to be a choir nun, new girl, or a *conversa?*"

"I'm sorry," Giulia said. "I don't know what those are."

"A choir nun is a noblewoman," Alessia said in a patient voice, as if Giulia were a small and very stupid child. "We wear the black veil, and say the Holy Offices, and hold the positions of authority. A *conversa* is a commoner. They wear the white veil, and do the servants' work."

"I don't know which I am. No one told me."

Alessia sighed. "Surely you know whether you're noble or common."

Giulia felt the stresses of the long day flare abruptly into anger. "My father was Count Federico di Assulo Borromeo of Milan," she snapped. "My mother was a seamstress in his household. So why don't you tell me, if you can, whether I am noble or common?"

"Well, it's obvious, isn't it." Alessia's lip curled. "I knew you were too coarse to be noble, with that big nose of yours."

"My nose is from my father. That's one part of me

that is noble beyond a doubt."

A flush had risen to Alessia's cheeks, visible even in the dim candlelight. "You'll have to do something about your pride, new girl, if you want to get along here. We don't like girls who have ideas above their station."

She turned on her heel and stalked back to her friends. Beside Giulia, the game-players were snickering.

"Coarse indeed," said the one who'd said hello. "She should talk, with her ugly horse-face."

"You're in for it now," said the other. She was as homely as her friend was pretty, with small mistrustful eyes. "She's not used to being talked back to."

"I'm Isotta," said the pretty one. "That's Bice. We're *conversae* too."

"I'm Giulia."

"We know," Isotta said. "You can join our game, if you want."

Later, after Suor Margarita had returned to supervise the removing of habits, the saying of prayers, and the blowing out of candles, Giulia lay on her back, staring up at the shadowed ceiling. The window shutters had been opened to let in the cool night air; if she tipped back her head, she could see, through the window above her bed, a slice of sky dusted with pinpoint stars.

Exhausted as she was, she couldn't fall asleep in this unfamiliar place. For nearly all her life, she'd felt alone among the people who surrounded her.

Now she was alone in a different way—alone among strangers. She had always felt she did not belong at Palazzo Borromeo, but at least it had been home. At least there had been two people who loved her. She pictured Annalena's face, and Maestro's. She thought, as she hadn't for a long time, of the way her mother used to smooth her hair back before she slept.

The tears she'd fought all day came at last. She buried her face in her hard pillow so the others wouldn't hear.

CHAPTER 7

❖ A Small Blue Flame ❖

The bell for Prime began to ring just after dawn, join-
ing other bells in monasteries and nunneries all over
Padua. Prime was the third of the eight Holy Offices,
or prayer services, that gave structure to the monastic
day, but at Santa Marta the nuns had a special dispen-
sation to combine it with Matins and Lauds, the two
night Offices, so they weren't forced to get up twice in
the middle of the night.

The bells brought Giulia awake, and to the knowledge, like a stone pressing on her chest, that four
weeks had passed and she was still a prisoner at Santa
Marta.

She got out of bed. Around her in the half-light of early morning, the other novices yawned, stretched, and rubbed their eyes. Suor Margarita came bustling in, clapping her hands, the signal for the girls to line up at the washbasin. Alessia, closest to her final vows, was first, while Giulia, the most recently arrived, brought up the rear. Not much water remained by the time her turn came, the other girls having splashed much of it out onto the floor. She washed her face, neck, and hands, then returned to her bed and took her scratchy novice dress out of the trousseau chest where she folded it at night.

Pulling it on over her chemise, she was aware of the talisman against her skin. She had retrieved it, along with the pouch that held her horoscope frag-ment, the night after her arrival, counting slowly to a thousand after the candles were blown out, then slipping out of bed and creeping to the fireplace, dreading all the while that one of the girls would wake. She could wear the pouch and talisman in safety, for they were hidden by the high neck of her chemise. There was no danger of anyone glimpsing them when she was undressing either—except for the vestition ceremony, no one at Santa Marta ever saw anyone else unclothed. A novice slept in her chemise, washed without taking it off, and changed it once a week by putting a new chemise over her head while unlacing the old one and letting it slip over her shoulders and fall at her feet.

Giulia bound up her hair as best she could—she had yet to perfect the trick of knotting the kerchief-ends so her braid wouldn't fall out—then made her bed according to Suor Margarita's exacting requirements, tugging the blanket smooth, placing the pillow just so. The novice mistress also expected her girls to sweep the floors, fetch the wash water, and empty the chamber pots—something that caused grumbling, because in other convents such work was done by the *conversae*, the servant nuns, at least for the girls of noble blood. Suor Margarita supervised, pacing between the beds, clapping her hands or snapping her fingers at any sign of dawdling or whispering. Giulia had been certain she was going to hate Suor Margarita, but for all her attention to discipline, the novice mistress was not unkind. The other night, when Paola had had the toothache, she'd come in three times to change the girl's compresses.

Suor Margarita clapped her hands again. The novices assembled for the walk to the refectory. Another clap, and they left the dormitory, hurrying through the corridors, hands clasped at their waists and eyes downcast, like a line of ducklings behind a mother duck. Others made way for them: black-veiled choir nuns returning from singing Prime, a lone *conversa* lugging a pile of linens so high she could hardly see over it.

The sun had risen by the time they reached the refectory, its first rays slanting through the east-facing windows. The refectory was the biggest room at Santa Marta, with whitewashed walls and a vaulted ceiling hung with a forest of chandeliers. Tables and benches to accommodate nearly one hundred and fifty nuns and novices were arranged across the red tile floor.

Suor Margarita led the way to the novices' table. Giulia's seat faced the dais at the head of the room, where Madre Damiana and the other nuns of high authority sat. Above the dais, an enormous fresco of the Last Supper spanned the wall, its rightmost third hidden behind a canvas-draped scaffolding. In the portion Giulia was able to see, the painted disciples enjoyed themselves at the banquet, lifting glasses, throwing back their heads in laughter, leaning toward one another to exchange words or gestures. Their poses were stylized, but their faces were the faces of real people, each one individual and distinct. Jesus sat in their midst, sad amid the revelry, knowing what his companions did not yet understand. All the colors were beautiful, but Giulia thought the sapphire blue of Jesus' cloak was most beautiful of all, a color so deep and yet so clear that it seemed to shine with its own inner light.

The fresco wasn't the first painting Giulia had seen. There were the faded hunting scenes in the antechambers of Palazzo Borromeo, the altarpiece in the family's chapel, and the small, jewel-like Annunciation in her father's study, which he'd let her look at whenever she visited him. But none of them had been anything like this fresco—a painting that did not simply depict a series of images, but told a story, speaking to the heart and mind as well as to the eyes. Each time Giulia looked at it, she noticed something new: the angle of a disciple's gesture, the nuance of another's expression, the bruises on the apricots in the dish by Jesus' right hand, the dog peeping from under the tablecloth, the fact that the chandeliers, as well as the ceiling and windows, were exactly like those of the real refectory around her, so that each meal eaten here took on a little of the sanctity of that ancient, holy Supper. Looking at the fresco made her fingers burn, the way they did when she saw something she especially wanted to draw. She couldn't bear, sometimes, how much she missed her sketchbook.

Madre Damiana entered at last, austere in her white robes, accompanied by her second-in-command and the rest of her administrators. The *conversae* who worked in the kitchen brought in the meal: fresh bread and butter, hot soup, and water to drink, cold from the well. It was plain, like all the food at Santa Marta, but well-prepared and plentiful.

The refectory filled with the sounds of spoons clinking on crockery, mugs thumping on tables, and the voice of the nun at the lectern, reading excerpts from the life of Marta, the convent's patron saint. With Suor Margarita distracted by her meal, Giulia was able at last to tug at her kerchief, which she had tied too tight. Around her, the other girls were also taking advantage of the novice mistress's temporary lapse of attention. Bettina and Barbara traded whispers. Bice and Isotta, always playing games, stole spoonfuls from each other's bowls. Alessia sat among her acolytes—Costanza, and Nelia, and Elisabetta, and Paola—managing to look pious even while chewing. Everyone ignored Lisa, who had a hunched back and spoke as if her mouth were full of pebbles.

They ignored Giulia too. It didn't have to be that way—Bice and Isotta would have welcomed her, if she'd cared to join them. But though she'd been grateful for their acceptance the first night, she had not tried to make friends with them. She was used to being on her own, and anyway, it was safer. She didn't want to slip and let down her guard, even for a second. No one must ever guess the hatred she felt for this place. No one must ever suspect her burning determination to be free.

The meal ended, and the nuns separated to their work. For Giulia, this meant Suor Columba's sewing room. If there were a more inappropriately named nun at Santa Marta, Giulia hadn't met her. No one could be less like a dove than skinny old Columba, with her slash of a mouth and her wintry eyes and her willow switch, always ready to slice at the arms or shoulders of seamstresses who displeased her. She ran the sewing room like the tyrant of her own tiny city-state. Even the older nuns feared her.

Today the work was bedsheets, to be hemmed, seamed, and darned. Such simple sewing was far below Giulia's skill—at Palazzo Borromeo she'd been a garment maker, working with complicated patterns and rich fabrics. But at Santa Marta, only the choir nuns were allowed to do fine needlework. And unlike the novices of noble blood, who worked only in the morning and spent their afternoons in the schoolroom, learning the duties they would follow once they became choir nuns, Giulia, a *conversa*, had to sit stitching all day long, with only an hour's break for noon prayers and the midday meal. There wasn't even the relief of conversation, for Suor Columba and her willow switch strictly enforced the Little Silence.

The morning crawled by. Giulia finished a hem, knotted her thread and bit it off, picked up another sheet. And another. And another. Growing up, she'd often cursed her sewing duties for the time they took away from the drawing and reading and daydreaming she preferred—but if being the Count's bastard had its disadvantages, there had also been compensations, one of which was that as long as she got her work done, she could come and go more or less as she pleased. Not until now had she fully appreciated that freedom. At Santa Marta there was no freedom at all, only rules: rules for behavior, rules for speech, rules for everything except perhaps breathing. Even worse was the sameness, every day exactly like the one before—the same waking up, the same stitching, the same meals in the refectory, the same hour of recreation—all of it marked, at the same intervals, by the same bells for the same Holy Offices.

It had been the end of April when Giulia arrived. Now it was the end of May. Just four weeks—yet it felt like four years. She wondered sometimes, with a catch of panic, whether she could bear the time until the talisman set her free.

The bell rang at last for Sext, the noon service. Giulia stood and stretched her back, which ached from the hours on the hard bench, then made her way to the novice wing for midday prayers. Afterward, she lined up with the others for the walk to the refectory, where she ate her meal and then prepared to return to the sewing room.

As she stepped through the refectory door, a nun she had never seen before caught her arm.

"Come," the nun said. She had smooth olive skin and wide brown eyes, and looked very young—not much older, perhaps, than Giulia herself. She wore the black veil of a noblewoman.

"But what—" Giulia stopped, remembering the Little Silence.

The young nun smiled and beckoned, then turned, her shoulder dipping. For a moment Giulia thought she had stumbled—but then she saw that the nun limped, as if one leg were shorter than the other.

The nun led the way through a maze of corridors. Giulia followed, the brief pleasure of escaping the sewing room fast chilling into apprehension. They had left the parts of the convent she knew, and she had no idea where she was being taken. Had she done something wrong?

The room into which Giulia's escort ushered her at last was enormous. One whole side of it was open to the air, facing a sunny courtyard—the same court-yard, Giulia realized, that she'd seen on her first day at Santa Marta, for there was the chapel, snugged up against the wall. In the flooding light, two black-veiled nuns sat before small desks or lecterns. Two more nuns worked at a long drafting table strewn with paper, pens, inkpots, and other drawing materials. They raised their heads briefly as Giulia and her guide entered, then bent back to their labor.

Another table was crowded with glass vessels, pottery bowls, and flasks and bottles of every description. Here, a fifth nun was grinding something in a mortar, her sleeves tied back, her habit covered by a bibbed apron. She wore a white *conversa's* veil.

Giulia's escort continued into the chamber, but Giulia stopped short at the threshold. The bright space smelled of dust and raw wood and plaster, and of other things, musty and unfamiliar. What kind of place was this?

The nun at the mortar put down her pestle and came forward, cleaning her hands on her apron.

"Angela, you may go back to work." The young nun dipped her head in acknowledgment and limped toward the table. "Giulia, welcome! I'm Suor Humilità, the mistress of this workshop. Come, let's talk."

She led the way toward a door on the chamber's far side. Giulia followed, more confused than ever. A workshop? With a *conversa* as its mistress?

Beyond the door lay a small chamber furnished with another paper-strewn table, a large cabinet, and a pair of chairs.

"Sit," Suor Humilità said. Giulia obeyed. The nun rummaged among the documents on the table. She was a short, stocky woman, not young but not old either, with a wide mouth, apple-pink cheeks, and deep-set eyes as dark as olive pits.

"Ah!" she exclaimed, extracting a sheet of paper.

She held it out. "Is this yours?"

It was one of the drawings Giulia had brought with her from Milan: the *cortile* of Palazzo Borromeo, looking down from Maestro's window. She stared at it, shocked. Had they discovered her mattress hiding place?

"Child." The nun sat down beside her. "You have done nothing wrong. I just need to be sure that this is from your hand." She touched the initials at the bottom of the sketch. "G.B. Giulia Borromeo. Yes?"

There was no point denying it. Giulia nodded. "Where . . . how did you find it?"

"It was in the box you brought with you."

"The box?" She'd been sure she had removed all her drawings.

"The abbess herself discovered it. Who taught you to draw?"

"No one, Suor."

"No one?" The small dark eyes were uncomfortably keen. "You had no painters in your family? No drawing master?"

"No, Suor. I've always just . . . drawn, ever since I can remember."

"Well, God has given you talent, and I'd like to have the use of it. I want you to become an apprentice in my workshop, to train to be a painter."

"A painter? But women can't be painters!" Giulia caught herself. "I'm sorry. It's just that—I mean, I've never heard—"

"Ah, child. Women can be many things—if only in the convent." Suor Humilità rose and took Giulia's arm. "Come, I'll show you."

She led Giulia back into the big room and over to the drafting table.

"Lucida and Perpetua, my journeymen. They are well beyond their apprenticeships, but not yet masters." Suor Perpetua, white-veiled, nodded; Suor Lucida, in choir-nun black, flashed a dimpled smile. "Many of the paintings we make here are for the glory and beauty of Santa Marta. But we're in demand elsewhere as well, God be praised. Paintings from my workshop hang in holy places all over Padua, and beyond it too."

Giulia heard the pride in Suor Humilità's voice— the sort of pride nuns were not supposed to have, at least according to Suor Margarita.

"Lucida and Perpetua are making studies for an altarpiece for the monastery of San Giustina. And over here"—she drew Giulia toward the lecterns—"are my two master painters, Domenica and Benedicta. They are working on a private commission, six paintings of scenes from the life of Santa Barbara."

The two artists—one tall and stern, the other tiny and ancient—were working on wood panels. On each of these, a scene had been drawn in ink or charcoal and overlaid with shadows and highlights in shades of brown. The painters were layering color atop this monochrome, fleshing out the figures and the background around the saint, who was already complete. The saint was slender, with elegant hands and long golden hair, clad in a dress of profound, glowing blue.

"Oh!" Giulia exclaimed. "The blue! It's the same

blue as in the painting in the refectory, isn't it?"

Suor Humilità's wide mouth curved in a smile. "You've got a good eye, child. That certainly is my blue. It's my own invention. I took more care with it than I did with the gold of Our Lord's halo, for the blue is rarer."

"*You* painted the fresco?" Giulia spoke before she thought, but Suor Humilità did not seem insulted.

"Indeed I did. With my artists' help, of course."

Giulia was awed. She'd assumed the fresco was the work of some famous artist—a male artist, of course. "It's the most beautiful thing I've ever seen."

"All of us give glory to God in our own way," Suor Humilità said, pleased. "My way, the way of every woman in this room, is the painter's way. God gives us this beautiful world, and we give it back to Him, humbly and with gratitude, in our painting."

Giulia could have stood for hours watching the details take shape under the artists' skillful brushes, but Suor Humilità pulled her away, toward the table where the young nun who had come to fetch her was carefully scooping a dark powder from the mortar onto a marble slab.

"This is where we prepare our pigments. Angela has just finished grinding charred animal bones, which she will mix with water and make into a pigment that we call bone black."

Suor Angela looked up and smiled, then went back to her work.

"So, Giulia Borromeo. What do you say, now that you've seen my little kingdom? Will you join us?"

"But the sewing room—"

"You'll never sew another stitch, unless you want to. Come, say yes, for Angela's sake! I know she's been longing for another apprentice to help her grind colors."

Giulia felt as if she were dreaming, as if she were still lying on her crackly straw mattress and any moment would be roused by the ringing of Prime. It wasn't just the bewildering suddenness with which this had happened. It wasn't just the prospect of being able to draw again, much as she wanted that—oh, how she wanted it! It was this workshop of women— women artists, creating paintings and altarpieces as if they were men. Before today, she had never imagined such a thing was possible.

Suor Humilità was waiting.

"Yes," Giulia said. "Oh, yes."

Suor Humilità's sudden smile was like the sun. She seized both Giulia's hands in hers. "Then tomorrow, we'll get started!"

In the dormitory that evening, the novices talked and laughed in the daily hour of recreation—all but Lisa, who looked on longingly from a distance, and Giulia, who sat on her bed, her head free at last of the hated kerchief.

She was aware of Isotta and Bice, playing another of their games on the bed by hers. They hadn't bothered to invite her to join them tonight. She was aware also of Alessia and her clique, gathered in their usual spot by the window. Alessia was eating nuts; she always seemed to have a supply on hand, sometimes sharing them with the others, but more often consuming them all herself. Alessia was a bully—she reminded Giulia of Piero, except that she forced others to do her dirty work, looking on while Nelia or Costanza or Elisabetta trod on heels or whispered taunts or pulled the hair of the girls they disliked. Giulia was nursing a bruise on her arm where Nelia had pinched her last night at supper.

Just now, though, Giulia's thoughts were far from Alessia and her cronies. She could hardly believe her good fortune. No more sewing room drudgery, no more switch-cuts from Suor Columba. She'd be free to draw again—maybe even to learn something about painting. Most amazing of all, she would be in the company of painters—real painters! Even if they were nuns.

When her father had been alive, he'd summoned her to his study every year. He always asked the same questions—was she healthy? Happy in her work? Treated well?—and she always gave the same dutiful answers, wondering if he really paid attention to anything she said. When they were done, he would allow her to stand for a little while before the small painting of the Annunciation that hung on the wall. It had seemed, then, the most beautiful thing in the world. How had the artist made the colors so bright and clear? The faces of the Madonna and the angel Gabriel so otherworldly, and yet so real? What would it be like to have the skill to create something so exquisite? Giulia had sometimes let herself daydream about that, about what it might be like to apprentice in a painter's workshop, though she knew it was stupid even to think about such things. Girls could draw, if they were permitted. But they could not become painters, any more than they could become astrologers or scholars or merchants. Like most everything else in the world, that was reserved for men.

Yet here, as real as life, were women painters— six of them, a whole workshop full. How had that come about? Who had established the workshop, who had taught them? She tried to imagine living as these artists did—forever prisoned within convent walls, yet following pursuits few worldly women could aspire to.

What had Suor Humilità said? *Women can be many things, if only in the convent.*

She remembered how the workshop mistress had seized her hands and smiled, and felt a stir of guilt. She knew the offer of apprenticeship hadn't really been an offer, in the sense of something that could be refused. Novices didn't choose, they only obeyed—she could not have said no even if she had wanted to. And she hadn't wanted to. Still, she felt uncomfortable. For of course she could never really be Suor Humilità's apprentice. She was leaving Santa Marta.

I'll work hard, she promised herself. *While I'm here, however long or short a time that is, I'll strive each day to do my best.*

Her presence might be false. But her work would be true.

She shifted around on her bed so she could lean her elbows on the windowsill. Moonlight silvered the clipped grass of the garden court, and the sky was thick with stars. She gazed up at them, twinkling jewel-points against the blackness of the farthest celestial sphere, moving in their slow dance around the Earth. Had she really overlooked the *cortile* drawing when she removed the others from the cedar box? Or had it been something more than her own carelessness that put the drawing in Madre Damiana's hands? She felt the talisman, heavy at her throat. Could this astonishing stroke of luck be the spirit's doing? Was the workshop of women, somehow, the way to escape Santa Marta?

She caught her breath. From the bed nearby, Bice glanced up, then returned to her game.

The bell rang for Compline, the final service of the day. Elsewhere in Santa Marta, the choir nuns were filing toward the nuns' chapel, partitioned from the larger church so that their singing could be heard, but no profane eye could spy them at their worship. The *conversae* were completing their final chores—hanging the last sheets in the laundry, laying the last tables in the refectory. In a little while, the Great Silence would begin, the quiet that forbade any but the most essential words, and lasted until dawn.

As for the novices, it was bedtime. Suor Margarita paused in the doorway after the candles were blown out, making sure all was in order, her white habit gleaming in the dimness; then she turned and was gone.

That night, Giulia dreamed she was running on an

86

endless plain, her hair loose, her feet bare. Ahead of her danced a small blue flame—the luminous blue of Santa Barbara's dress, the shimmering blue of Jesus' cloak, the drowning blue of the sorcerer's robe, the unyielding blue of the talisman. On and on it led her, farther and farther, until she left the Earth entirely and began to rise through the planetary spheres. They were as clear as crystal and as permeable as water, and they sang as she passed through them, the flame drawing her on and on—never out of sight, yet never within reach.

When the bells woke her in the morning, she found, for the first time since her arrival, that she did not dread the day ahead.

CHAPTER 8

✤ The Workshop ✤

Suor Angela was waiting again outside the refectory. She smiled when Giulia emerged, the shy smile Giulia remembered from yesterday, then limped off down the hall.

"You don't have to walk behind me," she said after a moment, glancing over her shoulder, the one that dipped. "Nun or novice, it doesn't matter in our workshop. Apprentice and artist are the only ranks that count there, and you and I are both apprentices."

"You're an apprentice?" Giulia said, forgetting the Little Silence. She'd assumed, perhaps because of the black veil, that Suor Angela was a journeyman, like the two nuns at the table yesterday.

"Yes. I've been with the Maestra for three years now."

The Maestra. Suor Humilità, of course. It made Giulia think of Maestro and his untidy study, where she might be heading at this time of morning if she were still in Milan. Swallowing a surge of homesickness, she hurried to catch up.

The smell of the workshop greeted them at the threshold—a blend of familiar and unfamiliar scents, the mysterious odors of the painter's craft. Giulia breathed deeply as she entered. *Today, I'll sketch again.* The thrill of it ran through her like light.

Suor Domenica was already there, standing under one of the arches that opened onto the courtyard and removing the cloth that draped her lectern.

"Good morning, Domenica," Suor Angela said.

Suor Domenica glanced up. She was rod-straight and rake-thin, her ivory skin pulled tight over the bones of her face. Her brows were creased in what looked like a habitual frown.

"I'll need vermilion today. A good quantity, mind you."

"I ground it yesterday," the younger nun replied. "It's ready whenever you want it."

"Hmph. Well, prepare some tempera then. Perhaps now that we have an extra pair of hands, there will be more doing and less waiting."

Suor Domenica turned back to her lectern, folding the cloth that had covered it with precise, tight motions.

"You mustn't mind the way she talks," Suor Angela whispered. "She wears a prickly hair shirt under her habit, and it makes her awfully cross. Now, let's put on aprons and get to work."

Along the side wall, shelves stretched from floor to ceiling, holding a vast collection of jars, bowls, boxes, and other containers, many marked with neatly written labels. Nearby, bibbed aprons hung on pegs.

The two girls tied aprons over their habits. Suor Angela moved to the shelves, taking down a large flask, a big bowl, a smaller one, several palm-sized squares of fabric, a pair of spoons, and a metal pin. She led the way over to the preparation table. Its clutter had been cleared away, except for a clay jug of water and, strangely, a basket of speckled eggs.

"I'm going to show you how to mix tempera," Angela said, putting down what she carried. "I'll be showing you how to do a lot of things. If there's anything you don't understand, just ask. Questions are good. The Maestra says they're one of the best ways to learn."

"It's all right for me to talk?"

"Why wouldn't it be?"

"Suor Margarita says that novices must keep the Little Silence during the day, unless they are spoken to first."

"Oh my goodness!" Suor Angela laughed. "That wouldn't be at all practical, with everything we have to do and learn! Some of the other workshops keep the Little Silence, but we don't."

"There are other painting workshops?"

"No, no. The other workshops are for other things, embroidered altar cloths and linens for brides' trousseaux and ointments from our herb gardens. We're known for our herbals—people send all the way from Venice to buy them. Don't look so surprised!" The young nun laughed again. "Nuns aren't supposed to be worldly, but we must exist within the world, we must eat and be clothed and maintain our buildings and beautify our church. Santa Marta has an endowment, the same as all the big convents, but we need more than that to make ends meet."

"Oh," Giulia said, trying to grasp the idea of nuns as merchants.

"All our workshops do well, by God's grace, but Suor Humilità's workshop most of all. It's the only one of its kind, you know, perhaps in all the world. It was founded by Suor Catarina Altichieri more than fifty years ago. She had painting lessons as a child, and when she took vows at Santa Marta she was permitted to continue, and to train other sisters. Suor Catarina's paintings were only for Santa Marta, but when Suor Anna Sovato became the next Maestra, her work was so fine that other convents began to commission her. By the time Suor Anna retired, the workshop was known throughout Padua. Now, under our Maestra, our fame has spread even farther."

"I was wondering . . ." Giulia hesitated.

"What? You can ask me anything."

"Well, I was wondering how a *conversa* could become the mistress of a workshop. I thought only the noble nuns could do that."

"Ah." Suor Angela nodded. "Yes, that is unusual. But it's not easy to find women who can be trained to be good painters. We can't afford to overlook talent, whether it is held by a noblewoman or a commoner. As for Suor Humilità . . . commoner or not, no one else could have become Maestra. She is a genius. Do you know there's a color named after her?"

"The blue," Giulia guessed.

"That's right. Well, it's not actually named after her, but after the altarpiece where she first used it, for the cloak of our Lord Jesus Christ, as he endured His Passion in the Garden of Gethsemane. Passion blue, they call it, the most beautiful blue in Padua, maybe in the whole of the Veneto."

Passion blue. It seemed instantly right, as if there could be no other name for a color so profound, so luminously alive. In her mind's eye, Giulia saw the small blue flame that had danced through her dream last night.

"How old are you, Giulia?"

"I'm seventeen."

"And I'm nineteen!" Suor Angela clapped her hands. "We're almost of an age. How lovely!"

She sounded genuinely delighted, for all the world as if she were not a choir nun and Giulia merely a *conversa.* Giulia thought of Alessia and her contempt, of the servant nuns at their separate tables in the refectory. Could this workshop really be so different from the rest of Santa Marta?

"Oh dear. Domenica is glaring at us. We'd better get started." Suor Angela turned toward the table and took an egg from the basket. "Now, to make paint, you need something to bind the pigment—not just so you can paint with it, but so it will dry hard and won't fade. You can use oil, or"—she held up the egg—"you can use egg yolk mixed with water."

"*Egg yolk?*"

"Yes. It's called egg tempera. The Maestra doesn't use it very much these days, but she still prefers it for smaller panels like the Santa Barbara paintings. But regular egg tempera dries very fast. We are adding oil as well as water, so the artists will have more time to work."

Suor Angela cracked the egg on the edge of the big bowl. "You drain the white through your fingers, like this. Then you dry off the yolk." With a delicate, practiced motion, she rolled the yolk onto one of the fabric squares. "The yolk has a membrane, which must be broken with a pin—" She pierced the yolk and let it drain into the smaller bowl. "Now a spoon of water from the jug—and stir—and the same amount of oil." Taking a fresh spoon, she poured from the flask. "This is walnut oil. The Maestra likes it best. It must be added slowly, stirring all the time. Here. You try."

With her left hand Giulia tipped the spoon as Suor Angela had done, spinning a thread-thin stream of oil into the bowl, while with her right hand she stirred. It was harder than it looked to coordinate both actions. But soon the yolk smoothed and thickened.

"There. That's finished. You can take it to Domenica."

"How does it turn into paint?"

"The painter has her pigments ready in jars, and she mixes them with the yolk. Even with oil added to the egg, it can be done only a little at a time, or it will dry up."

Domenica accepted the bowl without thanks, setting it down on a table that also held brushes, a paint-caked rectangle of wood with a hole at one end, and several stoppered jars. "Get along," she snapped, when Giulia didn't move away at once. "You've too much to do to be standing idly about."

Disappointed, for she had hoped to see the paint being mixed, Giulia rejoined Suor Angela, who, despite her limp, had managed to drag a large wooden washtub into the courtyard and was tipping in buckets of water drawn from the fountain. "There's always washing up to do, so I keep this ready," she said. When the tub was full, they fetched brooms and began to sweep the floor, a task interrupted twice as the other artists arrived and called for materials—egg tempera for Suor Benedicta at her lectern, ink for Suor Perpetua at the drafting table. Suor Benedicta was elderly, with a face like a wizened apple; she smiled when Giulia handed her the egg mixture, revealing gums almost empty of teeth. Suor Perpetua, middle-aged and homely, her skin pitted with smallpox scars, greeted Giulia kindly. "We are all very happy you've joined us, my dear."

Suor Lucida was the last to appear, breezing into the workshop well after Terce, the midmorning Office. Suor Domenica's head came up like a hawk's.

"Oh dear," Angela whispered to Giulia over her broom. "There will be words now."

"How kind of you to grace us with your presence, Lucida." Suor Domenica's tone was icy.

"Good morning to you too, Domenica," Suor Lucida replied sweetly, settling herself on a stool at the drafting table.

"What excuse do you offer for your lateness?"

"I do not need to excuse myself, Domenica, but since you ask, I had preparations to attend to."

"And those preparations were more important than the work that waits for you here? Your frivolity is a disgrace."

Suor Lucida rolled her eyes. "Your censoriousness is a bore."

"The Maestra will know of this." Suor Domenica was rigid with anger. Beside her, Suor Benedicta painted on, as serenely as if she were alone. "I shall see to it."

"Please yourself." Suor Lucida shrugged. "Oh! I haven't said hello to our new apprentice yet!"

She jumped off her stool in a swirl of white robes.

"Welcome, Giulia!" Within the severe frame of her black veil, her face was lovely, her smile full of secret joy, as if she knew something wonderful and was just about to reveal it. Her habit was made not of wool or linen, but of lustrous silk, and instead of a cloth belt she wore a tooled leather girdle, cinched tight under her breasts, giving her robe more the look of a court gown than a nun's habit. "Don't mind Domenica, she lives to find fault. The rest of us are much more easygoing, I promise. Oh! You must come to my dinner party on Thursday! Everyone else is coming, except Domenica of course, she'd never do anything so *frivolous*. Say you'll come!"

Dinner party? Do nuns have dinner parties? "Thank you, but I don't know if I'm allowed."

"Oh, pish. Certainly you're allowed. I'll speak to the Maestra. Good, that's settled! And now I must get to work, or the good Lord only knows what tales Domenica will tell."

And she returned to her stool, trailing the scent of roses.

Giulia turned to Suor Angela. "Can I really go?"

"As long as the Maestra agrees. I'm sure she will."

"I didn't think . . . that is, I thought everyone ate in the refectory."

"Some of the wealthier sisters have their own *conversae* to cook for them." Suor Angela began sweeping again. "Lucida is a Cornaro—so is Madre Damiana, actually, Lucida is her niece—and they're one of the richest families in Padua. Domenica thinks she's too worldly, and even the Maestra gets angry with her sometimes." Suor Angela glanced toward the drafting table, where Suor Lucida was chatting to Suor Perpetua, exactly as if the homely nun did not wear a white veil and Suor Lucida a black. "But she has such a generous heart."

Later, after they had finished the sweeping, prepared yet more egg yolks, and torn up a dozen frayed sheets for rags, the girls knelt by the washtub, scrubbing egg-encrusted bowls. It was baking hot; the near-noon sun lay like iron on Giulia's back and shoulders, making her heavy dress more uncomfortable than ever. She was thirsty, and though she had wadded up her skirts as a cushion against the stone, her knees were starting to hurt.

"Suor Angela," she said after several minutes of splashing.

"I'm just Angela." The young nun looked up to smile. "We don't use titles here."

"Um, Angela. When will we be allowed to draw?"

"We have drawing time with the Maestra every day, after the midday meal. And we can draw as we like if our other work is done."

"Oh. I thought—" Giulia stopped.

"What?"

"I just thought I'd be spending more time sketching." Giulia set a clean bowl upside down on the flagstones to dry. "Or watching the painters. Just . . . learning."

"Instead of washing up?" Suor Angela—Angela—sat back on her heels, wiping sweat from her forehead with a forearm that was just as wet. "There's more to being an artist than drawing and painting. To use color, you must understand where it comes from and how it's made. To work on a wood panel or on a plaster wall, you must know how the wood is prepared and the plaster laid. To run a workshop, you need to know every bit of its operation, down to the sweeping of the floors. You must be able to do it all before you can let apprentices like us do it for you, or you'll never truly be mistress of your craft."

"Don't you mind? I mean ... you're a noblewoman. Sweeping floors can't be what you're used to."

"Oh my goodness, Giulia, I'm not noble!" Angela laughed. "My father is a silk merchant. It's for the very large dowry he gave to Santa Marta that I wear the black veil, not for my blue blood."

"Oh," Giulia said. "I didn't know."

"Anyway, you're right. Noblewoman I may not be, but I grew up like one, with servants to wait on my slightest wish. Before the Maestra brought me into her workshop, I'd never so much as folded my own linen, let alone dusted a shelf or scrubbed a floor. I had to learn not just the making of paint and the techniques of drawing, but how to do those things as well." She dropped her eyes. "You must think that's silly."

"No," Giulia said honestly. "I was a servant, but I worked in the sewing room. I never scrubbed a floor either. And I had ... privileges, because of my father."

"Why because of your father?"

"My father was Count Federico di Assulo Borromeo of Milan." Giulia met Angela's gaze, feeling the color rise in her cheeks. "My mother was his seamstress. I'm illegitimate. My father never acknowledged me, but he let me live under his roof and do more or less as I pleased, as long as I got my sewing finished."

"Oh my goodness, Giulia!" There wasn't a trace, in Angela's voice or face, of the contempt that Alessia and her clique had shown. "That's funny, that you'd ask if I'm a noblewoman, when you're the one with noble blood!"

"Not in any way that matters."

"Well, that may be." Angela leaned over the washtub again. "But we are all God's servants. The meanest task, done with devotion, is as pleasing to our Lord as the highest work of art. So I give thanks for what I do for the Maestra, even if it makes my back ache and my leg hurt, for I know I will one day paint pictures that will speak God's glory to all who see them. What could be more wonderful?"

Giulia looked at the other girl, up to her elbows in cloudy water, sweat dampening the edges of her wimple, her soft mouth curved in a smile. A sudden, surprising envy gripped her—for Angela's serenity, her calm certainty of her place in the world.

She picked up another dirty bowl and went back to work.

At the bell for Sext, the noon Holy Office, Domenica, Benedicta, Lucida, and Angela departed for the nuns' chapel. Sext was the only daytime Office they were required to attend—to avoid interrupting their work, they had special exemption from Terce and None, the midmorning and midafternoon Offices.

With less difficulty than she'd feared, Giulia found her way back to the novice wing, where the other novices were gathered for the daily prayer service. Angela was waiting to escort her back to the workshop once the midday meal was done.

As they left the refectory, Giulia saw an unusual group approaching—unusual, because one of its members was male, and not wearing the clothing of a priest. He was escorted by two elderly nuns, as if he were a prisoner under guard. With an odd little shock, Giulia realized that this was the same young man who had turned to stare at her on the day she arrived at Santa Marta. She'd gotten only a glimpse, then, but she remembered his long curly hair and his wide mouth.

He looked at her today too, or rather at her and Angela, a brash, assessing glance—and then he winked.

Without thinking, Giulia turned to watch him go past.

"Giulia!" Angela whispered. "You are too bold!"

Hastily, Giulia turned away.

"I thought men weren't allowed in Santa Marta," she said, when they reached the workshop.

"They aren't." Angela's pretty face was disapproving. "That was an extremely disrespectful young man. I should report him to Madre Damiana."

"Why is he here, then?"

"Things need to be built or fixed sometimes, and when we can't do it ourselves we have no choice but to bring in those who can. He must be the craftsman who's repairing the refectory fresco. Tiles blew off the roof in February and rain got in. The Maestra is afraid the plaster will come off the wall."

That explained the scaffolding. "So . . . he's here all the time?"

"Until the repair is finished. Well, except for when we are having meals, that wouldn't be proper. Look, there's the Maestra." Giulia turned; Suor Humilità was just coming in from the corridor. "It's time for our lesson."

"My two apprentices!" Humilità came toward them, smiling. "How are you settling in, Giulia? Is Angela taking good care of you?"

"Yes, Suor Humilità. Maestra, I mean."

"Excellent! Come."

Humilità led the way over to a portion of the workshop marked out by benches. There, shelves and cabinets held a strange jumble of objects: household and kitchen items, seashells, cushions, bits of armor, several plumed hats, a gilt crown and scepter, stuffed birds and animals, even a gruesome-looking collection of human skulls. Beneath the shelves, chests contained secular clothing, cloaks and gowns and other garments in modern and antique styles. These, Angela had explained, were the costumes worn by the models Humilità used for her paintings. There were also several life-size statues of saints in wood and stone, and a number of marble busts.

A tableau had been arranged on a table: a clay cup, a glass flask half-full of water, a pottery dish heaped with apricots. Humilità set Angela to drawing it, then sat down by Giulia.

"So," she said. "I already know you have talent,

Giulia, but today I want to test it." She handed Giulia a sheaf of paper, a tablet of wood to rest it on, and a stick of charcoal wired to a wooden holder, then sat back and folded her arms. "Draw me that stuffed fox over there."

Giulia was not used to drawing while anyone was watching; especially, she was not used to being judged. The sketch went wrong almost at once.

"May I try again?"

"As many times as you like."

It went wrong again. And again. But it felt so good to have paper under her hand and charcoal in her fingers; and on the fourth try the rhythm of it came to her, and she forgot Humilità on the bench beside her, forgot the sounds and smells of the workshop around her, saw only the fox, knew only the flow of image from eye to hand, the transformation of one reality into another.

Humilità did not comment on the finished drawing. "Now San Sebastiano." She pointed to the statue of the saint.

Giulia drew him, his arrow-pierced body contorted with suffering, his head thrown back in agony. She drew a stuffed bird, a skull, a glass dish, the court viewed through the arches of the loggia. All the while Humilità watched, her dark eyes intent, her expression giving nothing away. It was intimidating to be the focus of such concentrated regard—but also oddly thrilling. No one had ever paid so much attention to her drawing, not even Maestro.

"Now I want you to draw from memory," Humilità

said. "Draw me someone you know well."

Giulia's hand moved almost of itself to shape Maestro's features. She drew him as she remembered him best, hunched over his worktable in his felt cap and his frayed-at-the-collar doublet, a quill in his fingers and an ink pot close by. Finished, she sat looking down at him, feeling the press of tears behind her eyes.

"Who is he?" Humilità asked.

Giulia drew a deep breath. "Maestro Bruni. My teacher."

"You love him." It wasn't a question. "I can see it there, on the paper. Now, one last test. Draw me someone from your imagination. Someone you have never met."

Giulia put charcoal to paper and sketched a head. She added a torso, then a pair of arms and two long legs. She dressed him in striped hose and a loose-sleeved shirt, then gave him hair, curling long onto his shoulders. Last, she gave him features—eyes, nose, a wide smiling mouth.

"Who would he be, if you knew him?" Humilità asked.

"I don't know."

It was a lie. A hundred times over the years Giulia had drawn this man, wearing a hundred different faces, mostly imaginary but sometimes taken from life: the man in her daydream, the man she would marry. Today, she had borrowed the face of the brash young man in the corridor. As she thought of him, she was conscious of the talisman, the stone as warm as a promise against her skin.

"It's interesting that both your choices are male."
Humilità took the portraits, holding them at arm's
length. "Not quite proper for a pledged novice,
perhaps."

"Oh. I'm sorry, Maestra, I didn't mean—"

"No, no. It's a good thing! The paintings we make
here must include men, our Lord Jesus Christ among
them. The drawing of men poses difficulty for any
woman, who for the preservation of her virtue isn't
supposed to look upon the unclothed male form"—
there was a distinct edge to Humilità's voice—"but
especially for nuns, who cannot look at any man at all,
apart from priests and members of their own families. That is why we have those busts and statues over
there. They are a poor substitute for flesh and blood,
but all we are allowed." She returned the portraits to
Giulia. "But you have a natural sense for the male
form. These are very good."

Not till Humilità's praise was given did Giulia realize how very much she had wanted it. "Thank you,
Maestra."

"Now, you have some bad habits, which isn't surprising considering that you are self-trained. I will
be addressing those in our lessons. We shall also
have to teach you about anatomy, as much at least as
a nun is allowed to know." That edge again. "Angela
will train you in the manual tasks, preparing pigments and making gesso and all the rest. Benedicta
will help you with color lore. You must completely
master color before you begin to paint, and that will
take time. But as you are already so far along in your

drawing skills, I see no reason why you shouldn't start to work with paint in, oh . . ." She considered. "Two years, perhaps."

"Two *years?*" The words were out before Giulia could stop them. Humilità's eyebrows rose.

"That's not long, child, did you but know it. Perpetua was four years just learning color. Angela has been with me three years, and is still not ready to put her brush to a commission."

"I'm sorry, Maestra." Giulia knew it was foolish to be disappointed. "It's just that it seems like such a long time."

"You've much to learn, and about much more than color." Humilità's dark eyes bored uncomfortably into Giulia's. "Now go sit by Angela, and do as she's doing, and I will be with you both in a little while. Oh, and I've arranged for you to accompany us to Lucida's supper on Thursday."

"Thank you, Maestra."

Angela had nearly finished her drawing—a very good drawing, Giulia noted—and soon put down her charcoal. She sat watching as Giulia, working quickly, roughed in the objects on the table and began to add detail.

"You're awfully good, Giulia. I can see why the Maestra was so excited when she found out about you."

Giulia looked up. "Was she really?"

"Oh my goodness, yes. She showed us all your drawing. You're the first novice she's ever taken as an apprentice, did you know?"

"No, I didn't."

"Well, it's true. I'm one of the youngest she's chosen, but I'd made my final vows almost a year before she took me on."

Humilità returned from speaking to Domenica and Benedicta at their lecterns, and for the next hour the girls drew under her supervision. She was a challenging teacher, able with a single question or observation to turn an assumption inside out or flip a perception on its head. Maestro, too, had been that way, though he'd been gentler with it.

Later, while Angela prepared yet more tempera, Giulia knelt again at the washtub. The egg mixture spoiled quickly in the heat, and the clotted yolk smelled foul as she scraped it down the drain beside the fountain. Yet she felt none of the discontent of the morning. Perhaps it was being able to draw again. Perhaps it was *what* she had drawn. In her mind's eye, she saw her sketch of the man who was her heart's desire, wearing a borrowed face—imaginary now, but soon to be real.

"This is the beginning, Mama," she breathed to the dirty water, the egg-crusted bowls. "This is how I will get free."

CHAPTER 9

❖ The Repairer of Frescoes ❖

There were several things, Giulia realized, that she should have asked the sorcerer on the night he made the talisman. How long the spirit would take to find her husband, of course—but also how she would recognize him when he arrived, and whether she should wait for him to find her or make some kind of effort to seek him out. Since she had no answers, it seemed to her that taking action was better than waiting. Surely it made sense to give the spirit as many opportunities as possible.

So the moment she learned about the young craftsman who was repairing the fresco, she was determined to find a way to visit him.

Her chance came three days after she became part of the workshop, on the morning of Lucida's dinner party. The evening before, she and Angela had sealed twenty slender twigs into a clay pot and placed the pot in one of the kitchen bread ovens, so the twigs could bake into charcoal overnight. When she arrived at the workshop the following morning, she volunteered to fetch the pot.

"Can you find the kitchen on your own?" Angela, tying on her apron, sounded distracted.

"I think so."

"Well, don't take too long. I'm going to show you how to make gesso today. We must get a start on the panels for the San Giustina commission."

Santa Marta's main building was shaped like a long narrow box, with the kitchen and the refectory and the living quarters ranged along the south side, and the workshops and the store rooms and the chapter hall along the north. Humilità's workshop was on the north side; to reach the kitchen, Giulia had to cross a garden court, then walk all the way to the back. It seemed to take forever; she was breathless with nerves, afraid that the nuns she passed would somehow be able to read her intentions on her face. She reached the kitchen at last, and waited while one of the cooks fetched the pot of charcoal sticks, wrapping it in a cloth to protect her hands. Its heat warmed her palms through the fabric as she approached the refectory. Two nuns were ahead of her. She dawdled until they turned the corner, then, glancing back to make sure no one was about, she trotted to the refectory door and slipped inside.

She'd worried that there might be nuns stationed as chaperones, but the sun-drenched room was empty. She could hear tapping sounds, though, coming from behind the canvas that shrouded the scaffold. Balancing the clay pot in one hand, she smoothed down her dress and pushed at her kerchief so a little of her hair showed. Her pulse beating in her throat, she approached the scaffold.

The canvas covered the scaffold's length, but not its sides. As she rounded the edge, she could see him: the young man who had winked. He was doing something with a hammer at the fresco's top. She stopped. Should she speak? Wait for him to notice her?

As she stood there, irresolute, he turned and saw her.

"Saints!" He took a step back. "Where did you come from?"

"I'm sorry. I didn't mean to startle you."

"Is that for me?" He pointed to the pot.

"Oh! No. No, it's just something . . . I mean, no. It's for someone else."

"I see." From the height of the scaffold, he looked down at her. He wore russet hose and a loose shirt under a workman's smock, the collar open to show a smooth throat, the sleeves rolled above sinewy forearms. His nose was crooked, as if it had been broken long ago. His long light hair curled onto his shoulders. "Well, was there something you wanted?"

Get hold of yourself. He's going to think you're a half-wit. "I was, um, curious. About what you're doing to the fresco."

"Ah. Well, I'm repairing it. Water got in behind it, and I'm stabilizing it so it won't fall off the wall." He smiled, and Giulia, who had been thinking he wasn't particularly good looking, realized she was wrong. "Would you like to see?"

"Yes. If you wouldn't mind."

"Not a bit. Come up the ladder."

Giulia set the pot down on the nearest table. He waited, arms folded, as she began to climb, bunching up her skirt so she wouldn't trip over the hem. When she reached the top, he extended his hand to help her. His fingers were rough, his grip firm, and he held her hand for longer than he needed to before he let go.

The scaffold was composed of thick planks laid across a wooden framework. Bounded on one side by the fresco, enclosed on the other by the canvas, the effect was of a narrow hallway. Some light filtered in from above, but most of the illumination came from lanterns hung on brackets attached to the scaffold posts.

"They're not going to call the watch to take me away, are they?" he said. "For talking to a . . . what are you? Not a nun."

"I'm a novice. I don't actually know what they'd do." She'd considered the punishment she might receive if she were discovered, but it hadn't occurred to her that he might be penalized also. "I was careful. No one saw me come in."

"Well, where's the fun in life if we don't take chances, eh? As long as you stay clear of those two old crows who lead me around at meal times, making sure

I don't steal anyone's virtue." His smile was wicked. "I'm Ormanno, by the way. Ormanno Trovatelli."

"Giulia Borromeo."

"Pleased to meet you, Giulia Borromeo."

He was only a little taller than she was. She hardly had to tilt her head at all to look into his eyes. Like his hair, they were light, an icy shade of blue. They moved from her face to her throat, a frankly appraising gaze. She felt herself beginning to blush. *Is he the one? Is he my heart's desire?* She'd wondered if the talisman might give her a sign of some kind. But all she felt was the uncomfortable thumping of her heart.

"You know," he said, "I have the strangest feeling I've seen you before."

"You have. Twice."

He snapped his fingers. "I remember now. The corridor, a few days ago. You were with that pretty nun."

"Yes. You winked at us."

"That was wrong, I know it." He grinned. "But I couldn't resist, you were both staring at me so. And the other time?"

"In the street, about a month ago. You were coming out of the church. I was just about to go in the convent door. There was a woman with me, and a big carriage—"

"The carriage! I remember. That was you?" Giulia nodded. His eyebrows rose. "You didn't seem pleased about it, if you don't mind me saying."

"I wasn't." Giulia took a deep breath. "I'm not at Santa Marta by choice. I was forced."

"By your family?"

"Not exactly. But I don't plan on staying. I don't intend to become a nun."

"Well." His eyes moved over her again, more slowly this time. "If I'd been wondering why a novice would climb a ladder to flirt with a man who winked at her in a corridor, I suppose that would be my answer."

Giulia felt her blush deepen.

"So," he said. "The fresco." Turning, he stepped toward the scaffold's far end. "You can see over here how the plaster has begun to crack. And there are stains, see? Mostly mineral deposits, but some black mold as well. So over here"—he moved in the other direction, forcing her to retreat before him—"I've used bronze tacks to fix the plaster to the wall. I have to be careful where I place them, for I don't want to spoil the images or create further cracking. With the mineral deposits, you can't remove them completely without damaging the plaster, so I've been scraping away as much as I dare and then trying to make them less visible."

The teasing manner was gone. He was a professional now, a man engaged with, and proud of, his work. For the first time, Giulia turned her attention to the fresco. In this part of it, three disciples leaned toward one another behind the table, and a fourth sat at the table's front, his back to the viewer, his hand outstretched to take a fig from a platter. The figures were bigger than she'd realized, several times life-size, rendered with an astonishing wealth of detail. Close to, she could see what was not apparent from a distance: the grainy texture of the plaster, the slight unevennesses of hue where color was spread over a large area. To the left, beyond the scaffold, Jesus' face was beautiful and sad, His cloak a breathtaking sweep of Passion blue.

"How will you make them less visible?" she asked.

"I'm rubbing them with a mix of oil, tallow, a little chalk, and a few other things."

"Won't the tallow darken over time?"

"I'm hoping not. This is my own formula—better than my master's, though he'd never admit it. The mold I'm washing away, though I can't get it completely clean. Some of the stains may need to be overpainted."

"What a shame, that so much has been spoiled."

"Not spoiled. I'm very good at what I do. By the time I'm finished, only Maestra Humilità and I will know where the repairs were." He looked at her, his icy eyes—which really weren't icy at all, but bright, like stars—appraising her again, though not quite as before. "You're really interested, aren't you. Not just pretending."

"Why should I pretend?"

He shrugged. "Most girls would. To be polite, or"—he smiled—"to flirt."

"Well, I'm not most girls. I'm interested in everything about painting. In fact, I'm Maestra Humilità's . . . well, I'm her apprentice." It felt peculiar to say it—true and not true at the same time.

"Her apprentice, eh? I thought you didn't intend to be a nun."

"I don't. But . . . but I've always drawn, ever since I can remember, and I want to learn, and I can learn from her. I *will* learn from her. As much as I can, for however long I'm here."

It was more truth than she'd told anyone since the sorcerer.

"Your Maestra doesn't know this, I'm guessing."

Giulia felt a sudden alarm. "You won't say anything, will you?"

"Never a word." He grinned. "Although—"

He broke off, holding up his hand. From below came the sound of footsteps. They stood motionless as the steps paused, moved on, paused again, moved on again. Giulia had almost forgotten the risk of what she was doing—but now she remembered and held her breath.

The footsteps faded away. Ormanno stepped to the scaffold's edge and peered around the canvas.

"Gone," he said.

"Who was it?"

"One of the cooks. They come in before meals to lay the tables." He turned toward her again. "Maybe you should be going, Giulia. I don't want to make trouble for you. Or me either, for that matter."

"Yes," said Giulia. "I suppose I should."

"You might come back and see me. Though I won't be here much longer—the work is nearly done."

"I'll try. Or . . . you could come see me." Giulia could hardly believe her boldness. Yet if he were the talisman's choice, it wasn't bold at all, but inevitable. "There's a parlor where we're allowed to receive visitors. You can say—you can say you're my cousin Federico, from Milan."

"Do you really have a cousin named Federico?"

"No. But they don't know that."

"You've got secrets, Giulia Borromeo. I like a girl with secrets." He made a little bow. "Good-bye, then."

"Good-bye."

For a moment she waited. Shouldn't there be something else? But he did not move, and the silence began to stretch, so, reluctantly, she stepped toward the ladder. He stood watching as she climbed down. Ordinary concerns, suspended while she'd been with him, began to return. How long had she been gone? Too long, probably. She would have to make up a story about getting lost after all.

"Psst! Giulia! Don't forget your jar."

She realized that she'd been about to walk off without the pot of charcoal. She turned to retrieve it. From above, Ormanno raised his hand in farewell. As she crossed to the refectory door, she imagined she could feel his eyes—but when she looked back, he had vanished, at work again behind the canvas.

CHAPTER 10

❖ A Golden Evening ❖

Angela did not question Giulia's story about losing her way. She set to work at once showing Giulia how to cook gesso—a foul-smelling concoction of water, chalk, and glue—over the workshop's brazier, and then how to brush it, while still warm, onto the three enormous wooden panels laid out on sawhorses.

The San Giustina commission was to be an altar-piece, a triptych, with the central panel depicting the Crucifixion and the two side panels the thieves crucified alongside Christ. Applying the gesso was a painstaking process, for great care had to be taken not to introduce air bubbles. Once the gesso was dry, it must be burnished to velvet smoothness with pumice stones, after which another coat would be laid on.

"We'll need at least six coats," Angela said. "Maybe more. The Maestra is very particular, and this is an important commission."

At sunset, the four choir nuns left to sing Vespers. Normally the Vespers bell was a signal for Giulia to return to the novice dormitory, but today, because of Lucida's supper party, she waited in the workshop with Humilità and Perpetua, who as *conversae* were not allowed to participate in Holy Offices. She wasn't surprised, when Lucida and Angela and Benedicta returned, to see that Domenica was not with them.

They left the workshop. Humilità led the way toward the back of the convent, setting a slow pace to accommodate old Benedicta, who steadied herself on Perpetua's arm. They arrived at last at a loggia whose arches overlooked another garden courtyard. Dark had not yet completely fallen, and in the twilight Giulia could see winding gravel paths and flower beds massed with rose bushes and lavender. In the middle lay a round pool, from which a single jet of water leaped toward the sky. The rising moon caught the drops as they reached their apex and began to fall, like a spill of ice.

"It's the prettiest court in Santa Marta," said Angela. "Don't you think so? The abbess's residence is here, and the hereditary cells."

"Hereditary cells?"

"They're not really cells, although we call them that. Many of the great families have been sending women to Santa Marta for generations. Some have built their own residences."

Humilità led them toward the courtyard's far side, where a row of small tile-roofed houses crowded against one another like a child's toy blocks. At the endmost house, beyond which Giulia could see the shadowy mass of trees of the convent's orchard, Humilità knocked. The door flew open, spilling golden light.

"Welcome!" Lucida cried. Over her white habit she had thrown a sleeveless mantle of shimmering bronze brocade, lined with copper-colored silk. "Come in! Everything's ready."

Standing candelabra illuminated the interior of the little house. The floor was plain terracotta, the walls of undressed stone, but exotic rugs cushioned the tiles, and rich-hued tapestries softened the walls. Small footstools and dainty tables flanked pillow-piled benches. An exquisite painting of Madonna and Child stood on a shelf in a corner, with a cushioned kneeler underneath.

"Come." Lucida took Giulia's arm. "You must sit by me."

Opposite the door stood a dining table, its polished boards set with glass goblets and gleaming plates. More candles burned in holders at the table's center. Lucida pulled out a chair for Giulia, then seated herself at the table's head.

"Maestra," she said. "Will you give us a blessing?"

Lucida extended her hands. Gems winked on her fingers—Giulia didn't remember, earlier, that she had been wearing rings. Around the table the women joined hands and bowed their heads.

"Almighty God," Humilità said, "who redeemed the world through Your Son, Jesus Christ, bless us as we partake of Your bounty this night. Make us always mindful of Your glory, which speaks to us in all things. Amen."

"Amen," the others chorused.

Lucida clapped her hands. Through a door at one side of the room came a middle-aged *conversa*, carrying a tray laden with steaming bowls.

"It's chestnut soup," Lucida said, taking up her spoon. "Made to a family recipe. I hope you enjoy it."

The soup was delicious, savory with spice and thick with cream. The mixed salad with green onions, roast pigeon in puff pastry, and pasta dressed with garlic and butter were delicious too. To drink there was wine, poured by Lucida's *conversa* from dusty bottles. Giulia had sampled leftovers from her father's table, courtesy of Annalena, but she'd never consumed an entire meal of such delicacy. Nor had she known that nuns were allowed to drink wine. *But then,* she thought, *almost everything in this house is something I thought nuns weren't allowed.* From the talk she had heard in the novice dormitory, she knew that choir nuns lived more comfortably than *conversae*—much more comfortably, in many cases—but she had never imagined such opulence.

Lucida clearly enjoyed the role of hostess and was attentive to her guests' comfort. For Benedicta, who with her missing teeth could not chew, she had arranged a special dish of mashed artichoke hearts in citron sauce. As they ate, the women talked—about the completion of the Santa Barbara commission, about upcoming feast days and other convent affairs. Giulia knew nothing of these goings-on; amid this intimate little group, with its web of established relationships, she was an outsider. Yet, somehow, she did not feel excluded. Lucida smiled often in her direction, and Angela and Humilità broke off what they were saying to explain things for her. The wine helped too. She was only sipping, but even so she could feel it going to her head, making the strange, golden evening more than ever like a dream.

The *conversa* cleared away the main course and brought in plates of apricots, grapes, cheeses, and little cakes. For Benedicta, there was a bowl of stewed figs in honey.

"I'll wager Domenica is fasting tonight, to make up for our gluttony." Lucida selected an apricot. "I wish her joy in it, the sour old crow."

"You should be kinder, Lucida," Perpetua said. The light of the candles flattered her homely features, masking the disfiguring pockmarks on her cheeks. "She's had a hard time of it."

"Yes, yes, I know." Lucida finished her apricot and licked her fingers. "But just because she was made to suffer doesn't give her the right to make others miserable."

"It's a sad story." Angela turned to Giulia. "She was engaged to a young man, but then her father died and her uncle inherited the estate. He had daughters of his own to dower, and decided Domenica should go to Santa Marta instead of marrying. She ran away to her fiancé, but he was afraid and returned her to her uncle, who sent her here."

Giulia, listening, felt a shudder of recognition.

"She made her vows." Perpetua took up the story. "Not long after, she got permission to go to her nephew's christening, with her sisters as chaperones. Somehow, she managed to escape. Her uncle's sons went after her and brought her back. She got sick after that. Nearly died." Perpetua shook her head. "When she was well again, she was the opposite of what she'd been. A conversion. Few now are more devoted."

"Devoted?" Lucida made a face. "With her hair shirts and her self-flagellation and her fasting—really, it's distasteful. Do you know, Giulia, Domenica puts bitter aloe in her food so she won't enjoy it? My aunt Damiana has had to reprimand her for her excesses. And she's not the only one. There's Claudia, who sleeps without blankets in the winter, and Felicita, who puts pebbles in her shoes, and Innocentia, who wears a studded chain around her waist. Sometimes she gets infections, and Madonna, how she smells! God has given us this beautiful world for our use and enjoyment. I don't see how it honors Him to be miserable on purpose."

"Are there many like Domenica?" Giulia asked. "Brought here against their will, I mean?"

"Oh yes," Lucida said. "There are too many women in the world, and what can families do with those they cannot marry off, except send them to a convent? Take me, for instance. My father was able to dower my two older sisters for noble marriages, but for me he could afford only a nun's dowry. All my life I've known I must be a nun." She pulled a grape off its stem and popped it into her mouth. "Though to be fair, I am not like some others who are put here by their families' decree, for I never wanted to be subject to a husband's authority. Besides, who knows what kind of odious idiot my father would have chosen for me?"

"He might have chosen a handsome idiot," Humilità said, smiling.

"Ha! You should see my poor sisters' husbands. One is as fat as a goose and just as stupid, and the other's twenty years older with warts all over his face. No. I am where I was meant to be. Thanks to my father's indulgence in hiring a drawing master for my sisters and me when we were children, I have work that delights me. My family may visit me as often as they choose, or"—she slanted a smile in Giulia's direction—"as often as *I* choose. I live my own life in my own house, and need not bow to the will of my father or the whims of my brothers or the desires of a husband. I am Christ's bride, and no human man may command me!" For an instant, her bright face was fierce. "Nor do I need to fear dying in childbed, as my mother did. I am not one of those who sees Santa Marta as a prison." She bit into one of the little cakes. "For me, it is the greatest freedom a woman can possess."

There is freedom here, if you are willing to seek it. Madre Damiana had said that, on Giulia's first day.

"My mother died in childbirth too," Perpetua said. "I always had a mortal fear of it."

"Is that why you became a nun?" Giulia asked.

"Bless you, no." Perpetua's smile showed her crooked teeth. "My father was a tailor, but his shop burned down in a fire and he couldn't support us all. He brought me to be a *conversa* here at Santa Marta. They needed seamstresses, so they were willing to take me without a dowry."

"So it wasn't your choice?"

"Choice didn't come into it, dear. It was the convent or starve. I was grateful for the shelter, and for the work that gave it to me. I'd be grateful still, even if it hadn't been God's plan for me to serve Him in another way. My father taught me to make pictures of the clothes he made, so patrons could see them and choose, and the Maestra who was here before our Maestra discovered I could draw. That's how I came into the workshop."

"I never wanted to be anything but a nun," said Angela softly. "To give myself to God, safe and apart from the temptations of the world. Besides." She gave a small, self-conscious laugh. "What man would want a wife with a withered leg?"

Giulia looked at Angela. She had been impressed

by how little Angela's limp impeded her, and had assumed she must not mind it. But that laugh said something quite different.

"What about you, Benedicta?" Lucida turned to the elderly nun. "What brought you to Santa Marta?"

"Oh, my dear," Benedicta replied in her cracked old voice, "it's been so long I've quite forgotten. After so many years, anyway, what does it matter?" She cackled. "That's God's little joke. We all come in differently, but we all go out the same."

"That leaves you, Maestra," Lucida said. "Tell Giulia why you became a nun."

"My father is a painter—"

"A *famous* painter," Lucida interrupted.

"He has a workshop here in Padua. He saw my ability and couldn't bear to waste it, so he trained me like an apprentice, for all I was a girl. When I was fourteen, he arranged for me to join the workshop here. I could not have become a painter otherwise. The world does not allow such things for women. Like Lucida, I always knew I would go to Santa Marta."

"And it's our good fortune that you did," Angela said.

"By God's grace," Humilità replied.

"And your hard work," said Perpetua.

"*All* our hard work." Humilità smiled at Lucida. "Even yours, my willful butterfly."

Lucida laughed. "What about you, Giulia?" She turned her dancing smile Giulia's way. "Don't be afraid to tell the truth. It won't go farther than this room."

"My father died," Giulia said—careful, aware of the loosening influence of the wine and the danger of saying too much. "And his wife wanted me gone. I'm illegitimate, you see, and he gave me his protection, but she had no reason to continue that. So she arranged for me to be sent here."

"To become a painter," Angela said.

"No. She meant me to be a seamstress, the way I was at home. She hated me. She'd never have done anything to benefit me." With effort, Giulia stopped herself. *Careful, careful.*

"Well, whatever her intent, God guided her choice," Humilità said. "There is nowhere better in the world you could have come. You are meant to be here, my dear. I have no doubt of it."

The candle flames glinted in her small dark eyes, and on the wine goblet she held. Giulia felt a chill, as if a cold hand had been laid above her heart.

From elsewhere in the convent, bells began to ring.

"Compline," Humilità said. "We must return Giulia to her dormitory."

"How quickly the time has passed!" Lucida exclaimed.

"Angela, would you escort Giulia, please?"

"Of course, Maestra."

Angela got to her feet, her shoulder dipping. Giulia pushed back her chair and stood. The wine rushed to her head; she had to catch at the edge of the table to steady herself.

"Thank you so much for inviting me."

"It was entirely my pleasure!" Lucida jumped up and came around the table to kiss Giulia on both cheeks. "We shall have many such suppers!"

Giulia looked back as she and Angela passed through the door. The candle-lit table was a heart of brightness in a room whose edges shaded into shadow. Humilità and Perpetua still sat, for *conversae* did not sing Vespers, while Lucida bent toward old Benedicta, helping her to her feet, her face as lovely as a Madonna's in the golden light.

It was a painting. Giulia knew this, with a soul-deep thrill that set her fingers burning. And she knew, against all odds or certainties, that she would one day paint this scene—these women, this light, this moment—and preserve it forever.

Outside, stars winked down from an inky sky. As they crossed the court, Angela linked her arm through Giulia's, making Giulia jump.

"I'm sorry," Angela said, withdrawing.

"You startled me, that's all."

"Oh. Well, then."

Angela put her arm back. Giulia could feel the dip and halt of her limp.

"I'm glad you've come, Giulia. I think we're going to be good friends, don't you?"

"Yes," Giulia said, because it was the only way to answer such a question. It wasn't the truth—how could it be? She would be gone soon. But it wasn't a lie either. She liked Angela. For someone who had never had friends her own age, it was a feeling as unaccustomed as the pressure of Angela's arm against her own.

Angela left her at the entrance to the novice wing. Suor Margarita was waiting in the dormitory doorway, her hands hidden in her sleeves as usual.

"Good," she said when she saw Giulia. "You're back on time."

"Yes, Suor Margarita. Thank you for allowing me to go."

Suor Margarita pursed her lips. "I did *not* allow it. My girls receive no special privileges. But I was overruled."

"I'm . . . I'm sorry."

"Well." The novice mistress softened a little. "I know it was not your doing." She turned abruptly toward the dormitory. "Girls! Girls!" She clapped her hands for attention. "Quiet now, I have something to say to you!" They obeyed, setting down their games, turning from their conversations. "You may have noticed that Giulia was not with us tonight. She has been chosen for a special honor—she has joined the workshop of Suor Humilità, where she will learn to be a painter, to the glory of God and our Savior Jesus Christ. Her duties may sometimes take her away from us, so if you do not always see her at table in the refectory, or during recreation hour, that is why."

"But, Suor Margarita!" Alessia, standing by the window with her clique as usual, stepped forward, an expression of outrage on her face. "She's a *conversa!*"

"Yes, Alessia, that fact is known to me."

"Why should a commoner get such favor, when there are noble girls who could be chosen?"

"Perhaps," said Suor Margarita in an icy tone, "because Giulia has abilities they do not."

"But Suor Margarita—"

"That is enough, Alessia. I believe it would be instructive for you to contemplate the sin of envy tomorrow, while working with Bice in the kitchen."

Alessia's mouth opened; for a moment Giulia thought she would defy the novice mistress. But then she clamped her lips together and was silent.

"To bed now, girls." Suor Margarita clapped her hands again. "Quickly, quickly!"

Isotta was giggling as Giulia returned to her bed and began untying her kerchief.

"Ooooh, Alessia in the kitchen! Getting her noble fingers dirty!"

"Laugh away," grumbled Bice. "I'm the one who's stuck with her."

"Poor you," Giulia offered, trying to be sympathetic.

"And lucky *you*." Bice eyed her. "I wouldn't mind lounging around all day painting pictures."

"It's not like that. Most of what I do is sweeping and mopping and washing up."

"Better than the kitchen, though. Or cleaning out the chicken house. But then, you've noble blood. S'pose they couldn't have you down on your knees like us regular *conversae*."

"It's not like that," Giulia said again, but Bice only shrugged.

The girls folded their gowns and kerchiefs into their trousseau chests and gathered at the washbasin, Alessia first as always. Returning, she brushed up against Giulia, who was last in line.

"You don't deserve it, new girl," she whispered, seizing Giulia's braid and wrapping it viciously around her fist. "I've got my eye on you."

Another yank, and she was gone. Giulia put her hand to her smarting scalp. Lisa, in front of her, twisted around to give her a sympathetic look.

"She's so mean," Lisa said in her thick voice, her tongue garbling "s" into "z" and dropping the ends of words so that it was hard to understand her. "Her and the others. I hate them all."

"It doesn't matter." Giulia gave Lisa a little smile. She felt sorry for the crippled girl, who was not only the most frequent focus of Alessia's bullying, but was disliked and ignored by everyone else as well.

After the candles had been blown out, Giulia lay open-eyed, listening to the breathing of the other girls. She thought of the beauty she had felt and seen in the golden glow of Lucida's supper table. She thought of the lush garden courts, the jewel-like chapel where her vestition ceremony had been held, the graceful architecture, the plentiful food. All of it was so different, so completely different from anything she had expected to find at Santa Marta. She thought of the stories she had heard tonight, the circumstances that had brought each of the artists to the veil. She had imagined that all nuns must be like her, forced against their will, or else like Angela, willingly pledging their lives to God. But she was beginning to see that there were many variations of willing and unwilling—as many, possibly, as there were nuns.

She wrapped her fingers around the talisman, as she always did before sleep, and sank into deep blue dreams.

CHAPTER II

✤ Pigments and Horoscopes ✤

The following Tuesday when Giulia arrived in the refectory for the evening meal, the scaffold was gone. The whole of the fresco was visible now, in all its glory—not just the figures that had been hidden, but the harmony of the design, the way the positioning of the disciples on either side of Jesus emphasized His solitude.

For a few weeks, she waited to be summoned to the visitors' parlor to receive her "cousin." But by the end of June, she'd accepted that Ormanno was not coming. She struggled to put him out of her mind. She'd liked him, liked his smile and his seriousness about his work and the lingering way he had looked at her. He had seemed to like her too—just, apparently, not enough.

He wasn't the one. But someone will be.

She had plenty to keep her busy in the workshop. Humilità expected the tile floor to be swept daily and scrubbed weekly, the shelves and cupboards to be kept in order, and the preparation areas to be cleared and equipment properly stowed at the end of each day. Giulia sometimes couldn't sleep for the aching of her knees or back or shoulders, sore from lifting or scrubbing or just the many hours spent on her feet. Suor Margarita sighed at the state of her hands, embedded with charcoal powder, cracked and rough from hours at the washtub, and scolded her for the stains at the hem of her dress, which was not quite covered by her apron.

But she also learned to fashion brushes out of squirrel hair and hog bristles, and to trim them to shape. She learned to transfer a cartoon, the drawing on which a painting was based, onto prepared wood panels by a technique called pouncing—pricking the lines of the drawing with a pin, laying the drawing atop the panel, rubbing with a coarse linen bag filled with charcoal, so that when the cartoon was removed the drawing was left behind. Perhaps most important, she began to study the making of paint and the uses and properties of the hundreds of ingredients from which paint was made: minerals, metals, clay, plant matter—even the crushed bodies of insects.

Turning these ingredients into usable pigment was exacting and tiring. Materials must be broken up and pounded to powder in a mortar, then ground with water on a porphyry slab until they became a silky paste. The finished pigments were placed in little pots and mixed with more water, ready for the artists to combine with tempera or oil to make them flow.

Some paints, such as bone black or red ochre, consisted of a single natural ingredient. Others, such as lead white or the yellow known as *giallo di napoli*, were compounded of several materials. Humilità bought some of these ready-made from apothecaries, but others she manufactured herself, or expected Angela and Giulia to mix for her. The recipes for doing so, along with formulas for tempera, gesso, primers, lacquers, and the purification of oils; instructions for achieving color effects; and techniques for making paint more malleable or more durable or more quick-drying, were collected in a leather-bound ledger with a brass clasp, which was kept in a locked box in one of the cabinets in Humilità's office.

"It's our most precious possession," Angela said, when she showed Giulia the book for the first time. Humilità was present that day, and had unlocked the box herself. "It contains the knowledge of all three of our Maestras, back to the workshop's founding. We must always take great care with it, so there is no chance it will ever be lost or stolen."

"Stolen?" Carefully, Giulia turned the pages,

crammed with writing, diagrams, and figures. Some
of the ink was so faded it was barely legible. The portion in Humilità's strong, angular script was twice as
long as the rest. "Would someone really do that?"

"Oh my goodness, yes!" Angela's brown eyes grew
wide. "When a workshop is famous, like ours, other
painters covet its techniques and recipes. That happened to the Maestra's own father. One of his apprentices copied a dozen of his recipes and sold them to
another workshop." She lowered her voice. "Just
because this is a house of God doesn't mean there
aren't venal women here who would use our secrets
for their own gain."

"Is Passion blue in the book?"

"All our recipes are in the book. But the most valuable ones are in cipher. I'll show you."

Angela pulled the book toward her and looked
through it till she found what she wanted, then
pushed it back to Giulia. The page was filled with an
apparently senseless jumble of letters and symbols,
written in Humilità's hand and broken into blocks.
Between each block, a square of color had been laid
down.

"The colors say which recipes they are, but only the
Maestra can read them, so only she can make them.
Here are more." Angela reached around Giulia to turn
more pages. "See? And here—"

"Passion blue." Giulia recognized it instantly. Even
in the form of a small painted square, it glinted like a
jewel. It had an entire page to itself.

"Yes. It's the only one the Maestra never lets us

see her make. When she needs to compound it, she comes to the workshop in the hour before dawn and locks the doors until she's finished."

A formula for color so valuable it was not just written in cipher, but only mixed in secret? Passion blue was beautiful, with its unique depth and luminosity—but surely there were only so many ingredients from which any paint could be made, and only so many ways of combining them. Would it be so hard for someone else to discover the secret? Would it matter so much if they did?

Before the workshop, Giulia had assumed that painters must be the sole authors of their work, just as she was the sole author of her drawings. But the workshop's commissions were almost all collaborative. Their composition was decided by Humilità, who also made the preliminary figure drawings and studies, as she was doing now for the San Giustina altarpiece commission. For the larger and more important works, she also created the cartoons and underdrawings—though for smaller pieces she often left that task to Domenica and Benedicta, the workshop's two master painters. Of the actual painting, she might do a great deal or relatively little, depending on her own interest and also on the provisions of the contracts that were drawn up for each commission.

Everything else was done by the other artists, each according to her own particular skill. Perpetua's talent was the depiction of natural things—trees and animals, rocks and rivers, stars and clouds. Landscapes were generally left to her. Lucida was a portraitist,

best at painting faces; she created devotional miniatures, tiny and exquisite representations of saints that,
when finished, were sent to another of Santa Marta's
workshops to be set in gilded frames and sold to the
public. Stern Domenica excelled at interiors, and at the
tricky mathematical discipline of perspective. Benedicta
was unmatched at painting drapery, rendering sensu-
ous shadows and lustrous highlights with amazing
authenticity.

Humilità encouraged Giulia to watch the painters if
she had no other tasks. Sometimes Giulia kept Angela
company as she worked on her practice painting, a small
Madonna and Child. Angela was talented—the painting
was lovely, with clear colors and graceful lines—but she
was an apprentice, not a master, and Giulia preferred
to stand by Benedicta's lectern. The elderly nun might
be missing her teeth and unsteady on her feet, but her
eyes and mind had lost none of their sharpness, and her
hand was firm. She seemed glad to share the vast trove
of knowledge she had accumulated over more than fifty
years of painting—especially her knowledge of color.

"Remember, my dear," she might say, putting the
final touches to a vermilion cloak, "color is two things—
itself, and what the light makes of it. This cloak is the
vermilion of brightness, the vermilion of shadow, and
the vermilion of everything in between. You must see all
those different vermilions if you are to paint them, yet
you must never forget that they are aspects of a single
color. One thing made out of many, and many things
that add up to one, like God's own creation."

Or, explaining why a mixture of blue and yellow

made a more stable green than the pigment known as *verderame*: "This is the great secret of color, child. Inside every color, other colors live. Thus we can create green from yellow and blue, or paint a purple robe by laying blue over a red ground. That's why a poppy is not simply red, it is yellow red, and an olive leaf is not merely green, it is gray green. There is no color for which this isn't so."

It was a new language, this color lore, opening a door on a new world of understanding. The more Giulia learned, the more she realized how delicate and demanding a skill it was. The wrong underpainting could spoil even the most exquisite pigment. The slightest error in preparation, the tiniest impurity, could make the difference between a color that was clear and one that was muddy, one that faded and one that lasted. The addition or subtraction of a single element could completely change a color's properties, and maintaining consistency of hue despite variations in ingredient quality was an art in itself. Giulia began to understand how hard it was to create a color as pure, as profound, as unfading as Passion blue. She began to grasp why, in the world of painters, such a thing was so valuable.

She imagined Humilità sometimes, alone in the workshop in the light of a single candle, combining ingredients like an alchemist. Like the sorcerer. He too must know things that were too precious to share with others. He too must have a book of secrets. She thought of his blue robe, and of the blue talisman, and of the blue flame that returned sometimes to dance in her dreams. Of Passion blue. So much blue . . . and so many secrets.

It never seemed to occur to Angela that she and Giulia would not become best friends. She told Giulia all about herself—her family, the house she had grown up in, her lifelong dream of devoting herself to God. She spoke of her indulgent father, who had wanted her to marry but in the end bowed to her heart's desire. She described her delicate mother, who had taught her the embroidery-patterning skills that, as a novice of sixteen, had brought her to Humilità's attention.

She took Giulia with her to the visitors' parlor to meet her older brother, Alberto, a slight young man with his sister's wide brown eyes who was in training to take over the family silk business. Giulia felt the weight of the talisman around her neck as she watched him through the bars of the iron grille that split the parlor in half, so that the nuns and their guests might never forget that they inhabited separate worlds. But though he was polite, she could tell, when his eyes turned to her, that it was her novice dress and kerchief he saw, not the girl inside them.

Angela was fascinated by Giulia's life in Milan, so different from her own, and wanted to know everything about it. Talking about herself was not something Giulia was used to. Not since her mother died had she had anyone to confide in—Annalena had always been too busy or too tired, and Maestro, who would talk for hours about scholarly subjects, was uncomfortable with anything that carried too much emotion. She'd gotten used to being solitary, to keeping things to herself. More than that, here at Santa Marta, she was afraid of letting down her guard.

But to her surprise, she discovered that she enjoyed answering Angela's questions. Gradually, she found herself speaking of things that were more intimate: her love of drawing, the misery Clara and Piero had made of her childhood (though she didn't mention the horoscope or what Piero had done to it), her memories of her mother. She told Angela about the Secret Hour, the precious time at the end of the workday when she and her mother would latch the door of their little room, open up the cedar box, and admire its contents—the beautiful trousseau, the topaz necklace, the gifts from Giulia's father. It was a happy memory. But the box and everything in it were gone now, and the wave of grief and loss that rose in Giulia as she spoke took her by surprise. She had to stop, biting her lips against the tears that wanted to fall. Angela said nothing, only laid a gentle hand on her shoulder.

On a hot afternoon in the middle of July, Angela and Giulia gave the drawing area its monthly cleaning, dusting the statues and busts, emptying the shelves and cabinets so they could tidy them properly. Reaching into the back of one of the cabinets to scoop out a heap of broken pottery, Giulia felt something more substantial underneath. She pulled it out and realized, to her astonishment, that she had found an astrologer's astrolabe.

She sat back on her heels, examining it. It was crude compared to the fine astrolabes Maestro had owned, made of plain brass and bare of chasing or ornamentation. It was also badly tarnished. But it had all its parts, and the disks and pointers still turned, if rather stiffly.

"What's that?" asked Angela.

"An astrolabe." Giulia ran her finger around its edge, the familiar feel of it bringing a stab of homesickness. "What a strange thing to find. I wonder how it got here."

"What's an astro—astro—"

"Astrolabe. Astrologers use them to cast horoscopes."

"My father had horoscopes cast for Alberto and me when we were born. Mine says I will be close to God all my life and live to a great old age. Alberto's says he will be wealthy and have many children." Angela frowned, setting a wooden box back in its place. "Did your Maestro Bruni teach you astrology too, along with history and geography and Latin?"

"Not exactly." Giulia had wanted very much to learn. She never quite lost hope that she might remember her birth date—and even if she never did, she wanted to understand how lives could be written in, and read from, the stars. But astrology was the only knowledge Maestro ever refused her. His art could only be passed on to an apprentice—and that, of course, she could never be. "I was often there while he worked, though, and I transcribed hundreds of charts and interpretations for him. And he let me read any of his books I wanted. I learned quite a lot on my own."

"Like what?"

"Oh . . . how Creation is shaped, like a great hollow ball, with the stars on the inside and the Earth at the center and the spheres of the planets in between. And I know the powers and aspects of the seven planets, and the meaning of the twelve signs of the zodiac, and the names of the stars and constellations and their place in the night sky. And I can use this astrolabe. Well, not as a real astrologer could, but I've done some horary horoscopes. They're simpler than the others, because all you have to do is answer a question."

"What kind of question?"

"Any kind you like."

"Oh, Giulia! Could I ask a question? Could you cast a horoscope for me?"

"Well—"

"We could do it right now!" Angela clapped her hands. "Domenica and the Maestra are away cleaning the paintings in the choir, and Lucida and Perpetua and Benedicta won't mind. Oh, say you'll do it, please!"

Giulia hesitated, but only for a moment. From the instant she had seen the astrolabe, she'd known she was going to use it.

She led the way into the midafternoon heat of the courtyard. She raised the astrolabe, letting the heavy disk of it hang from the ring at its top, turning it so it faced her edge on.

"Angela," she said. "What I find in your chart may

not be what you want to hear. Maestro always used to say, before he cast a horary chart, that when you asked the question you had to be ready to receive the answer you least desired."

Angela nodded, her bright face solemn. "I understand."

"Then ask."

Angela drew a deep breath. "When will the Maestra declare me a journeyman?"

Giulia adjusted the rotating bar on the astrolabe's back—the alidade—so that the sun's rays passed through the pinhole sights at either end, casting a point of light upon the flagstones of the courtyard. Having determined the altitude of the sun, she held the astrolabe flat on her palm and rotated first the rule—the pointer at the front—and then the rete—the perforated plate beneath—to match the measurement she had just taken. With the imprinted plate at the back—the tympan—the astrolabe now presented an exact picture of the heavens at the moment of Angela's question.

She led the way from the white-hot sunlight into the cooler shadow of the workshop. Lucida, working on one of her devotional miniatures, glanced up.

"What are you girls doing?"

"Giulia found an astrolabe on the shelves." Angela said. "It's a tool astrologers use. She's making me a horoscope."

"A horoscope?" Lucida's face lit up with interest. "I didn't know you had that skill, Giulia."

"Only a little skill," Giulia said. "I learned a bit from my tutor, that's all."

"Well, it is a dull day and my hand is tired." Lucida put down her brush. "I am ready to be diverted."

"What will the Maestra say?" asked Perpetua anxiously from the drafting table.

"The Maestra isn't here. Nor, saints be praised, is Domenica."

"I don't know, Lucida. It seems very worldly."

"And did not God make the world? And the stars, which speak His will?" Lucida laughed. "Besides, it will be fun!"

Perpetua's face spoke her doubt, but she didn't object as Giulia sat down opposite, placing the astrolabe carefully on the table. Lucida and Angela came to stand at her back, one by each shoulder. Across the room Benedicta painted on, as though she were alone.

On the back of a piece of used paper, Giulia wrote Angela's question, then scribed a freehand circle. With six quick strokes, she slashed the circle into twelve segments, one for each of the twelve houses, and marked each house with its associated zodiac sign. The others watched as she began to enter the measurements she'd taken. At last she put down her quill.

"What does it say?" Angela breathed.

"Well . . ." Giulia surveyed the chart. She'd told Lucida the truth: She was a novice, or even less, in the art of interpretation. But the chart seemed free of the ambiguous planetary placements and relationships that often made them difficult to read. "The first house rules the querent, the person asking the question." She pointed to it as she spoke. "The house that rules the quesited—the question—is always different, depending on what's being asked. For your question, Angela, I think it would be the fifth house, which rules painting, poetry, and the arts. Um . . . now, the Sun is in the first house, which usually means that things will happen quickly. In the fifth house is Jupiter, which represents a friend or teacher, someone who can help. And Jupiter and the Sun are in conjunction, which is favorable for the outcome. So I think . . . I think the answer to your question is 'Soon.'"

"Oh, Giulia, that's what I was hoping! Thank you!"

"Now you must do one for me," said Lucida. "And for Perpetua too. And for Benedicta. We all must have a chart!"

For the next hour, Giulia cast horoscopes. Lucida wanted to know whether her sister Sophronia's baby would be a boy or a girl (probably a boy). Angela asked how the business venture her brother Alberto was currently involved in would turn out (badly; despite the warning she'd given earlier, Giulia did not want to say so, and told Angela that the chart was too complicated to interpret). Perpetua, giving in at last to Lucida's urging, asked whether the tooth that was paining her would improve (Giulia, apologetic, had to tell her no, which made the homely nun sigh). Only Benedicta refused to join in.

"Questions are for the young," she said, not pausing in her work. "At my age, there may not be time enough for answers, and if that's so, I do not want to know it."

"What about you, Giulia?" asked Angela. "Don't you have a question?"

"Yes, but . . . it's getting late."

"Nonsense," Lucida exclaimed. "You've answered our questions. It wouldn't be fair for you not to ask one of your own."

Giulia hesitated. Her own question pressed behind her lips. But she how could speak it in front of the others?

"My question is . . . well, it's private."

"A *secret* question! How mysterious!" Lucida was delighted. "Go on, then. We'll block our ears."

Under the iron fist of the sun, Giulia held up the astrolabe and breathed her question to the air, investing it with all the strength of her hope and desire. Returning to the workshop, she felt both anticipation and dread. She could almost hear Maestro's voice: *Be prepared, when you ask the question, to receive the answer you least desire.*

She transcribed her measurements, holding her mind away from the symbols' meaning. Not until the last one had been set down did she allow herself to look at the chart with an astrologer's eye, or as much of one as she possessed.

"That can't be right."

"Oh dear," said Angela. "Isn't it the answer you wanted?"

"I think I must have cast it wrong. The measurements don't make sense."

"Can you ask again?"

"No." Giulia crumpled up the paper. "You can't ask

the same question more than once in a single day."

"Oh, Giulia, what a shame!"

"We've been at this long enough, anyway," Perpetua said. "We should all be getting back to work."

"Thank you, Giulia." Lucida smiled her lovely smile. "It has been a most entertaining hour. We'll do it again, I hope."

Giulia gathered up the horoscopes and placed them on the brazier, where they quickly caught fire and curled into ash. The astrolabe she returned to its cabinet, pushing it to the back where she had found it, and could find it again.

"You know so many things, Giulia," Angela said, as they returned to tidying the shelves.

"Not so many, really. Not compared with someone like Maestro."

"More than me. More than most of the nuns here. And you've had such an exciting life, living in a big house with all those people, reading books and making drawings, learning astrology, going about on your own like a boy. I never met anyone like you before."

Giulia was silent, astonished by this description of herself. She'd known her life was unusual, but it had never occurred to her to think of it as exciting. She'd only seen it as something to escape.

Angela set the glass vessel she had just finished cleaning carefully inside a cabinet. "You must think I'm awfully dull."

"No, Angela! Of course I don't."

"But I've never done anything interesting."

"Angela, you're the kindest girl I've ever known.

You grew up in a home of your own. You have a family, a mother and father and brother who love you. I always wanted those things. I always wondered what it was like to have a place . . . a place where I belonged."

"But you *do* belong, Giulia. Here at Santa Marta." Angela's soft mouth curved in a smile. "We are your family now, we painters. We are your sisters."

Giulia looked quickly down at the piece of crockery she was polishing.

As she went about her tasks that afternoon, she was aware that for almost the entire time she'd been casting horoscopes, she had not once thought of escaping Santa Marta. She'd forgotten she was a prisoner.

That night Giulia dreamed of the small blue flame that had visited her just after she became Humilità's apprentice. She had dreamed it now a dozen times or more, always the same way: fleeing before her, never allowing her to catch it or even to draw close. She'd begun to believe it was Anasurymboriel—though whether the spirit was actually touching her sleep, or she was just dreaming that it was, she didn't know.

As always, the dream woke her. She lay on her back, her eyes open on the dimness of the ceiling, the other girls stirring and breathing around her. She thought of the chart she had cast for herself that afternoon. She'd tried to be meticulous—yet somehow she had made a mistake. It was the only possible explanation.

She had asked: *When will I receive my heart's desire?*

And the chart had replied, or seemed to: *It is already yours.*

That made no sense. It had to be an error, though she could not remember anything in the casting or the transcription she might have gotten wrong.

It didn't matter. She knew where the astrolabe was. She'd find a way to ask again.

She closed her hand around the talisman and shut her eyes, willing herself to dream of Anasurymboriel. But when she fell asleep, her jumbled dreams contained no blue at all.

CHAPTER 12

❖ Plautilla and Alessandro ❖

Maestro had had another saying: *The art of the horary chart lies not just in the making, but in the questioning.* It was not enough simply to ask—one must find the *right* questions, the ones that would unlock the most illuminating answers.

Giulia decided that her mistake had been to ask a question that was too vague.

A week later, on a morning when the choir nuns were called to a meeting in the chapter room and Humilità was still away cleaning the choir paintings, Giulia dug out the astrolabe and brought it into the court again. This time she was explicit: *When will I meet the man who will be my husband?* The result was a chart that seemed to show a long span of time and a great deal of opposition. Another error—it had to be, for the only alternative was that the talisman would fail, and that was impossible.

Unwilling to give up, she returned to the courtyard and asked a different question: *When will I escape from Santa Marta?* This time, the answer was clear: Before winter.

She caught her breath. She'd steeled herself for a much worse answer, or for no answer at all.

"That's enough now, Giulia." From across the drafting table, Perpetua gave vent at last to her disapproval. "Perhaps there's no harm in such games, but you have more important things to do."

"Yes, Perpetua."

Giulia burned the charts, as she had the others, and went back to sweeping. *Before winter,* she thought as her broom whisked the tiles, stirring up little clouds of dust. *Four months, or maybe five, and I'll be gone.*

When she'd first come to the workshop, that would have seemed an impossible amount of time to endure. Now it seemed hardly any time at all. She could almost imagine she was sorry it wasn't a little longer—for the sake of the learning, and for Angela.

Almost.

On July twenty-ninth, Santa Marta celebrated the feast of its patron saint. All work was suspended. A special Mass was held, and even the *conversae* and the novices were allowed to take Communion and to confess.

Giulia had dreaded confession—she could not possibly reveal the sorcerer and the talisman, the sin she had no intention of renouncing. When her turn came to kneel before the grille set into the wall that divided the nuns' chapel from the public part of the church, she whispered to the priest on the other side everything except that. He made no comment as she confessed her anger at the Countess, her reluctance to become a nun, her loathing of Alessia; she had the sense, even through the heavy lattice of the grille, that he was not really listening. When she was done, he mumbled a penance and an absolution, the words running together so she could hardly understand them, and sent her on her way.

She knelt before the chapel's crucifix with the other penitents, her hands clasped together, but did not pray. She salved her conscience by promising herself that she would say the penance later, when she had gained her heart's desire and no longer wore the talisman around her neck. She would make a full confession then too. Until that time, she had no choice but to live with the burden of her sin—even if it were an additional sin to do so.

Afterward, in the beautifully decorated refectory, there was a magnificent meal—especially appropriate for this feast day, since Santa Marta was the patron saint of cooks. When the eating was done, the tables and benches were pushed back and a group of nuns presented a play about Santa Marta's life, written by one of the sisters. It was reverent but also very funny, with nuns in costumes (some of which Giulia recognized from the workshop) impersonating men as well as women. Sitting at the back of the room with the novices, Giulia was able to escape her dark mood for a while, and laugh along with the others.

The next day, work began in earnest on the San Giustina commission. Giulia and Angela had finished gessoing and burnishing the three huge panels the previous week; now, with Humilità, Perpetua, Lucida, and Domenica, they wrestled the panels onto the wooden support structures that Domenica, who was as handy with hammer and nails as any man, had built to hold them, facing the light of the workshop's open wall. It was a nerve-racking job, for the panels were very heavy, made of joined planks that might split if dropped. The painters got them into place without mishap, finishing just as the bell rang for Sext.

Returning from the midday meal, Giulia found Angela already at work on the long list of colors Humilità and the other painters would need in the coming days—except of course for Passion blue, which Humilità, as always, prepared in secret. Perpetua and Lucida sat together at the drafting table. Lucida was in the midst of a story.

". . . and Nicolosia's father shut her up in her room as punishment for her defiance. And the next morning, what do you think? Nicolosia was gone! Her family was terrified she'd been abducted by some villain, but when they questioned her maid—oh, Perpetua—" Lucida broke off, pushing a little basket toward the older nun. "Do take another almond ball."

"Lucida, you are such a tease!" Perpetua exclaimed.

"I don't want an almond ball—I want the rest of the story!"

Lucida laughed. "Giulia, have some almond balls! They're from Signorelli—the best in Padua."

Giulia finished tying on her apron, then went to take a handful of the little sweets, which she brought over to the preparation table to share with Angela. The candies were wonderful, filling her mouth with the richness of sugar and the crunch of almonds. Lucida's sisters always brought a delicacy of some sort on their weekly visits to Santa Marta. They also brought gossip, and Lucida carried both back with her to the workshop, entertaining her fellow artists with tales of the Paduan nobility. Giulia marveled, sometimes, that she'd ever thought that nuns knew nothing of the world beyond their walls. Santa Marta's brick and mortar might close off physical passage, but to news and information, they were as permeable as water.

"At first the maid pretended she knew nothing," Lucida went on with her story. "But in the end she confessed—Nicolosia had eloped! With Deodato Mantegna! He came in the middle of the night and put a ladder to her window."

"No!" Perpetua leaned back in astonishment.

"By the time they were found, they were already married. Now Deodato's family is insisting that Nicolosia's family pay a dowry, and Nicolosia's family is seeking to have the marriage annulled."

"If she's clever, she'll get herself with child," said Benedicta from her lectern. "Then no one will be able to pretend the marriage wasn't consummated."

"Benedicta!" said Perpetua, scandalized. Beside Giulia, Angela giggled.

"That's exactly what they're hoping won't happen, obviously," Lucida said. "But there's another problem. Nicolosia had been affianced to Erasmo da Carrara since she was ten years old. Now her family owes the Carraras a bride. But their only other daughter is Nicolosia's sister Catarina, who is a nun at Santa Anna."

"Oh, what a dilemma!" Perpetua clasped her hands. "What will they do?"

"My sister Maria says they will remove Catarina from the convent and give her to Erasmo."

"Remove her?" Perpetua was horrified. "They can't do that! She is the bride of Our Lord Jesus Christ!"

"It wouldn't be the first time. Forty or fifty years ago, at . . . oh, Maria told me the convent's name but I've forgotten . . . at any rate, there were two daughters, the older was affianced and the younger took vows. The older sister died before the wedding, and they removed the younger so she could take her sister's place. It required special intervention by the Church, but it was a noble family, and so it was done." Lucida shook her head. "The sister begged to be allowed to resume her vows. When her family refused, she threw herself from her bedroom window. She didn't die, but it cost her the use of her limbs. Of course she couldn't be married in such a state, so her family sent her back to the convent, where she lived out her life in the infirmary. In the end she got her wish. And her family got nothing, except for grief and scandal."

"Oh, that poor girl!" Angela said. "To be crippled so!"

"I know a scandal," said Benedicta from her lectern.

"You, Benedicta?"

"Who better, Lucida, since it happened fifty years ago, right here at Santa Marta. A nun who was taken from the convent—by her own will, though, not another's."

Giulia, who had finished her almond balls and was at the shelves gathering supplies, felt a chill ripple down her back. Normally she only half-listened to these gossip sessions; the names of the people and places meant nothing to her. But now, all at once, she was fully alert.

"Here?" said Perpetua. "Surely not."

"My teeth may be gone," said Benedicta tartly, "but I've still got my memory. It happened not long after I took my vows. There was a young nun named Plautilla, whose brother loved her dearly and came frequently to visit. Often he brought his friend Alessandro. Somehow, Alessandro and Plautilla fell in love. They took to meeting secretly in the orchard. There was a broken spot in the convent's western wall, at the very back where it ran beside the canal. Alessandro climbed into the orchard that way, and they met under the trees."

Giulia turned. A breach in those impregnable walls?

"He must have loved her greatly, to take such a risk," Lucida said.

"He loved her thoroughly, at any rate." Benedicta cackled, rocking a little on her stool. "Oh, what a scandal, when Plautilla was found to be with child! The abbess didn't want it known, for fear the Cardinal would hear of it and curtail our privileges. So she kept it secret, meaning to smuggle the baby out to be adopted when it finally came. But then . . ." Benedicta leaned forward. "On a night when the moon was full, Plautilla disappeared. Poof!" She threw up her hands. "Just like that. As for Alessandro . . . that very same night, he vanished from the city."

"He came for her!" Giulia hadn't meant to say anything. "He came over the wall!"

"That's what I've always believed, my dear."

"What happened?" Angela asked. "Was she ever found?"

"They were never heard from again." Benedicta smiled her sweet, toothless smile. "Quite a love story, eh?"

"Love story!" Perpetua was indignant. "A disgrace, you mean! No, I don't believe it. How could we not know about such a thing, if it really happened?"

"Because," Benedicta said, "the abbess decided it should be forgotten. She had the break in the wall bricked up, good as new, and she ordered us never to speak of it. But you can't forget a thing like that, can you?" She sighed, her wizened old face suddenly sad. "We're almost all gone, those of us who were nuns then. Strange to think of it now."

"Those bricks have fallen in again," Lucida said thoughtfully. "I walk sometimes in the orchard, and there's a gap in the wall, at the very back along the canal, just as you said. I told my aunt about it. She said she knew, but there were repairs that were more pressing."

"That's the problem with suppressing stories." Benedicta cackled again, her momentary sadness gone. "Sometimes they hold lessons we should remember."

"What lessons?" demanded a new voice. It was Humilità, entering in her usual vigorous manner, with Domenica beside her. Behind them walked one of the local servant women who came in daily to help in the kitchens.

"We were just gossiping," Lucida said. "It's my fault, Maestra. My sisters brought me sweets and I was sharing them, and we fell to talking."

"Well, no harm done. Serena"—Humilità addressed the servant—"you may prepare over by the benches. The rest of you, to work! You too, my butterfly, but not before you give me a few of those—what are they? Ginger comfits?"

"Almond balls. From Signorelli." Lucida held out the basket. "Domenica, won't you have some? A little sugar might do you good."

Domenica swept past as if she hadn't heard. Humilità, digging into the basket, shook her head.

"Lucida, Lucida." She turned. "Come, girls. Time for our lesson."

Humilità was a demanding teacher, intolerant of anything less than what she judged to be her pupils' best. She expected Giulia and Angela not just to draw, but to *think* about what they drew—evaluating every line, considering every choice—and to be able to explain, after finishing a picture, exactly why they had drawn it as they did. She gave praise where she judged it due, but never softened her criticism to spare the girls' feelings.

Giulia had always drawn instinctively, choosing whatever subjects took her interest, the images flowing from eye to hand as water flowed downhill—a swift, almost alchemical transformation that she had never tried, or wanted, to put into words. She found it hard to draw when the subject was selected for her. It was hard also to be forced to explain the process, to have her mistakes and successes picked apart like a piece of embroidery, until, as it seemed to her, there was nothing left. She was a better artist than Angela (she knew this without vanity), yet she was more often the focus of Humilità's criticism, and less often the subject of her approval. It was impossible, sometimes, not to feel aggrieved.

Yet Humilità was a master. Giulia was always aware of it, and never more so than in the lessons, when Humilità's passion poured from her like heat or light. She couldn't deny that, over the past weeks, her own technique had improved. She craved Humilità's praise, even as she resented the workshop mistress for how stingy she was with it.

Today was to be a life class, quill and ink on rose-colored paper. The model, Serena, pulled off her gown and shoes and shook out her long red hair. Humilità arranged her on a stool, the hem of her chemise drawn up and one sleeve pulled down, exposing her plump bare legs and one smooth naked shoulder. Strictly speaking, such posing was forbidden; it was sinful for a woman to look upon uncovered flesh, even another woman's. "But how can you draw people in their clothes, if you don't know what they look like out of them?" Humilità, explaining this to Giulia, had demanded. "So we do it anyway."

Serena was a lovely subject, but Giulia couldn't concentrate. Benedicta's story, the nun and her lover who had met in the orchard and escaped through the gap in the wall, would not leave her mind. She was uncomfortably aware of the silent, judging presence of Humilità, pacing slowly at her pupils' backs, pausing every now and then to peer over their shoulders. When, about halfway through her drawing, she carelessly filled her quill too full and made a blot on the paper, she braced herself for a reprimand. But all Humilità said was, "Start over."

When the lesson was done, Humilità motioned for Giulia to stay. "Your mind was somewhere else today."

"I'm sorry, Maestra. I'll do better tomorrow."

"See that you do. I have something to tell you. You may know that I have permission to visit my father's studio four times a year to obtain supplies. The day after tomorrow is my summer visit. Each time I go, I take one of my artists with me. This time it will be you."

"Me?" Giulia said. "Going out? Into the city?"

Humilità smiled. "Since my father's studio is not inside these walls, yes, we will go out. I have written him to expect us. Does that suit you?"

"Oh, yes, Maestra! Thank you!"

"It will be a good learning experience for you, to see the running of a larger workshop. Now go along, work is waiting for us both."

She strode off to begin transferring the cartoons for the San Giustina commission to the scaffolded panels, a task she would not allow any of the others to help with. Giulia returned to the preparation table.

"She's taking you to her father's studio, isn't she," Angela said, measuring finished pigment into a jar.

"Yes," Giulia replied, hardly believing it.

"Wait till you see it." Angela smiled. "It's so big! And so busy! There's nearly a score of apprentices and journeymen, and they make all kinds of things, sculptures and silver goods and gold jewelry, not just paintings."

"Silver goods and jewelry? Really?"

"The Maestra's father can fresco a chapel, and furnish it too. He's famous, you know—all the great and noble of Padua are his patrons. Paintings and goods from his workshop are in houses and holy places all over the city. And he dotes on our Maestra. You'll see."

Returning to the dormitory with the other novices for recreation hour, Giulia discovered that her bedclothes—which she'd left perfectly tucked in as Suor Margarita required—had been pulled askew, her pillow tossed to the floor. She sighed. In addition to pinching, hair-yanking, and mockery, Alessia and her friends occasionally sneaked back to the dormitory to leave nasty surprises for the other girls.

Suor Margarita noticed, of course, and sent Giulia to do penance with Lisa at the fireplace. Lisa, who was being punished for knocking over her soup bowl, gave Giulia a sympathetic look as Giulia knelt down.

"It was Costanza," she mumbled. "Your bed. I saw her. But really it was Alessia."

"It always is." The others treated Lisa as if she were slow-witted, but to Giulia it was clear that she was not stupid at all.

"I'm going to pray she gets warts."

Lisa went back to muttering the Paternoster. Giulia clasped her hands as if in prayer and closed her eyes. She could hear the giggles of Alessia and her clique, but for once she didn't care. *I'm going out the day after tomorrow. Out of Santa Marta, out into the city.* She could feel herself yearning toward that freedom, like a sunflower twisting to the light.

She thought of the horoscope she had cast. Before winter, it had said. The day after tomorrow wouldn't be the day she escaped. But something would happen. She was sure of it.

"It's my chance, Mama," she whispered, so softly only she could hear. "Everything is about to change."

CHAPTER 13

❖ The City of Painters ❖

On the appointed day, Giulia arrived at the saint's door right after breakfast. No one was there, and for a few uncomfortable moments she feared that she had somehow mistaken Humilità's meaning or that there had been a change of plans. But then Humilità appeared, striding along the loggia in her purposeful way. She wore a black cloak over her white habit and carried a covered basket.

"Are you ready, Giulia?"

"Oh yes," Giulia breathed.

Humilità rapped briskly on the saint's door. The lock scraped and the door swung open on the cool dimness of the vestibule. Giulia vividly remembered her panic the one and only time she had crossed this threshold—but today she was going in the opposite direction. Her heart pounded with excitement, not dread.

The doorkeeper pulled open the outer door, and Humilità led the way into the heat and light of the street.

"Take my arm, Giulia." Behind them, the door thumped closed. "There will be crowds, and I don't want to lose you."

Giulia had not seen much of Padua on the day of her arrival, for Cristina had insisted on keeping the carriage's window covers closed. Now, as she and Humilità walked, she craned her neck to look up at the houses that rose two, three, even four stories on either side, their plaster fronts tinted cream and gold and pink. Balconies jutted overhead; windows spilled drying laundry or held pots of brightly colored flowers. On nearly every block, arcaded walkways along the house fronts allowed pedestrians to stay clear of the carts and riders that thronged the street. The clatter of wheels and hooves echoed in the confined spaces; the air smelled of animals, refuse, smoke, and, distantly, the stagnant water of the canals.

Giulia breathed deeply, savoring the bustle and the noise, the sight of buildings that were not cloisters and people who were not nuns. Humilità set a quick pace, expertly navigating a succession of narrow, twisty avenues. Pedestrians made way for them, bowing or crossing themselves; a few offered alms, which Humilità accepted with a nod and a blessing and dropped into her basket.

Ahead, Giulia saw a dazzle of sunlight. A roaring swelled beneath the din of traffic: the sound of a great crowd. The houses and arcades fell away, and they emerged into a huge light-filled piazza, packed with market stalls and teeming with people. Beyond the stalls rose one of the most extraordinary buildings Giulia had ever seen, overtopping the surrounding houses and extending almost the entire width of the piazza. It was fronted at ground level by a columned arcade; above the arcade, a graceful loggia ran the full length of the second floor, and above that, red brick walls supported the dome of an immense roof, shaped like a great barrel sawed in half.

"That's the Palazzo della Ragione, the Palace of Justice," Humilità said. "It's a marvel of engineering—that roof is self-supporting, there's not a single column holding it up. Padua's courts meet on the upper level, and below is the market, the Piazza della Fruitta on this side, the Piazza dell'Erbe on the other. But it's not just fruits and vegetables. In the Padua market, you can buy nearly anything."

They plunged into the market, past stalls heaped high with every kind of fruit, with great cheese wheels and baskets of spices and metal and leather goods and cloth. The air was rich with the odors of all these things, clamorous with the voices of vendors crying their wares and customers haggling over prices. Humilità paused at a stall arrayed with fat rounds of bread, and one offering velvety apricots and dusky plums, and one selling pots of soft cheese. She insisted on paying for her purchases, even when the merchants would have provided them as charity.

With the items tucked into her basket, she steered Giulia into the shadow of the Palazzo's ground-level arcade and sat down on one of the benches there, motioning Giulia to do the same.

"I used to come here with my mother when I was a girl," she said, settling the folds of her cloak. "It seemed like the most wondrous place in the world."

"My mother used to take me to the market too, when she needed special fabrics or embroidery thread." Giulia smiled, remembering. "She always bought me a sugar pig."

"Your mother was a seamstress?"

Giulia nodded. "She taught me to sew. I was never good at it, though. Not the way she was."

"Were you very young when she died?"

"I was seven." After all these years, it was still hard to say.

"I was eight."

Giulia looked at Humilità, surprised, but the workshop mistress was bending forward, rummaging in her basket.

"Here." She pulled out several sheets of paper and two sticks of charcoal. "I always sit here awhile and draw, on my outside days. You can do the same, if you like." She handed Giulia the paper and one of the charcoal sticks. "Today isn't a lesson, so you may please yourself."

She took out her sketchbook, which she carried everywhere in her waist pouch, as Giulia once had done, and set to work.

Giulia drew a woman lugging a heavy oil jar, a child hanging on his mother's skirts, crows wheeling against the cloudless sky. But the bustle of the market was distracting, and after a little while she set her paper aside. It was very hot, even in the shade of the arcade; her chemise was damp under her scratchy novice dress. How did Humilità stand it, with her wimple and veil, her heavy habit and enveloping cloak? Passersby cast them curious looks. At first shyly and then more boldly, Giulia looked back. But their eyes, especially those of the young men, always slid away. Like Alberto, they saw only the ugly novice uniform.

But someone will see more, she told herself. *This is my day, and it has only just begun.*

She looked at Humilità. The workshop mistress was not sketching scenes or figures, but filling page after page with faces. Giulia was fascinated by the workshop mistress's swiftness, the sureness with which she captured features and expressions.

At last Humilità sighed, put down her charcoal, and stretched her arms.

"That's enough for now, I think." She turned over the sheets she had filled. "I can draw from imagination, but I prefer to work from life, and I can't use the same nuns' faces over and over again. And how, in the drawing of men's faces, can one find inspiration inside a convent? So I bring my book"—she closed the cover and patted it—"on each of my outside days, and add to it as I can. When I need a fresh face, I have it."

"I used to carry a sketchbook," Giulia said. "And charcoal. My fingers were always black with it."

"I too, when I was a child. My mother used to scold me, though it never did any good. Where is your sketchbook now?"

"I had to . . . leave it." Giulia thought of the gap inside the chimney where it was hidden.

"In Milan?"

"Not exactly. But it isn't with me any longer."

Humilità's dark gaze was keen. She was not the stern instructor now, or the energetic workshop mistress, but something else, something Giulia had not seen before.

"You wouldn't be at Santa Marta, would you, Giulia, if you had your choice."

Dismayed, Giulia looked down at her clasped hands. She'd thought she was doing a better job of pretending.

"I understand. Truly, I do. Forced vocations are a common evil."

"Everyone says that." Giulia looked up. "But then why are they allowed?"

Humilità sighed. "Because they benefit the fathers and brothers who don't wish to support a woman who cannot marry, a woman who is mad or ugly or disfigured or simply inconvenient."

Inconvenient, Giulia thought. *Yes, that's me.* "Not always fathers and brothers. It was my father's wife who sent me here."

"Giulia, I know it isn't easy. To sacrifice the world and its delights, to accept a life within walls—no, that is not easy. As artists, too, it is more difficult, for we are not in the world, and can only imagine it in our work"—she gestured to her sketchbook—"with a little help if we're lucky." Her voice held the edge it acquired when she spoke of something that angered or frustrated her. "But God knows better than we do what we're fit for. Your father's wife may have had ill reasons for sending you to Santa Marta, but she did God's will nonetheless."

"I saw nothing of God in what she did to me."

"All things happen for a reason. Santa Marta is the one place in the world where you can become what God made you: a painter. In time, you will understand that."

Giulia said nothing. She could not tell the truth, and didn't want to lie.

Humilità set her sketchbook aside and shifted on the bench so she could look into Giulia's face.

"I have made my workshop famous," she said. "I know pride is a sin, yet I confess it—I am proud. I thank God every day that He created me what I am, that He has allowed me to do what I most love and thus give Him glory. Padua is a city of painters—Giotto, Lippi, Altichiero, Mantegna—all have left their mark here, and so will I. But of all the gifts God has given me, there's one I haven't had. Can you guess what it is?"

Giulia shook her head.

"An heir. Someone to take my place when I die, or grow too old to hold my brush. Someone to pass my secrets to. Someone to carry on my work." She paused. "Perhaps you, Giulia."

Giulia was astonished. "Me?"

"I'm hard on you, I know. But only because I see the promise in you." Humilità reached out and took both Giulia's hands in hers. "You have so much talent, child. It is wild and undisciplined, but if you can learn to master it, if you will let me train you as I know I can, you will become a true artist. Perhaps even a great one. One whose name may be remembered."

Unbidden, the words of the horoscope fragment came into Giulia's mind: *She shall not take another's name, nor shall she bear her own at the end of life. . . .*

"I know that your vocation has been forced. I know you fear the vows a nun must make. But Giulia, those vows will not give you only a nun's life. They will give you a painter's life. An *artist's* life. And I promise you that a true vocation awaits you there. I promise you that I will show you how to find it."

Her grip on Giulia's hands tightened, almost painfully. Then she let go and rose to her feet.

"Come, it must be near noon. We should be getting on. Give me your charcoal and paper."

Giulia handed them over. She took Humilità's arm again. They left the market, entering the tangle of streets once more.

This time, Giulia barely noticed where they were going. Humilità's excitement over her *cortile* drawing . . . being brought into the workshop, as no other novice ever had been . . . the rigorous and sometimes harsh instruction . . . she had never thought to put those things together, to imagine what they might add up to. Humilità, master painter, leader of the only workshop of women in the world, thought that she, Giulia, might become a great artist! Even, perhaps, workshop mistress in her turn!

All at once she could see that future, like a road stretching out before her. The years of training. Becoming a journeyman like Lucida, then a master like Benedicta. Her work displayed in private chapels and in public places, where hundreds of eyes, maybe thousands of eyes, would see it. A life spent painting—an artist's life, as Humilità had said.

But I'd have to become a nun. I'd have to spend the rest of my life at Santa Marta.

And just like that, the vision died. She wanted to paint—yes, she wanted that, though she hadn't really understood how much until now. But she did not want to live as Humilità did, cloistered within walls, ruled by bells, surrounded by sisters, only sisters—never a husband or a lover, never children. Never a home of her own. Painting or no painting, she could not find a vocation for that kind of life. She did not *want* such a vocation. She hated Santa Marta.

Or did she?

An awful confusion swept her. At her side, Humilità strode purposefully along, a look of satisfaction on her face. For a moment, childishly, Giulia was angry with her—for making such impossible promises, for invoking such an impossible future. But then she remembered her own deception, how every day she cheated Humilità's trust by falsely playing the part of a true apprentice.

"Is anything the matter, Giulia?"

"No, Maestra."

It changes nothing. What she told me changes nothing.

She struggled to believe it.

Chapter 14

❖ The Balcony ❖

They stopped at last before a well-kept three-story house, with an arched doorway beneath its shady arcade.

"I was born in this house," Humilità said. "My mother died in it."

She stood a moment, gazing up at the balconied front, then shook her head as if shaking off a thought and stepped forward to bang the iron knocker. The door was opened by a stout elderly woman, her plain brown dress tied up at one side to reveal a bright scarlet underskirt.

Her look of suspicion vanished when she saw

Humilità. "Violetta!" she cried. "Oh, my pet! You're home!"

She held out her arms. The two women embraced. Humilità pulled away and put a hand on Giulia's shoulder.

"This is Giulia Borromeo, my pupil. Giulia, this is Lorenza, who raised my brothers and me after our mother died."

"Welcome, Giulia." Lorenza offered a gap-toothed smile. "We're always glad to meet one of Violetta's girls."

"Lorenza refuses to use my religious name," said Humilità with affection, "no matter how I rebuke her."

"Well, my pet, it doesn't suit you."

"I see you still wear your red underskirt."

"The day I *don't* wear my red underskirt is the day you should remark upon it. Come in, come in. You're just in time for lunch."

Giulia glanced at her teacher as they entered. *Violetta?* Lorenza was right, Humilità didn't suit her, for she was anything but humble. But Violetta fit her even less.

Lorenza led them down a central hallway and into the kitchen, its windows and doors thrown open against the heat. Several women were preparing food; they dropped their tasks and crowded around, exchanging greetings and kisses. Once Giulia had been introduced and Humilità's basket unpacked, Lorenza led them through the kitchen door, into the courtyard beyond.

"I'll just go tell the master you're here."

The courtyard was enormous. Flagstone paving sloped toward a drain at the center, where a trio of boys knelt at a washtub. By the wall that formed the left-hand boundary, two men worked at a carpenter's table, surrounded by wood shavings and scraps. A single-story brick building rose on the right, with windows all along its front and huge openings cut into its peaked roof, their shutters flung back.

"My father's workshop." Humilità nodded toward the building. "When I was nine, he bought the house next to ours and knocked down the wall between the two courtyards so he could build the workshop onto the back."

"Will we go inside?" Giulia could hear the sound of voices and hammering and see figures passing before the windows. Some of the excitement she had felt that morning began to return.

"Yes indeed. My father employs nearly twenty apprentices and journeymen. Some of them live in that house"—She gestured toward the house next door. "My brothers and their families live with my father in this one, where we all grew up."

"Your brothers are painters too?"

"Gianfrancesco and Tiberio are. Fernando's talents tend more to business." Humilità smiled. "A good thing for my father. His fortunes have risen since Nando began to manage his affairs."

There was a small commotion inside the workshop, and a man burst through the door. He was as big as a bear, with a broad, craggy face and iron-gray curls swept back from a high forehead. His clothes were stained with paint, as were his hands, outstretched as he strode toward Humilità and Giulia.

"My favorite daughter!" he cried in a booming voice that seemed to fill the court. "Come to pay her old father a visit!"

He swept Humilità into his arms, lifting her off her feet like a child. Before that moment, Giulia could never have imagined anyone treating her strong-willed, dignified teacher so.

"Your *only* daughter, Papa." Humilità laughed as he set her down.

"That doesn't mean I can't have a favorite." He winked at Giulia. Humilità had his eyes—deep-set, dark as olive pits. "And I assume this lovely young lady is the new apprentice you wrote to me about."

"Yes." Humilità tugged at her wimple, which had been pulled askew. "Giulia Borromeo, this is my father, Matteo Moretti—artist, artisan, and chairman of the *Fraglia*, the Paduan painters' guild."

"I'm honored to meet you, sir." Giulia curtsied.

"The honor is entirely mine!" He made a little bow and smiled, displaying a perfect set of teeth. Gray hair and all, he was a good-looking man—but also, in his bigness and his loudness and something else that Giulia could not quite put her finger on, intimidating. "Violetta has never apprenticed a novice before. She must believe you have promise."

"Giulia has great talent, Papa. She's farther along than I was at her age, even though she's entirely self-trained."

"Saints protect us." Matteo cast his eyes heavenward.

"Another female genius. What is the world coming to?"

"Of all my brothers," Humilità said to Giulia, "none is my father's equal. He has long wondered what sin he committed, that God should give the greatest ability to his daughter."

She was smiling, but Giulia heard the edge in her voice. Her father laughed.

"You've made the best of it, haven't you, Violetta?"

"What of my brothers, Papa? Are they not with you?"

"Nando is away—"

"Oh, no!"

"Yes, my dear, I'm sorry, he was meant to be home but there was some difficulty with the delivery schedules and he had to extend his stay. But you'll see Gianfrancesco and Tiberio when they return later this afternoon. Come, ladies." Matteo Moretti gestured toward the stairway that rose from the side of the court to the second floor. "We'll lunch in my study."

The study was a big room with a low ceiling and several windows looking down onto the street below. There was a large worktable strewn with drawing and writing materials, at least a dozen chests and cabinets crammed with books and papers, and, at the windows, a dais for posing, with several lecterns set up nearby. Giulia was reminded of Maestro—not because this room was similar to Maestro's study, but because it spoke so clearly of a man completely dedicated to his craft.

Humilità's father directed them to a small table

laid for a meal. Lorenza and one of the women from the kitchen brought in bread, cheese, olives, a salad of artichokes, and the fruit Humilità had purchased at the market. Humilità and her father talked of family matters—the recent illness of her oldest brother, Tiberio; the engagement of her youngest, Gianfrancesco; her middle brother Fernando's spendthrift wife. Matteo Moretti spoke of the major commission he had recently received, to furnish and fresco the newly renovated chapel of a noble family, and Humilità described the completion of the Santa Barbara panels.

Giulia ate and listened. It was odd to see the confident workshop mistress flush as her father teased her, and even odder to hear him interrogate her about her work as if she were a journeyman, rather than a master painter. Was it hard for her to come home this way, Giulia wondered—to return to the world she had renounced, and then renounce it all over again when it was time to go? Despite the frustration with the convent's limitations that Humilità occasionally revealed, she had never said anything to suggest that her vocation had been anything but willing. Still, Giulia remembered her words, in the market, about sacrifice. She remembered how Humilità had stood looking up at her childhood home when they arrived.

Was Santa Marta really the only way she could paint? Couldn't her father have kept her with him?

"You should have seen it in its original form." The conversation had shifted to the San Giustina commission, and the unusually detailed contract the monastery had insisted on. "They wanted to specify the exact composition of the central panel, can you believe it?"

Matteo Moretti was frowning. "Why did you not write to me, Violetta? I could have advised you."

"I've been running a workshop for some years, Papa. I am quite capable of doing my own negotiating. I admit I made more concessions than I ordinarily would, but San Giustina is a prestigious monastery, and this will advance my workshop's reputation. A balance of interests. Didn't you teach me that?"

"I did, I did." Matteo leaned back in his chair and folded his arms. "What sort of concessions, if I may ask?"

"They want it complete by the middle of October so that it may be dedicated at the feast of All Saints in November. The requirements for the framing and gilding are extremely detailed—that's one of the things I want to talk to you about today. I must also use a large amount of Passion blue. The abbot wants to give glory to God with a magnificent altarpiece—but he also wants everyone to know how expensive it was."

"Naturally," Matteo said.

"And I'll be painting every figure in the central panel myself, and the thieves in the side panels as well."

"*Every* figure? Violetta, Violetta. That's why you have journeymen—to spare you that kind of labor. Particularly with such a close deadline."

"Never fear, Papa, the fee I demanded would please even you. Although my expenses will be higher than I anticipated. The cost for one of my blue's ingredients has gone up."

Her father raised his eyebrows. "Lapis lazuli? It's been some time since I purchased any. What's the increase?"

"Ah, Papa." Humilità shook her finger at him. "Did you really think you would catch me that way?" She turned to Giulia. "My father never tires of trying to trick me into telling him what's in Passion blue. He wants the recipe for himself, you see."

"And why not?" Matteo spread his arms. "Imagine the fame and fortune my workshop could command if I had the formula for that most mysterious of colors!"

"Your workshop already commands fame and fortune, Papa."

"Ah, but it could command so much more! Your blue wouldn't lose its secrecy, my dear—it would just become a *family* secret." He set his hands on his knees and leaned toward her over the table. "A good daughter would obey her father and share the recipe."

"I am *your* daughter," Humilità said. "Whom you taught to know her worth, and also how to hold her counsel."

Their dark eyes, so much alike, were locked. Giulia felt a change, like a breath of cold air sweeping through the stuffy room. Then Matteo threw back his head and laughed.

"Ah, Violetta, I never could make you do a thing you didn't want. But you can't blame me for trying."

"Can't I, Papa?" The edge was there again in Humilità's voice.

"You must pass it on to someone, you know."

"Why? Perhaps I would rather that it die with me."

Matteo shook his head. "You've a God-given gift, the equal of any man's. But only a woman could be so stubborn and capricious." He surveyed their empty plates. "I think we're finished here. Giulia, have you had enough?"

"Yes, sir. It was a delicious lunch."

"Good. I'll just go fetch my recipe book so we can discuss the gilding and anything else you might need. Excuse me a moment."

He disappeared through a door in the left-hand wall of the study, closing it behind him. There were scuffling sounds, then a muffled thump.

"He keeps his recipe book hidden under a loose floorboard under the window in his bedroom," Humilità said, her eyes on the door. "He thinks no one knows, but my brother Gianfrancesco found out when we were children. All four of us know what's in that book. We all know his secrets."

The words carried a strange bitterness. Giulia said nothing.

The door opened and Matteo came out again, holding a leather-bound ledger in his arms—very much like Humilità's own recipe book, but without a brass clasp.

"I doubt Giulia will find our discussions interesting," he said. "Perhaps she'd like to sit on the balcony and observe, as you used to do, my dear."

"That's a good idea, Papa." Humilità turned to Giulia. "When I was a child we all trained together, me alongside my brothers and the apprentices, as if I were a boy. As I grew older, though, that was no longer proper. So when my father built the workshop, he made a special place for me, so I could draw from life and yet be separate. You'll be able to see everything from there."

"Yes, Maestra." Giulia felt a thrill of anticipation. "May I draw too?"

"Of course."

The workshop was an enormous rectangular space, entirely open. From her stool on the balcony, which jutted out like the prow of a boat from one end, Giulia could indeed see everything, but was herself concealed from view unless someone looked up.

Much was familiar—the drafting tables, the shelves of pigment materials, the preparation area where apprentices were grinding colors, the mixed smells of smoke, wood, glue, and exotic materials. But much was strange, for as Angela had said, Matteo Moretti made not just paintings, but furniture and gold and silver goods—a full range of luxury items for the nobles and monasteries that were his patrons. The workshop was a chaotic hive of activity, with men and boys laboring at various tasks and rushing back and forth. Equipment and materials were everywhere, scattered on surfaces, tossed on the floor, pushed carelessly into corners along with piles of trash and debris. Despite the open doors and windows, dust opaqued the air. The din of tools and voices reminded Giulia of the clamor of the market.

In the center, where light streamed down through the roof openings, several painters worked on a large panel set up in front of a meticulously composed live tableau. A man knelt in prayer, clad only in a loincloth, his face raised as if in pain or ecstasy. Near him lay a woman, wrapped in a red robe that left her arms bare. Above them, suspended from a harness, a long-haired boy in flowing garments stretched down his arms, a huge pair of feathered wings bound to his back. Humilità used models and costumes too—there had been a procession of them lately, as she prepared for the San Giustina commission—but never anything so elaborate.

Obeying the familiar tingling in her fingers, Giulia took up the charcoal Humilità had left and began to sketch. At first she tried to draw the tableau as if she were standing on the floor below, but not only was that difficult, it didn't capture what she found interesting about the scene. She crumpled the paper and started again. She would draw exactly what she saw: not a man and a woman and an angel, but models posing and artists at their work.

It was stifling under the roof. Giulia's hands were sticky, and she had to pause to wipe sweat from her forehead with her sleeve. The talisman absorbed her body heat. She could feel the chain, a warmth at the back of her neck, and the stone, hot where it lay on the skin of her chest, just below the little pouch that held her horoscope fragment. Too hot, now she thought of it—hot enough to be uncomfortable. She put down the charcoal and curled her fingers around it—

"Giulia."

The voice, soft and urgent, came from behind her. It startled her so much that she jumped to her feet, letting out a yelp of fright.

She turned, and froze. Standing only a few steps away was the repairer of frescoes, Ormanno Trovatelli, whom she had never thought to see again. She stared at him, thunderstruck.

"I'm sorry," he said. "I didn't mean to scare you."

They were the words she'd spoken to him, the first time they met. "What are you . . ." She tried to catch her breath. "What are you doing here?"

"I work here."

"Here?"

"Of course." His hair curled around his face just as she recalled. His pale eyes were just as bright. "I'm a journeyman painter in Maestro Moretti's workshop."

She felt the talisman, hard against her palm. Later, it would seem to her that everything had gone clear, the way it had when she first put the necklace on: edges sharper, colors deeper, light more vivid. "You never said."

"Maestra Humilità always calls on her father's workshop for help when there's work she can't do herself. I assumed you knew."

"I thought . . . I just thought you were some sort of artisan."

"Well, I am. All painters are." His gaze slid away from hers, to the drawing that had fallen from her lap. "You dropped—" He bent and picked it up, then paused, his brows drawing together. "You've put in the harness he's hanging from. And the apprentices."

"I wanted to draw what's actually there. Not the story it's supposed to tell."

"It's good." He sounded surprised. "You're good."

He held it toward her. She took it. They looked at each other. She felt a breathless tension, like a tightening wire.

"Listen, Giulia." Ormanno's words came in a rush. "I've been thinking about you ever since we met. I know what you said about not wanting to be a nun, but still, you're a novice, inside convent walls, and I knew I should forget you. But I couldn't and that's the truth. When I saw you with your Maestra in the courtyard today, I had to try and talk to you again. I thought maybe you felt the same, but if I'm wrong, if I offend you by being here, just tell me and I'll go."

Giulia's heart had begun to pound. "You don't offend me."

"I'm glad." He seemed to hesitate. "You said . . . that day . . . that I could visit you. Did you mean it?"

Giulia's head was spinning. How long had she been waiting for this? Now it was happening, really happening. She felt as if she were tumbling downhill, too fast to think, too fast to stop. And she did not want to stop.

"Yes," she said.

"Then I will. I'll ask for you in the parlor. I'll say I'm your cousin Federico."

"You remembered."

"Of course."

"There's a chaperone. And there's a grille, you'll have to be on the other side of it. But . . ." *But the bars are far enough apart that hands can touch.* "We'll be able to talk to each other."

The intensity of his gaze burned across the space between them. "I wish there was a way we could meet like this. Without bars, I mean, or others watching."

And like a door opening in Giulia's mind, there it was. Benedicta's story.

"I know a way."

"Tell me."

"There's a break in the wall at the back of the convent, where it runs along the canal." Giulia had a sense of events slotting into place, as the panels of the San Giustina commission had slotted into their scaffolds. "It leads into the orchard. You could climb in that way, at night after everyone has gone to bed. I could meet you there."

"Is it safe?"

"The orchard is big, and it's well away from the main buildings. And the nuns sleep through the Great Silence. They don't get up in the night for Holy Offices. No one will know."

"And you? Can you leave your bed without being discovered?"

Giulia thought of the sleeping novices, of her bed directly below the open window, of the convent corridors, nearly deserted during the hours of the Great Silence. Of the spirit inside the talisman, bound to her heart's desire. "I think so. Can you?"

"I go as I please, night or day." He grinned with the teasing humor she remembered. "I've slipped out a few midnight windows, and climbed a wall or two in my time. But this will be a new adventure. I'll come tomorrow. Eleven o'clock."

"Eleven o'clock," she echoed.

"Giulia." His mobile face was serious again. "Are you sure?"

"Yes," she breathed.

Somehow, the distance between them had vanished. Their fingers met and clasped. His touch sent her blood racing; she felt the heat of it in her cheeks, her throat, the whole of her body. She imagined what it would be like to lean into his arms.

Footsteps sounded on the balcony stairs. They sprang apart just as the curtain across the doorway twitched aside. Matteo Moretti came through, followed by Humilità.

"What's the meaning of this?" Humilità stopped short.

"I'm sorry, Maestra Humilità," Ormanno said, turning smoothly to face her. "Your apprentice dropped her drawing over the railing. I was just returning it."

"Is this so, Giulia?"

"He gave me back my drawing, Maestra." Giulia's cheeks were burning. She couldn't meet her teacher's eyes.

"Well, it is highly improper. I would expect you to know better, Ormanno, given that you have only recently been inside the walls of Santa Marta."

"Apologize to my daughter for your forwardness,

boy," Matteo said harshly. "And to her apprentice."

"I apologize, Maestra," said Ormanno. "And to you, miss. Truly, I meant no offense."

"Now back to work." Matteo clapped his hands, as if dismissing a servant. "You've wasted more than enough of everyone's time."

Ormanno bowed, his face unreadable, then headed toward the curtain. He pulled it aside and was gone, leaving Giulia feeling hollow, as if something had been scooped out of her. She put her hand to her chest, over the lump of the talisman.

Anasurymboriel.

"He has a roving eye, that one. I will speak to him, Violetta, you may be sure of it."

"Please don't trouble yourself, Papa. It seems no harm was done."

"The conduct of my journeymen reflects on me. If I bring him with me on a commission, I don't want to fear he'll steal off to pester the daughters of the house."

Humilità and her father had finished their business. They escorted Giulia to the floor of the workshop, where she was introduced to Humilità's brothers: Gianfrancesco, a younger version of his father, and Tiberio, whose hollow cheeks spoke of his recent illness. Then Matteo walked them through the kitchen, where the workers clustered around again to say good-bye, and down the passage to the door.

"Write me about the progress of that commission," Matteo said. "I only hope you have not taken on more than you can fulfill."

"You needn't fear, Papa." Humilità's tone was sharp. "And you'll let me know of any difficulties with the frame."

"It is only a frame, Violetta."

He drew her to him and kissed her on the forehead. He gave Giulia a little bow; she curtsied and thanked him for his hospitality. Then she and Humilità stepped out into the street, as the door fell closed behind them.

Most of the afternoon had gone, and shadows lay long across the cobbles. Giulia felt as if she were walking an inch above the ground.

"Giulia," Humilità said after a few minutes. "You told the truth, didn't you? About that young man. He wasn't disturbing you?"

"No, Maestra."

"Because there are men who are . . . drawn to nuns. Some find allure in the fact that we are forbidden. Others imagine convents as secret brothels, with salacious doings behind their walls. Last year Madre Damiana had to summon the city watch to remove a man who was making lewd approaches in the visiting parlor. Unfortunately, there are nuns who encourage such behavior, whether it's because they are bored, or bitter, or lax in their vocation."

Giulia was glad it was dim under the arcade, so Humilità couldn't see her blushing. "It wasn't that way, Maestra. Really."

"Good."

"Maestra . . ." Giulia hesitated. "Do you think he . . .

the young man . . . do you think he's like that? Like those men?"

"I found no fault with his conduct when he was helping me repair the fresco, beyond a certain . . . inquisitiveness about my work, which I think perhaps was just a natural curiosity, given"—her tone became dry—"that in many ways I *am* a curiosity. Of course, four weeks is not a long acquaintance. But he did not strike me so. And he is very talented."

Questions pressed against Giulia's lips, but to ask them would be to give herself away, so she held her tongue. She saw Ormanno's face again, his long hair and his smile, his icy-bright eyes. Roving eyes, Matteo Moretti had said—but did that matter, now that his gaze was fixed on her? *Surely the talisman wouldn't bring me anyone like those men, those twisted men who dream of the forbidden.* She thought of the strange horoscope she had cast when she first found the astrolabe, the one that told her she already had her heart's desire. She'd thought her interpretation must be wrong, but it hadn't been, it hadn't been, for she had already met Ormanno in the refectory.

"What did you think of my father's workshop?" Humilità said.

"It's very different. So much bigger and noisier."

"An artist's workshop is the reflection of his soul. My father never does just one thing at a time—he is always going in ten directions at once."

Giulia thought of the tranquil order at Santa Marta, where nothing was hurried and everything was controlled. "The tableau was interesting," she said.

"With the angel in the harness."

"My father is known for composing the scenes he paints whole, rather than in parts or from studies. We don't have the space for that at Santa Marta. But a small workshop has its advantages. I'm always glad to return to my little kingdom. Which reminds me, I must rise early tomorrow. I must have a good supply of Passion blue on hand for the San Giustina panels."

For a little while they walked in silence. The sound and motion of the busy city swirled around them.

"It was an accident, you know." Humilità spoke so low that Giulia had to strain to hear her.

"What was, Maestra?"

"Passion blue. I was experimenting—I'm always experimenting with one thing and another. But finding the ingredient that makes the color what it is, that makes it more than simply blue—that was an accident. Even then, I knew I had created something extraordinary. That blue, my blue, more precious than other blues, which are the most precious of all colors." Humilità was quiet for the space of several steps. "Beware secrets, Giulia. All painters have secrets, but few are important enough for others to covet. Those that are, however they begin, always end as burdens."

Giulia felt the resonance of those words.

"Each time I see my father, he presses me. At first, I imagined it was a game between us. Now I wonder if it ever really was." She sighed. "Sometimes I think I should have given him the recipe when he asked me first. After all, I know his secrets, so in a way it would be a fair exchange.

But I did not, and that was my choice. And I will not give up Passion blue now—no, not to anyone."

The bitterness was there again, the same as in Matteo Moretti's study.

They walked on in silence. Giulia did her best to savor her last moments of freedom, but too soon the convent's high brick wall came in sight. Humilità knocked; the doorkeeper peered through the grate, then pulled the door open onto the dimness within. Giulia breathed deeply and thought of the talisman, and of the promise she had seen in Ormanno's smile. Those things kept her calm as they passed through the saint's door, back into Santa Marta.

That night, Giulia dreamed more vividly than ever before of the little blue flame. This time it did not flee, but hung trembling on the air, as if, like a true flame, it were pinned in place. When she reached toward it— slowly, as she might have done to capture a butterfly— it let her fold her hands around it.

She woke abruptly, the talisman heavy on her chest, Ormanno's face blazing in her mind's eye. She sat up, turning so she could lean her arms on the sill of the window above her bed. She no longer doubted that the dreams were real—that the flame was Anasurymboriel, speaking to her in her sleep. Not so very long ago, this might have frightened her. Not now. The sorcerer's promise was coming true. On that day in May when she climbed the ladder and stepped onto Ormanno's scaffold, her stars had already been turning toward a new pattern.

And yet.... An unwelcome tendril of doubt snaked its way into her mind. She had no experience with sorcery, no way to know what magic felt like when it was working. What if she were wrong? What if there was no magic? What if Ormanno's interest in her was no more than Matteo Moretti had said—a roving eye?

But then she thought of how the talisman had burned at his approach, and of the difference in her dream tonight. Of how they had encountered each other at Santa Marta three separate times—too many, surely, to be coincidence. Of the horoscope that told her she already had her heart's desire, and the one that predicted she would soon leave Santa Marta. Of the timing of Benedicta's story.

There are too many pieces, and they fit together too perfectly. It's the magic. It has to be.

Above her in the sky, a sliver of moon swam amid a sea of stars, frosty pinpoints against the blackness of the cosmos. She picked out the constellations: Lyra, Scorpio, Cygnus the swan. She could almost feel it, the great web of connection that bound everything together—the stars, and the planets, and the crystal spheres they rode upon, and the celestial spirits that inhabited them, and the Earth, and the beings who walked on it. And herself, one small stitch in a great tapestry, pulling against the grain, tugging the threads around her into a new configuration.

"It's happening, Mama," she whispered, imagining her words rising upward, like sparks. "It's really happening."

Part 3

Under the Summer Stars

✢✢✢✢✢✢

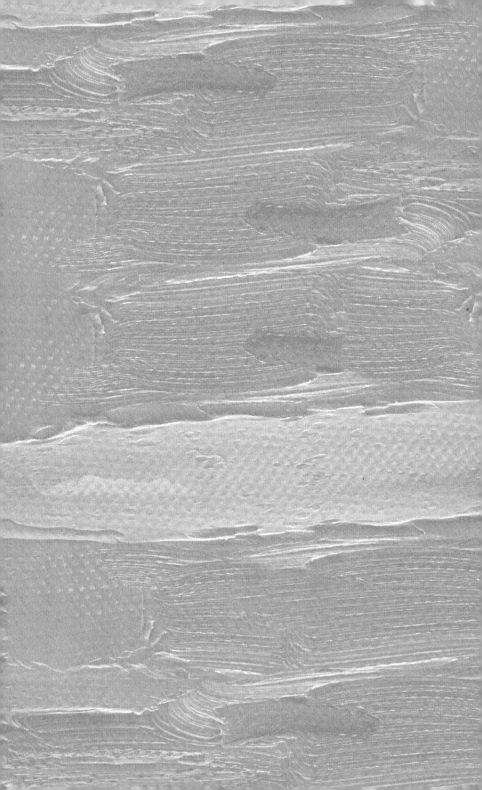

CHAPTER 15

✤ Ormanno ✤

. . . nine hundred ninety and nine, one thousand.

Giulia stopped counting and lay quiet, listening for a sign that any of the novices were still awake. She heard nothing. Suor Margarita, she hoped, was asleep as well; she'd counted to a thousand twice, slowly, after the novice mistress returned from singing Compline.

Now, she thought. *It's time.*

For just a moment, she could not move. She'd devised a plan, turning it over in her mind until every detail was as perfect as she could make it—but no plan was foolproof. What if one of the girls roused as she crept out the window? What if she encountered someone in the corridors? What if Suor Margarita came unexpectedly into the dormitory and saw Giulia's bed was empty?

She forced herself to slip out from under the covers. Each crackle of the mattress seemed impossibly loud. From beneath her pillow she drew her novice gown and sandals, which she had concealed after pretending to stow them as usual in her trousseau chest. She positioned her pillow under the sheet and blanket so that sleepy eyes might mistake it for her huddled form. If anyone realized she was gone, she hoped they would assume she'd gotten up to use the privy.

As silently as she could, Giulia climbed onto the windowsill, then dropped down into the grass. She paused to pull her gown on over her chemise, then set out at a run across the width of the lawn. The moon was just past full and the sky blazed with stars, bright enough to cast her shadow on the grass.

She entered the building again, dashing down corridors in which two out of every three torches had been extinguished for the night. Although she was now on the north side of the convent, away from the living quarters, this was the most dangerous part of the journey, for despite the special privilege that allowed Santa Marta's nuns to sleep through the night, some of the more devout sisters rose to sing the Holy Offices anyway. Giulia paused at each turning, surveying the way ahead before racing on, noiseless on her bare feet.

She reached the loggia that opened onto the garden court where Lucida lived. All the windows of the little houses were dark, but she felt horribly exposed on the gravel paths. Then she was in the orchard, beneath the dim shelter of the trees, with the pungent smell of windfall plums and apricots in her nostrils and the long grass damp underfoot. She paused to catch her breath and to tie on her sandals and tug her dress straight. It was unbecoming, there was nothing she could do about that, but she could at least fix her hair. She shook it out of its braid and combed her fingers through it. Should she leave it loose? *No. I don't want him to think me wanton.* She braided it up again, leaving a few strands to curl around her face.

From somewhere in the city, a bell tolled eleven.

She'd seen the orchard from a distance, when she and the others visited Lucida, but she had never actually entered it. She picked her way through the grass, hoping she was heading in the right direction. She smelled the stagnant water of the canal; the wall appeared at last, high and forbidding beyond the final rank of trees. There was no sign of a breach, but when she looked along the wall she thought she could see a gap some distance to her left. She hurried toward it— and there it was, just as Lucida had said, a spot where damp or age had eaten away the mortar and the bricks had crumbled into the canal, leaving a wide break that an agile man could easily scale from the other side.

She settled herself to wait in the shadow of the trees. The air was hot and very still. Between the wall and the trees lay a narrow stretch of open grass, lit silver by the moon. She thought of God, looking down on her in this moment, and turned her mind away, placing her hand on the talisman instead, waiting for it to give her a sign, to warm with Ormanno's approach.

She felt no change. But from the other side of the wall came the sound of oars, then a thud, then a scraping noise. A pause. A man's head and shoulders appeared above the fallen section. Giulia recognized Ormanno, his expression wary as he gazed around. For a moment Benedicta's story came into her mind: Alessandro, arriving to rescue Plautilla. Then Ormanno vaulted over the wall, effortless as a cat, and she forgot everything but him.

As if in a dream, she rose and went to meet him.

"You came." His smile melted the tension from his face.

"Did you think I wouldn't?"

"I wasn't sure." He surveyed her, as he had the first time they met. She had to force herself not to drop her eyes. "You're much prettier without that kerchief."

Giulia was glad of the moonlight, which washed the color from the world and concealed her blush.

"Are we really safe?" He looked around again at the trees and the night.

"As long as we stay here."

"Good." He turned, and she saw that he held a rope in his hand, its other end vanishing over the wall. He looped it around a jutting brick, tying it securely. "My boat," he explained. "Or rather, my friend's boat. He'd have my head if I let it drift away. I'd quite like to keep my head." He grinned. "Shall we sit? I've brought something for us to eat."

"Oh . . . yes. That would be nice."

He trod on the grass to flatten it, and they sat

down in the moonlight. From the bag he wore over his shoulder he produced a flask and a folded napkin.

"Wine and nut cakes. Stolen from my master's kitchen."

He uncorked the flask and held it toward her. She sipped—just for courtesy, her stomach was churning too much to allow for more. She was furious at herself for being so nervous. He was star-sent, bound to her by the talisman and Anasurymboriel's magic. Yet he was also a stranger, a man she knew absolutely nothing about— and right now, beyond the pulse-pounding closeness of him, that was what she was most aware of.

He took back the flask and drank, then smiled his teasing smile. The moon illuminated his fair hair, his crooked nose, his high forehead. It cast his starry eyes and the hollows of his cheeks into shadow.

"So tell me, Giulia. Who was it who forced you to come to Santa Marta?"

Giulia drew a deep breath. "My father's wife."

"Your father's wife? Not your mother?"

"No. My mother's dead. She died when I was seven." Anasurymboriel had chosen him for her; nothing she told him could make a difference. Still, the truth was hard to confess. "She was . . . she was never his wife. She was his seamstress. I'm illegitimate."

"Ah." He nodded. "Wrong side of the sheets, just like me."

"You're illegitimate too?"

"My mother left me outside the Erimitani monastery when I was a few days old. The monks say it's mostly girls without husbands who leave their babies that way. That's where my surname comes from. Trovatelli. The Found One." He tipped the flask back for another swallow, held it out to her again. "His seamstress, eh? So your father was a rich man?"

The wine tasted better this time. "My father was Count Federico di Assulo Borromeo of Milan."

"I see." He took back the flask, his brows rising. "A *very* rich man."

"He died last February. He was good to me while he was alive, he gave me shelter and work, and never cast me out even though his wife—the Countess—wanted him to. He tried to be good to me after his death as well, by leaving me a dowry. The Countess was bound by the provisions of his will and couldn't take it away from me, so she did the next best thing and used it to buy me a place at Santa Marta. That way she married me off, as my father intended, but not to a living man. And got rid of me into the bargain."

"Saints." Ormanno pulled his breath in through his teeth, shaking his head. "That's hard. Did she know you didn't want to be a nun?"

"I think that was the point."

"What a waste, locking such a pretty girl up inside a convent!"

The blood flooded Giulia's cheeks again.

"Didn't you have any family who could help you? Anyone you could go to instead?"

"No. There's no one. Now that my father . . . there's no one."

"So you're all alone in the world. Just like me." He nodded. His hair had fallen across his cheek; he tucked it behind his ear, a quick, practiced gesture. "Bastards, orphans, no family, no true home—we're two of a kind, Giulia. I had a feeling, the first time we talked. I don't know how, but I did. I think that must be why I couldn't forget you, even though I knew I should."

His pale eyes held hers. The intimacy of it made her speechless. Her heart was pounding again. Her body felt light and hot.

"Here." He offered her the napkin. "Have a cake. They're good."

She took one of the little cakes and nibbled at it. It tasted like dust. "You said you don't have a true home," she said. "But you live with Maestro Moretti, don't you?"

"That's a *place*. Not a home."

Giulia nodded. She understood the difference. "How did you become his apprentice? Did you always want to be a painter?"

"Saints, no. I barely knew what a painting was before I met him. No, he found me in the street."

"In the street?"

"I told you, I was a foundling. The monks treated me well enough, but the cloistered life, it wasn't for me. All the rules and the walls and the prayers six times a day. Not," he added, "that I've got anything against prayers. I was just tired of everything being the same, day after day."

Giulia felt a thrill of recognition. "I hate it too," she said. "The sameness."

"So I ran away. After a while I fell in with some

other foundlings. There was an older boy, he taught us how to beg and how to steal. He protected us. We were like brothers. It wasn't an easy life, but it wasn't the worst life either." He paused a moment, and she could tell he was remembering. "Then one day I tried to steal Matteo Moretti's purse. Instead of calling the watch, he brought me to his house. I was just a dirty street animal, all rags and scabs. He cleaned me up, gave me a bed and a place in his workshop. Training, once he saw I could draw. I've been with him . . . let's see, I was ten then. So nine years."

He's nineteen. She'd thought him older. "That was good of him, to take you in."

"You'd think so, wouldn't you." He gave an odd little laugh. "He's gotten the worth of it, believe me."

Giulia remembered how Matteo had spoken to Ormanno on the balcony, as if he were a servant. "Is he a hard master?"

"You could say that." Ormanno shrugged. "He is a good teacher, though. And his name is known, and not just in Padua either. I could leave here and go any-where, even to Rome itself, and any workshop would take me on, once they knew I was trained by Matteo Moretti."

"Are you planning to leave Padua, then?"

"One day. I want a workshop of my own. I'm not like some of the men I work with, content to sit in their master's shadow, never to shine with their own light. My—well, a girl I used to know, she always told me that I had a good place and should be content. It was foolish to strive for more, she said, and risk losing everything. But I think it's better to try and lose than to spend your life wanting and waiting. You've got to take the chances when they come to you."

"Yes," Giulia said. "I know."

"Oh?" He was teasing again. "You've taken a lot of chances in your life, then, have you?"

"Enough," Giulia said, stung. "Being here tonight, for one."

"Oh, I'm stupid." He was instantly contrite. "Forgive me, Giulia, my tongue sometimes runs ahead of my brains." He shook his head. "I don't even know why I'm telling you all this. Must be the wine."

"You haven't drunk so much."

"Haven't I?" He took a long swallow from the flask, then looked at her, tilting his head to one side. "What about you? You don't want to be a nun, but what *do* you want?"

"I want to marry," Giulia said boldly. "And have children. And paint."

"Paint?" His eyebrows rose.

"Women can be painters. Look at my Maestra."

"Hm," he said. "But if you leave Santa Marta, you'll have to leave your Maestra. How will you paint then?"

"I'll think of something." In fact, she already had. An idea had been born in her tonight, but she couldn't tell him that. Not yet.

"What's it like, anyway?" he asked. "Being the famous Maestra Humilità's pupil? In her secret workshop?"

"It's not secret."

"Oh, but it is, for no man has ever seen it."

"Well, I suppose, if you put it that way. . . ."

"How did you come to be her apprentice?"

"There was a chest I brought with me. They took it away when I arrived, but one of my drawings was inside. The abbess found it and gave it to Maestra Humilità. She decided she wanted to teach me."

"Is she a good teacher?"

"Yes. I've learned so much, even in just two months. Although it's hard sometimes. She can be . . . harsh, if she thinks I'm not trying hard enough."

"I got a sense of that, when I was working for her. Like her father." He paused. "Do you think she really painted it? The fresco, I mean?"

"What? Of course she painted it."

"It's just . . . well, there are rumors."

"What rumors?"

"Well, she's a woman. And no one has ever seen her paint. Some people say that my master has a hand in her work, though of course he swears it isn't true."

"Well, it's *not* true. *I've* seen her paint, and I can tell you that for certain." Giulia was surprised at how indignant she felt. "She's a master. A true master. You can take my word for it."

"Then I will."

He offered her the flask. She drank, feeling the warmth of it in her throat and belly. A breeze had sprung up, stirring the heavy air. She drank again. *Careful,* she thought, aware that she was starting to feel tipsy.

"How bright it is tonight." Ormanno was gazing up at the moon, his face and throat exposed to the silver light.

"It's harder to see the constellations when the moon is near-full." Giulia watched him. She felt breathless again; she wanted to touch his skin, to trace the crooked line of his nose, to tuck his hair behind his ears. It was brazen, she knew, but she couldn't help it.

"I don't know about constellations," he said. "They're all just stars to me."

"When were you born?"

"Why?

"Just tell me."

"November. Though I don't know the day."

"I don't know my birth day either." Another thing they had in common. "November . . . probably in Sagittarius. Sagittarius is the archer. There he is. You can see his bow, those three stars." She traced the bright points with her finger. "Those stars were shining on the night you were born. I was born under Pisces, the fish." She shook her head. "The journey from Milan seemed so far that I thought the stars would look different here, but they don't. They're just the same."

He was not watching the sky now, but her. "I've never met a girl before who knew the names of stars."

"I learned from a friend. An astrologer. He was my teacher, growing up."

"Does it matter?" He looked up again. "The stars you're born under?"

"Oh, yes. God writes His will for us in the skies of our birth. If you can read the heavens, you can know what He has decreed."

Or try to change it. She was aware of the talisman,

pulling at her neck. For the first time it occurred to her that if it had changed her stars, it must also have changed his. Or had it? Had God, knowing what she would do to defy her destiny, written her into Ormanno's fate? Was it all written, even the actions that changed the writing? The thought made her dizzy.

Far away in the city, the bell began to toll twelve.

"I should go," Ormanno said.

"Yes," Giulia said reluctantly. "Best for me to be getting back as well."

He corked the wine flask and stowed it and the empty napkin back in his bag, then got to his feet. She rose too.

"I'll come every Tuesday and Friday," he said. "At eleven, just like tonight. Can you get away that often?"

She nodded. In the flooding moonlight, they stood looking at each other. Hardly an arm's length divided them. As on the scaffolding, she realized that she was nearly as tall as he; she hardly had to tilt her head to meet his eyes. Would he kiss her? Surely he would kiss her.

"You really are a pretty girl."

He said it softly, so softly she almost didn't hear. He reached to touch her cheek. Instinctively, she stepped toward him, turning her face against his hand. He traced her jaw, drew his fingers down her throat, then tipped up her chin, and, leaning forward, set his lips softly on hers. The shock of it echoed through her. Heat flowed along her limbs. A fizzing dizziness burst inside her head.

He broke the kiss and pulled away. Involuntarily,

she followed—one small step, but he saw it and smiled, and for just a second there was something in his face that made her feel ashamed, made her feel she had given him too much, let him see too much.

He cupped her cheek again, and now she saw only warmth. "Till Friday."

He freed the rope and vaulted over the wall. She heard the scrape as he pushed the boat back into the canal, then the faint sound of dipping oars. Then silence.

On the way back through the convent, Giulia felt as weightless as a feather, invincible. She was careful, as she had been on the way out, but she knew she would meet no one. Anasurymboriel was protecting her, casting a cloak of magic over every step. She thought she could actually feel it, the faintest vibration against her skin, like the buzzing of a million bees.

Below the dormitory window she pulled off her gown, then slung it around her neck and climbed over the sill. The novices slept as if enchanted.

She slid into bed, huddling under the covers. Her body still glowed from Ormanno's kiss. She could still feel the touch of his hand against her face, the gentle pressure of his lips. His voice spoke inside her head: *We're two of a kind, you and I . . . two of a kind. . . .* It was true, they were alike; in their origins, their situations, neither with families, both alone in the world. And he was young . . . and handsome . . . and he was a painter. . . .

She closed her fingers around the talisman.

"Thank you," she whispered.

Never before had she addressed the spirit directly. If it were blasphemy, she no longer cared.

That night in her dreams, Anasurymboriel let her capture it again. It trembled against her palms, a moth-like fluttering. Its light leaked through her fingers—Passion blue, the profoundest blue there was. When finally she let it dart away, her hands were stained with its color. So real did the dream seem that when she woke, she was surprised to see her own pink skin.

CHAPTER 16

❖ To Wield the Rainbow ❖

The next morning, as if to make up for the night before, things began to go wrong almost at once.

Picking a moment when Suor Margarita was out of the room, Nelia pretended to stumble against Giulia's freshly made bed, contriving to drag all the covers to the floor. She made a mocking apology, then ran to join Alessia and the others. Giulia yanked the covers back into place, which made her late getting into line and earned her a reprimand from Suor Margarita.

In the refectory, she tipped her cup over, sending water flooding into her lap and the lap of Bice beside her. This time the annoyed novice mistress gave her not just a reprimand, but a penance: half an hour on her knees that evening. As she made her way to the workshop, the sodden cloth of her gown clinging to her legs, she was stopped by a fat old choir nun, who scolded her for the immodesty of the large wet stain as if she'd done it on purpose. And when she finally reached the workshop, she learned that Angela was ill with a stomach fever and Giulia would have no help assisting the artists that day.

Usually quick and efficient, she was able to get nothing right. She broke egg yolks, fumbled pigment recipes, forgot instructions. She dropped an entire bowl of lacquer, which Domenica had needed for the last of the Santa Barbara panels, splattering her sandaled feet, the front of her apron, and a huge area of the floor with clay fragments and sticky, smelly liquid. Domenica stood over her, scolding, as she cleaned it up, until at last Humilità intervened.

"Really, Giulia," she said, after she had sent Domenica back to work. "I don't know what has gotten into you. Are you sure you are not ill as well?"

"No, Maestra. I'm not ill."

But in a way she was. She felt as if she had a fever. No matter how she tried to keep her attention on what she was doing, the world around her would vanish and she would be in the orchard, under the stars, with Ormanno. She heard his voice again, felt the gentle brush of his fingers against her cheek and throat. He came to her in flashes: the tilt of his head, the way he tucked his hair behind his ears, his wide, wicked smile. Again and again she relived the kiss, the rush of heat and dizziness when his lips touched hers.

By the afternoon, she had managed to pull herself together, enough at least to focus on the daily drawing lesson, though she was aware she was not working well. Normally this would have brought sharp criticism from Humilità. But the workshop mistress seemed distracted. Her comments were uncharacteristically mild.

"That's enough," she said at last. "You're not at your best today, and truth to tell, nor am I."

It was an unusual admission for her to make. But she was visibly tired, her normally pink cheeks pale, her dark eyes puffy. She had finished transferring the San Giustina cartoons and had begun the underpainting, coming in before dawn, pausing only for the midday meal and the drawing lessons.

"I'm sorry, Maestra. I slept poorly last night."

"I too. But then I never sleep when I'm starting a painting. Too many ideas, too many images. They trouble my dreams." She let out her breath, not quite a sigh. "Especially with this painting. Especially this one."

All the artists had seen her studies for the altarpiece, and Lucida and Perpetua had contributed both faces and background details. But Humilità had created the cartoons in secret, and when she finally unrolled the finished drawings on the drafting table for the others to look at, there had been an awed hush. It was not just the masterly composition and the exquisite draftsmanship that held them silent, but the suffering the drawings depicted, so graphically rendered that it was difficult to look at—Jesus' brutally pierced palms and feet, the agony-stretched tendons of His neck, the thieves' pain-contorted limbs and faces, the Virgin's despair. Even Domenica had seemed affected, the harsh creases between her brows momentarily smoothed away.

"Because of Jesus' suffering?" Giulia asked now.

"That's one reason. I had to go deep into my soul to find those images. Very deep. It was not an easy journey." Humilità added, with a little of her usual tartness, "I wonder whether it has ever occurred to the abbot of San Giustina to consider the irony of commissioning such a work from a painter who barely ever sees the male form at all, much less that form unclothed."

"No one would know, Maestra. Your drawings . . . they are so real. As if you'd actually been there, at the foot of the Cross."

"Yes." Humilità nodded—not with pride, simply acknowledging a fact. "My father doesn't believe a woman is capable of painting the world as truly as a man can. But I *am* capable." She shifted on the bench, looking toward the huge panels in their scaffolds. "This painting will be my masterpiece. It won't hang in some private chapel, or in a convent to be viewed only by monks and nuns. It will hang above the altar in the great church of San Giustina, where anyone may see it. It will be the painting for which I am remembered—the one that will place my name beside Mantegna's, beside Lippi's. If that is pride, God forgive me." She crossed herself. "But I know it as I know these hands of mine."

She spread them before her, small and strong, the fingers marked with ink and paint.

"Maestra . . . may I ask you something?"

"Of course."

"Could you have become a painter, even if you hadn't come to Santa Marta?"

There was a pause. Giulia held her breath. It was a bold question. She knew there was a good chance Humilità would refuse to answer. But when the workshop mistress folded her hands and looked at Giulia, there was no anger in her face.

"Why do you ask?"

"It's just that I've been thinking, since we visited your father. . . . He trained you. He built you the balcony. Wouldn't he have let you stay with him and be part of his workshop? If you hadn't wanted to become a nun?"

"No. But not for the reason you might assume."

"Why, then?"

"My father is a great man. But he's not always a good one. He can tolerate no rivals, even among the men who work for him. I am a woman, and I would have been his rival. He couldn't bear to waste my talent, and so he trained me, but he also could not bear the challenge of it, and so he sent me to Santa Marta. It was the best choice, for both of us."

"So you wanted to go?"

"I wanted to be a painter." Humilità regarded

Giulia. "I think I know the source of these questions. It's our conversation in the market, yes? About your future?"

Giulia nodded.

"Even if my father were a different man, I would not have asked to stay with him. He might have been willing to accept me into his workshop, but I could never have had my *own* workshop. He might have been willing to make me a journeyman—but I could never have become Maestra. Not in a world of men. Not in his shadow. Santa Marta is the one place on Earth where I can fulfill the whole of the gift God gave me, where I can shine with my own light. Do you understand?"

Giulia nodded again, struck by how similar Humilità's words were to Ormanno's, last night.

"This is so for you as well, Giulia, with the difference that you do not have a father, even a jealous one, to start you on your way. For you, there is only here, with me." Her dark eyes held Giulia's. "Even if you do not yet realize it."

Giulia looked away, down at the half-finished drawing in her lap.

"Does that answer your question?"

"Yes, Maestra. Thank you."

"Never fear to ask questions, Giulia, even difficult ones. And now I must work." Humilità braced her hands on her knees and got to her feet. "Try to get through the rest of the day without dropping any more bowls."

The shortened lesson left Giulia with unexpected free time. Humilità allowed her apprentices to sketch as much as they liked as long as they got their work done, so she took some sheets of paper and a stick of red chalk into the court, and, sitting on the edge of the fountain, attempted to draw Ormanno's face. She had the idea of making a portrait she could give to him. But though she tried several times, the results did not satisfy her, and in the end she crumpled them all up and fed them to the brazier.

When the bell rang for Vespers, the choir nuns departed, leaving Giulia, Humilità, and Perpetua—all three *conversae*—alone in the workshop. Giulia finished the washing up, tipped the dirty water down the courtyard drain, and dragged the heavy washtub back to its place. Then she went to stand before the scaffolded panels to watch the painters.

Lamps and torches had been lit to supplement the fading evening light, amplified with an ingenious series of brass reflectors devised by Domenica. Humilità stood before the central panel, applying the shadows and highlights that would later be overpainted with color. The crowd, including the small portrait figures of San Giustina's abbot and several of his administrators, would be completed first. Next would be the figures in the foreground—the Virgin, Mary Magdalen, the disciple John. The Cross, with the pain-wracked form of the Savior upon it, would be last.

At the right-hand panel, Perpetua worked on the ground at the foot of the thief's cross. She, Lucida, and Domenica would share the painting of the backgrounds, the same in all three panels: stony earth, spiky shrubs and small dry grasses, distant desert hills and a threatening, cloud-clotted sky.

Over her weeks in the workshop, Giulia had observed the painters as often as she could, trying to learn not just from what they told her but from what she saw them do—noting their use of the different shapes and thicknesses of brushes, how they mixed prepared pigment with tempera or oil, how they applied the colors to the panels, how they layered and blended different paints to achieve the effect they wished. Color, its making and its employment, was a subject of almost infinite complexity. She could better understand, now, why there must be so much learning before an apprentice could begin to paint.

Yet, watching the artists bring scenes to life, she was often shaken by a profound sense of recognition— as if this were not new knowledge, but understanding that had always existed in some till-now undiscovered place inside herself. With all her desire and all her strength, she wanted to do as the painters did: to set brush to panel. To abandon chalk red and charcoal black, and wield the rainbow. To pluck moments from the flow of time and make them eternal. To pour her soul out onto the stark white of gessoed panels and bring another world to life.

I can do this, she thought at such times, feeling the familiar burning in her fingers. *I must do this.*

Now, watching the face of a Roman guard appear in monochrome under Humilità's expert brush, she thought of the question she had asked today, and heard again Humilità's judgment: *For you, there is only here, with me.* But she also sensed the stirring of the idea that had woken in her last night, under the changed stars that had guided Ormanno to her. Humilità was wrong. There *was* another way.

She felt the twisting of a familiar guilt. She'd been deceiving Humilità from the start—not by choice, though that didn't make the lie any less. But she knew now how she would escape—or at least, with whom. From today, she would truly be living a double life, lying not just by her intentions but by her actions.

In a way it was no different. But in another way it felt much worse.

I'll work harder than ever. I'll give everything I can. There will be nothing false about my work.

It was the same silent promise she had made on the night Humilità claimed her as an apprentice. This time, it felt hollow.

She turned away, and went to clear up the preparation area.

When Giulia reached the wall on Friday night, her heart racing with both anticipation and the fear that Ormanno might not have come, he was already waiting. He had brought wine again, and heavy dark grapes.

"Does Lorenza ever notice the things you steal from her kitchen?" Giulia asked.

He laughed. "Lorenza notices everything. But she always forgives me."

"Doesn't anyone wonder where you go at night?"

"They just assume I have a sweetheart." He

reached to tuck a strand of hair behind her ear. "And they're not wrong, are they?"

His touch stole her breath. "You've had many sweethearts, I'm guessing."

"None I've risked prison for."

"Prison?"

"Giulia, don't you know the penalties for men who corrupt nuns? Fines, prison, flogging. Sometimes all three."

Giulia was aghast. "I had no idea."

"Don't worry." He waved away her distress. "I've a mate on the city watch, he'd see me right if ever there was a problem. Besides." He smiled his teasing smile. "I don't mind a bit of danger. It makes it more exciting, don't you think?"

It was true. She laughed, exhilarated.

"Name the stars for me," Ormanno said. "The way you did the other night."

So she traced the constellations for him, and explained the spheres, and told him why the sun and moon revolved around the Earth. He seemed younger as he listened, his face upturned, his eyes following where she pointed.

When he grew tired of looking up, he stretched out in the grass. She lay down beside him, her shoulder touching his. Her heart beat high and fast. She was aware of his warmth, of his smell of wine and walnut oil and the faint tang of his sweat. The sky arched black and huge above them, the stars like diamond chips, the moon a misshapen silver coin. When he raised himself on one elbow and leaned down to kiss her, she closed her eyes and let herself fall into those depths, up and up, passing through the spheres as she did in dreams.

"What's that?" His hand, caressing her throat, had encountered the oval of the talisman beneath her gown.

"Just a necklace. Something I brought with me from home."

"Didn't you say they took all that away from you?"

"Yes. I smuggled it in."

He laughed softly. "I can see you were never meant to be a nun."

He kissed her again, more insistently this time, opening her mouth with his tongue. His fingers moved from her throat to her breast, and she gasped against his lips. He traced the swell of her hip, the length of her thigh. But when he stroked the fabric of her dress above her knee and slipped his hand beneath it, she tensed and caught his arm.

"No," she whispered.

He drew back at once. "I'm sorry."

"It's just . . ." She sat up, pulling away from him. "I don't . . . I mean I've never . . ."

"No. It's my fault. The girls I've been with . . . well, they weren't like you. I forgot that. It won't happen again." He held out his arm. "Come. We'll just lie together in the grass."

She hesitated, then curled up beside him. His arm closed carefully around her. His body was long and warm against her own; his chest rose and fell under her cheek, and she could hear the steady thumping of his heart. Would it matter if she let him do as he wanted? They were meant for each other, after all. But something in her was not ready.

There are men who are drawn to nuns. Humilità's voice spoke inside her mind. She pushed it away.

They lay chastely until the midnight bell struck. Then he got up and helped her to her feet. She patted down her rumpled dress and hair while he packed the wine flask into his bag.

"I'll walk you to the edge of the orchard," he said.

"Oh. I don't think that would be a good idea."

"But everyone's asleep, aren't they? I just want to see a little of where my orchard girl lives."

The endearment made her catch her breath.

She led him back beneath the trees. The moonlight fell between the branches, painting a ghostly mosaic on the grass. Entirely naturally, her hand fell into his. He was careful to keep a little distance between them as they walked.

Beneath the final rank of trees she pulled him to a stop.

"What are those buildings in front of us?" he whispered.

"The residences of the wealthy nuns. There's a beautiful garden in the middle, with a fountain."

"Let's go closer."

"No!" She tightened her grip on his fingers. "No. We shouldn't be reckless."

"You're right." He raised her hand to his lips, kissed the back of it and then the palm. "You go on, then."

"Good night, Ormanno." It thrilled her to say his name.

"Good night, my orchard girl."

She turned when she reached the other side of the courtyard. He was standing where she had left him, watching her go—she could just see the glimmer of his white shirt, the pale blur of his face. He lifted his hand. She raised hers, then slipped into the shadow of the loggia.

CHAPTER 17

❖ Orchard Girl ❖

Before the orchard, Anasurymboriel had only touched Giulia's dreams, never her waking hours. But now, on the nights she stole out to meet Ormanno, she felt the spirit's magic all around her—a vibration of the air, a stirring against her skin, and occasionally, faintly, a profound sweet scent, like the flower-smell that had filled the sorcerer's rooms on the night he made the talisman. That did not mean she was reckless—she still counted twice to a thousand before she left the dormitory, still paused at the turnings of hallways to make sure no one was about. But she trusted the spirit's protection. As long as she took care, she knew she would not be discovered.

Ormanno always arrived before her. As she slipped from her bed and raced like a shadow through Santa Marta's nightbound corridors, she played a game with herself: Would he be leaning against the wall? Sitting cross-legged on the grass? Lounging against a tree trunk? Each time she saw him, she felt for an instant that she'd pulled him from her imagination, a dream-man. She had to go to him and touch him to make sure he was real.

He never failed to bring wine and something good to eat, and, as the moon waned, a candle to give them light. The little flame was too weak to illuminate very much, but it made the dark around them darker, isolating them in a tiny world of their own.

As they ate and drank, they talked, learning about one another. She told him stories of her life in Milan—though, as with Angela, she did not mention her lost horoscope or the sorcerer or Anasurymboriel. One day she would confess those things. One day, he would learn that they had not found each other just by chance. But not yet. *Not till I'm out of Santa Marta. Not till we're married.*

She was hungry for knowledge about him too—what it had been like to be a foundling, to live by his wits on the street. The tales he told were stark with suffering and privation—the rivalry with other gangs, the casual brutality of the city watch, the times he had nearly starved to death. A hard life, as he had said, from which Matteo Moretti had delivered him. But not all the memories were bad ones. She could see that he still felt affection for the little gang of orphan boys who had been his only family. Some of them were gone, lost to hunger or disease, but some, like him, had survived and found a safer life. He never mentioned it, but she suspected he was still in touch with them.

"I ran away from my master three times," he told her, on the fourth night they met. "Back to my mates, back to the streets. I hated the workshop—the rules and the discipline, the other apprentices and the way they jeered at me for being a foundling. But it changed me—living in a comfortable house, eating as much as I wanted, knowing where I'd sleep each night. Finding out I could draw. In the end, I always went back."

"And he always took you in again." Giulia reached for a handful of the almonds he had brought. Rain had fallen earlier in the day and the grass was damp, the stars obscured by clouds.

"Not from charity," Ormanno said. "He knew my talents. He had plans for me."

"What kind of plans?"

"Just . . . plans." He gestured to his paint-marked shirt, which spoke his craft as clear as words. "The third time I came back, he told me I had to choose— him or the streets. I chose him. Or rather, I chose what he could offer me. It seemed a fair exchange." He took a swallow from the wine flask. "I don't regret it. I might be dead now if he hadn't found me. He gave me my life's work—I'd never have known I could paint if it wasn't for him. But . . ."

"But?"

"But I am tired of being at his command. Of working to his rules. We journeymen can do nothing of our own. We must use only his recipes, only his techniques, even in our own paintings that aren't part of the workshop's official commissions. And we aren't supposed to solicit private commissions for ourselves. Of course," he added, "that hasn't stopped me, though he'd be furious if he knew. But I have my own ideas, my own recipes, so many things I want to try—how else can I test them?"

He'd told her about his experiments with unusual lighting and unconventional angles in the portraits he had painted, as well as his fascination with the technical aspects of the painter's art—formulating new pigment and gesso and lacquer recipes, working out methods of purifying oils so they did not darken too much in drying. She loved this glimpse of the intelligence that lay beneath his off-hand manner. She was also growing to understand his intolerance of obstacles, his blazing impatience with anything that held him back.

"Like your formula for removing fresco stains," she said.

"Exactly. One thing I'll say for your Maestra, she is not afraid of trying something new. But for my master, the old way is always the best way. Take oil, for instance. If I had my choice, I'd use nothing else—it dries more slowly, so you can work bigger areas, and it blends more readily, so you can create more subtle color effects. It's impossible to paint like that with tempera. But unless a client demands it, my master won't have it. Tempera it must be, or at most, tempera with oil overglazes."

"The Maestra says that in twenty years no one will use tempera at all anymore."

"And she's right!" Ormanno flung down the wine flask. "He is jealous, too. To keep our places, we must never let him guess we might become his equals. Can you imagine what it's like to always hold yourself back? To never really know what you're capable of because you can never explore the limits of what you can do? To always be pretending to be less than you are? Can you even *imagine* it?"

"Is it truly that bad?"

"Yes." His voice was bleak. "It truly is. Time was I didn't mind so much. I owed him, after all, and that was fair, even though he never let me forget it. But it chafes me now, oh, how it chafes me! I need to move on. I want to belong to myself. I want my own workshop, with my own patrons and my own pupils and my own methods, and no one to tell me how to paint or what subjects to choose. I'm saving every penny I can. But it's not enough. It's not nearly enough."

"You'll find a way." Giulia reached across the candle, put her hand on his arm. She could feel the tension in him, the frustration. "You'll have your workshop. You were born to be a painter, Ormanno."

He shook his head. "How can you know that? You haven't even seen my work."

"You've told me so much about it. I don't need to see it to understand how much you love it. Besides, the Maestra said you're very talented."

He frowned. "She said that?"

"Yes."

She'd meant to please him, but he only pressed his lips together and changed the subject—which was odd, because he seemed fascinated by Humilità and her workshop, and was normally eager to ask question after question. Now and then Giulia remembered what Humilità had said about his curiosity, but she could see no harm in answering—he was a painter, after all, so why should he not be curious about another painter's workshop, especially one as unusual as Humilità's?

She was careful never to mention the pigment recipes she and Angela compounded, or the formulas and techniques described in Humilità's leather-bound book. But she spoke of old Benedicta's marvelous color wisdom, Lucida's lovely miniatures, Humilità's demanding lessons, the workshop's unhurried work routines. When he wondered how women could manage the heavier physical tasks, she told him about Domenica and her carpentry, and described the elegant scaffold the stern nun had built for the San Giustina altarpiece.

"The rumors are flying about that altarpiece," he said. "They say it's the most expensive ever commissioned by a Paduan monastery."

"That should please the abbot. The Maestra says he wants everyone to know what a costly gift he gave to God. He's in the painting, you know, kneeling by the Cross."

"Patrons often want to be painted in."

"Ormanno . . ." Giulia hesitated. "The first night you came here, you said there are rumors that the Maestra doesn't paint her own paintings."

"Just rumors, Giulia."

"Are people saying that about the altarpiece?"

"They may be."

"But why? Why would anyone think that?"

"Giulia . . ." He paused, choosing his words. "I know you respect your Maestra. As do I, from the little I know of her. But she is a woman, and women are . . . well, they are women, they are fickle and full of emotion and caprice. Women don't have the temperament for the demands of painting any more than they do for science or the law."

All her life Giulia had understood this to be so. It was why she could read books but never be a scholar. It was why Maestro could not teach her astrology. Yet hearing Ormanno say it, something rose in her, an instinctive denial.

"That's not true. Every day in the workshop, I see it's not true. Women *can* be painters. And if they can be painters—" She caught her breath. "They can be anything."

Not until the moment she said it had she realized she believed it.

"Of course there are exceptions," Ormanno said patiently. "There are always exceptions. That's why your Maestra is a marvel—not just for the paintings she makes, but that she makes them at all. And marvels aren't necessarily easy to accept. There's always someone who is jealous. There's always someone who won't believe. That's where the rumors come from.

Do you see?"

"Yes. But it isn't right."

He smiled at her, tilting his head the way he did when he was teasing or flirting. "Do you ever think of staying?"

"What, at Santa Marta? Ormanno, I've told you, I can't be a nun."

"But you want to paint. You can do that here."

"I can do it somewhere else too."

"Can you?"

"Of course I can." She tried not to let him see how much the question dismayed her.

"Your Maestra thinks highly of you. She told my master so. Maybe you could even be Maestra yourself one day. Have you thought of that?"

Giulia couldn't speak. He was boxing her in, just as Humilità had—painting and the convent, or the world and everything else, but not both.

"My master has a book of secrets," he said. "It's hidden in his rooms, none of us know where. When he takes it out for us to use, for color recipes and so on, he has his manservant stand guard to make sure we only see the page he chooses. He'd never pass his secrets on to those of us who work for him—his secrets are only for his sons, who will inherit his work-shop. When I realized that, I knew someday I'd have to leave him. But you—" He leaned forward a little, looking into her eyes. "You could have everything. All the secrets. All the things your Maestra keeps hidden."

"She doesn't keep things hidden," Giulia said stiffly, though it wasn't true.

"So she doesn't have a book of secrets?"

Giulia thought of the pages in Humilità's book that were written in cipher. "She has a book of *recipes*. It's locked in a chest in a cabinet in her study, but she gives it to Angela and me when we need it, and no one has to watch us when we use it."

"She trusts you, then."

"Of course she does."

"Even to mix Passion blue?"

"Only the Maestra mixes Passion blue. Only she can read that recipe."

"It's written down, then? In the book?"

"All her recipes are written down. Ormanno, I don't want to talk about this anymore."

"I'm sorry, my orchard girl, have I made you unhappy?"

"No, of course not."

But he *had* made her unhappy, and when she returned to the dormitory she lay awake, staring at the shadowed ceiling and thinking about what he had said. If he really thought women were unfit to paint . . . if he really believed something that she herself, soul-deep, knew to be false . . . and yet he'd admitted that there were exceptions. He'd dismissed the stupid rumor about Humilità. Perhaps after all it wasn't so surprising he should say such things, never having known any women painters.

But he knows me now. I can change his mind.

She thought about Matteo Moretti's recipe book. How odd that she should know where it was hidden, and Ormanno should not.

She brought the astrolabe to their next meeting, smuggled out of the workshop in her sleeve, along with paper and a charcoal stick. She thought he might like to ask about his workshop, or the money he needed. But when she explained the making of horary charts, he shook his head.

"No. No, I don't want to do that."

"Why not?"

"The stars are beautiful. I love it when you name them for me. But I'd rather that they just stay stars."

"But don't you want your questions answered?"

"If the stars have blessed me, why spoil the joy of discovering it by finding out ahead of time? And if they've damned me, why worry before it happens, since there's nothing I can do?"

"But there *is* something you can do. The stars tell what *may* happen—not necessarily what *will* happen. If you know what's coming, you can change it. At least you can be prepared."

"But what if I try to change things and fail? Do I curse the stars for troubling me, or myself for failing, or both? No. I'd rather find out as I go along. We wouldn't do half of what we do if we knew how it'd turn out, and what would life be like if we never took chances? Like you climbing up on the scaffolding, the day we met."

That wasn't chance. But Giulia held her tongue.

"I know something better we can do."

He pulled her into his arms. She'd been nervous with him after the second night. As much as she assured herself that Anasurymboriel would not bring

231

her a man who wanted only to ravish her, she could not silence the small part of herself that feared he was just such a man: the kind of man who coveted forbidden women. But she craved his touch, the way his embrace made her body go hot and light, the way his kiss made her heart beat and her head spin. And he'd been so careful with her since—at first only kissing her good night, and then later, when she felt more comfortable, holding her as if she were made of glass. She could feel his arousal as he lay against her, and it made her dizzy to know how much he wanted her. But, true to his word, he did not act on it.

They parted at midnight, as usual. Giulia ran lightly through the silent corridors, the astrolabe heavy in her sleeve. Outside the dormitory, she pulled off her dress and bundled it and the astrolabe together. She started to lift them onto the windowsill—but then, gripped by a sudden impulse, she freed the astrolabe from the folds of her gown and held it to the stars.

"When will Ormanno ask me to marry him?" she whispered into the hushed night.

She rotated the astrolabe's disks and pointers to match the star-sighting. The moon was waxing again but its light was faint, and she had to hold the astrolabe close to her face to see. Finished, she climbed through the window and into bed, concealing the astrolabe beneath her pillow.

Late the next afternoon, she stole a few moments from her work to carry the astrolabe into the court. Pretending she was sketching, she began to transcribe her measurements. But something about what she was doing felt wrong. After only a moment she put the charcoal down.

What was it Ormanno had said last night? *We wouldn't do half the things we do if we knew how they'd turn out.* But she *did* know how things would turn out. She had the promise of the talisman, and the chart she'd cast in July, which had told her she would be free before winter. It was almost September now. Did she really need to know more than that?

Unbidden, she heard Maestro's voice: *Be prepared, when you ask the question, to receive the answer you least desire.*

She crumpled the paper and spun the astrolabe's moving parts to erase her measurements. Then she put the astrolabe back where it belonged and returned to work.

CHAPTER 18

❖ Proposals ❖

September arrived, with no lessening of summer's heat. In the workshop, Giulia and Angela began gessoing a pair of panels for the private commission that would follow completion of the San Giustina altarpiece. Lucida gave another dinner party. Perpetua's bad tooth became infected and one side of her face swelled up like a water skin. Despite her pain, she refused to visit the infirmary until Humilità, exasperated, ordered her to get it seen to.

Giulia had vowed she would work harder than ever—and she kept her promise, fulfilling her responsibilities with meticulous attention, taking on more of the heavy labor to spare Angela's leg, throwing herself into the drawing lessons as never before. She did her best to lose herself in her tasks— to try, when she was in the workshop, to truly be a part of it. But Ormanno was always in her thoughts, a presence underlying every moment, a secret she must be careful every second to guard. Even with Anasurymboriel's protection, she knew her own carelessness might still betray her.

She should be happy now, she knew. She had her heart's desire, or almost. These were her last days at Santa Marta. Yet she hated having to be so vigilant all the time. She hated having to invent explanations for her absentmindedness or her clumsiness, when thoughts of Ormanno distracted her. She hated suddenly remembering, when Benedicta spoke of color lore or Lucida offered the sweets her sisters brought or Perpetua smiled and thanked her for fetching something, that she was deceiving them. Especially, she hated imagining how betrayed Humilità would feel, how wounded Angela would be, when they discovered she was gone. She had to struggle sometimes to meet the other painters' eyes, for fear of what they might read on her face.

This is how it has to be, she told herself when guilt caught at her throat or knotted her stomach. She had chosen her path on the day she left Milan, and there was no other way to get to the end of it. She'd never expected it would be easy. She'd accepted the burden of sin she was taking on. It was just that she'd thought that all the difficulty would lie in her actions—not in their consequences. She hadn't expected to hurt anyone but herself.

So she worked even harder, filling every free moment with activity. If nothing else, she hoped the others would remember that when she was gone, and know she had not been completely false.

Just past dawn on the second Friday in September, Giulia stood at the end of the novices' wash line, waiting while Lisa poured water into the basin. As the crippled girl bent to wet her face, a burst of giggles made Giulia glance around. Alessia and her cronies were watching Costanza, who was standing over Lisa's bed, a bowl in her hands. Finished with whatever she was doing, she dropped the bowl out the window, then trotted over to Alessia. She whispered to the older girl, provoking a fresh explosion of stifled laughter.

Giulia turned away before they saw her looking. "Lisa," she whispered. "Lisa!"

Lisa jerked around, water dripping from her face and hands. "What?"

"Shhh! Keep your voice down. I just saw Costanza put something in your bed."

"What?" Lisa was incapable of whispering. "What did she put there?"

"I don't know. Lisa, wait—"

But Lisa was already pushing past her. The crippled girl bent over the bed. An expression of horror spread across her face. Clumsily, she began yanking at the sheets. Elisabetta and Nelia and Costanza doubled over with laughter; Alessia stood straight, glaring at Giulia.

"What's the meaning of this?" Suor Margarita came striding in. "Saints preserve us, Lisa, what are you doing?"

"It wasn't me!" Lisa was crying now, great gasping sobs. She pointed at her sheets, half on the bed, half on the floor. "My sheets—Costanza—"

"Lisa soiled her bed, Suor Margarita," said Alessia. Behind her, her followers tried to control their mirth. The other novices, some of whom had seen what had happened, the rest able to guess, looked on—grateful, no doubt, that Lisa was the scapegoat and not them. "She's very upset about it."

"What? Lisa, is this true?"

"I didn't!" Lisa cried, almost unintelligible in her distress. "I didn't!"

Suor Margarita ripped the sheets entirely off the bed, and stooped to sniff the mattress. She straightened quickly.

"Lying is a sin, Lisa, indeed it is. Roll up those sheets and carry them to the laundry while I think what to do with you."

"But Suor Margarita, I didn't—"

"Do as I say! And you girls over by the window—" She turned on Alessia and the others. "Stop your sniggering. This is no laughing matter."

Lisa bent to obey, sobbing. Her shame and misery were pitiful to see. Giulia felt something take hold of her, a kind of clearheaded rage.

"Suor Margarita."

The novice mistress turned, impatient. "What is it, Giulia?"

"It wasn't Lisa."

An echoing silence greeted this announcement. Lisa stopped sobbing and stared at Giulia with her mouth open.

"It was Costanza. I saw her pouring . . . whatever it was . . . into Lisa's bed."

"You're a liar!" Costanza cried. "You didn't see anything!"

"And I saw Costanza and Alessia talking afterward. Alessia told her to do it."

"Alessia. Is this true?"

"She's lying, Suor Margarita." Alessia's sallow features were tense with rage. "She's a commoner who's jealous of her betters. She's trying to make trouble for me."

"Costanza used a bowl," Giulia said. "She threw it out the window when she was done."

Costanza's mouth opened. The expression on her face spoke her guilt as clearly as words.

Suor Margarita stepped to the window and looked out. For a long moment she did not move. Then she turned. In her face was the promise of punishment.

"Costanza. Alessia. Go and wait for me in the schoolroom."

"But Suor Margarita, it was Costanza." Alessia ignored Costanza's gasp of betrayal. "You can't punish me for what she did."

"Do not tell me what I can and cannot do." Suor Margarita's tone was ominously level. "I have had enough of you, Alessia, and more than enough. There's no filthy thing these girls do that you don't have your hand in, and well I know it."

"My father will hear of this." An ugly flush had risen into Alessia's cheeks.

"Indeed he will. I will write myself to tell him. Now get to the schoolroom. And not another word."

Alessia turned, her head high, and stalked from the dormitory. Costanza followed, weeping.

"Saints' mercy, Lisa." Suor Margarita sounded tired now. "What are you still blubbering for? Roll up the sheets and put them in the corner. I'll see to them, and to a new mattress. The rest of you, finish dressing and line up! Quickly, quickly!"

The novices unfroze themselves and obeyed. Giulia tied on her kerchief and went to stand in line behind Lisa. The crippled girl turned. Her eyes were swollen, her nose still running.

"Thank you," she mumbled. "For saying what you did."

"You're welcome."

"My sisters hated me too, but at least they ignored me most of the time. I thought it'd be different in the convent."

"It won't always be like this, Lisa."

"Yes, it will," said Lisa bleakly. "There'll always be someone like Alessia." She looked at Giulia. "Why are you nice to me? Why aren't you mean like the others?"

Giulia dropped her eyes. "I know what it's like to be the one who doesn't fit."

"You? But you're pretty. And clever." Lisa wiped her

nose on her sleeve. "You'll be in trouble now. She'll be wanting to get even."

"Hush, you two." Suor Margarita came bustling toward them. "Or there'll be a penance for you as well."

Lisa turned away. The novice mistress clapped her hands, and the girls set out for the refectory.

Alessia and Costanza were not at the midday meal, nor at supper. When the other novices returned from the refectory, the two girls were kneeling before the hearth. For the next seven days, Suor Margarita announced, they would live on bread and water and spend the whole of the recreation hour in prayer, begging God to grant them charity.

When the Compline bell began to ring, Costanza went straight to her bed, her head down. But Alessia made it a point to walk by Giulia, slowing as she passed and turning on her a look of such concentrated venom that Giulia had to look away.

She knew it would be wiser to remain in the dormitory that night, but there was no question of missing Ormanno's visit. For caution's sake, she added an extra thousand to her usual count.

The sky was clear and the moon was close to full again. They did not really need the candle, but Ormanno lit it anyway, and set out the wine flask and the small early apples he had brought.

"I have a present for you." From her sleeve, Giulia took a roll of paper. "I drew your portrait."

He unrolled it and held the candle to it so he could see.

"You don't like it," she said when he did not speak, feeling the first acid touch of disappointment.

"Is that really how I look?"

She had drawn him in profile, gazing up, his eyes wide and his lips a little parted, as he looked when she named the stars for him. She had sketched him dozens of times over the past weeks, but this was the only attempt that had satisfied her.

"It's how I see you."

He glanced at her, then back at the portrait. "It's very good. You're . . . very good."

"You don't like it, I can tell. Give it back."

She reached for it, but he snatched it away, rolling it up again. "No. You made it for me and I'm keeping it. Giulia . . ."

"Yes?"

He hesitated. She held her breath. Would tonight be the night?

"There's something I've been meaning to tell you. I'm leaving Padua."

The shock was instant and horrible. "What? Why?"

"It's time for me to move on. To become my own master. We've talked about this, Giulia. You know how I feel."

This isn't happening. Giulia held herself motionless, trying not to burst into tears. *It isn't true.*

"The thing is . . . the thing is, Giulia . . . when I came up onto the balcony that day, I thought you were just a pretty girl. I thought . . . a bit of fun, something to boast about to my mates, since you said you weren't for the veil. I never meant it to be serious.

But I've never met a girl like you, a girl who knows the names of stars. And . . . the thing is . . . well, what I want to ask . . . will you come with me, Giulia? When I leave Padua?"

Giulia's heart seemed to turn over in her chest. The edges of her vision flashed blue. She opened her mouth, but nothing came out.

"I know I'm not much of a catch," Ormanno continued. "A foundling, a thief, a journeyman painter with no reputation of his own. I know you're too good for me—you're educated, you have noble blood. But you're alone in the world, same as me, you've been abandoned by the people who should have cared for you, same as me, and that makes us more alike than not. I don't have much now. But one day I will have everything, and I swear that I can make you—"

"Yes." She flung herself into his arms, oversetting the candle and nearly him as well. "Yes, yes, yes."

He held her tightly. "Yes?"

"Yes. I love you." It felt wonderful, and terrifying, to say it at last. "I'd go anywhere with you."

"My orchard girl."

A little later, he pulled away. The candle had gone out in the grass. There was only the moon to see by, and the vast ocean of stars wheeling overhead.

"I'd like to leave this very night," he said. "But there's something I need to do first. It'll be another week, maybe two."

"Where will we go?"

"Florence. There are many painters there. I'm

sure I can make my way. It's a beautiful city, or so I hear."

"I don't care, so long as we're together."

He smoothed a curl of hair behind her ear. "You're happy, then?"

"Oh yes."

"I won't expect you to stop drawing, you know."

"I don't just want to draw. I want to paint."

"I can teach you a little, if you like." He was still stroking her hair.

"I don't only want to learn, Ormanno. You'll have your workshop. I can be part of it. We can be painters together."

His face stilled. His fingers fell away.

"Ormanno—just listen to me." She reached after him, catching his hands. "I know what the world thinks of woman painters, and I know you think it too, even though you've seen my Maestra's work and know the rumors about her are false. But I can prove you're wrong. Give me the chance to prove it to you. It doesn't have to happen right away. I'm not ready yet, I won't be for some time. But one day I *will* be ready." She caught her breath, feeling the desire in her, the core of fire that was her talent, eager to blaze up and be seen. "I know it's never been done before. But you've told me about your experiments, about how you want to break with tradition and try new things. Well, this is something new."

"Giulia—" He broke off. "How long have you been thinking about this?"

"Since the first night you came here."

His brows drew together. "You were that sure of me?"

"I've known . . . how I felt about you . . . since that day on the balcony. I hoped you felt the same."

"Giulia." He pulled his hands away. "I've already told you I don't expect you to stop drawing. You can do that to your heart's content in your spare time. But a woman in my workshop—" He shook his head. "You have to see that's not possible. I could never build a reputation or attract patrons. I'd be laughed at. I'd be treated as a curiosity."

"But I'm good. You said it yourself. Could you look at the drawing I gave you tonight and say whether a man or a woman had made it?"

"No," he said slowly. "I couldn't. But don't you see— it doesn't matter what I think. It's what other people think. I have to consider my future. *Our* future."

"But it's the painting that matters! The painting, not what people *think!*"

"It is hardly so simple, Giulia. Painting is an art, but a workshop is a business. There has to be a balance."

"You're afraid." She knew she shouldn't say it. But her plan was unraveling, falling to pieces, and she could not stop the words. "You're just afraid!"

"Enough." His temper snapped. "If you are so bound to be part of a workshop, there is one right here at Santa Marta that would be glad to keep you."

"So now you want me to stay here?" The tears she had been fighting spilled over. "You've changed your mind? Is that what you're saying?"

"No!" He caught her in his arms. She resisted, her own arms stiff at her sides, but he held her tight and after a moment she stopped struggling. "No. I want you with me. I do. I just . . . you can't expect . . . ah, Giulia, Giulia!" His voice strained with frustration, and with his effort to contain it. "I don't want to quarrel with you. I don't want to disagree."

"I don't want to quarrel either."

"Then let's not. We don't need to talk about this now, do we? Can't we leave it for another time?"

"What other time?"

"When we're away. When we're safe."

She drew back so she could look into his face. "Will you think about it? Will you at least do that?"

He pulled her close again. "I'll think about it."

"Do you promise?"

He let out his breath, not quite a sigh. "I promise."

He released her and got to his feet, though the midnight bell had not yet rung. He reached down his hand and she allowed him to draw her up.

"I'll come on Friday," he said. "I should know by then when we can leave. Good night, my orchard girl."

He kissed her chastely on the forehead, then untied the rope that held the boat and climbed over the wall. She listened until she heard the sound of his oars. As she turned to go, she thought she glimpsed a spark of blue, glimmering in the shadows beneath the trees. But then she blinked, and it was gone.

In the dormitory, huddled in her bed with the covers

pulled over her head, she realized that she had made a mistake. She should never have told him her idea about the workshop. It was too sudden, too soon. After all, he'd only seen two of her drawings. Why should he have faith in her on the basis of that? She should have held her tongue till they were away, till they'd had time together and he'd had a chance to see what she could do.

I can still make it right. She would bide her time, saying nothing more about the workshop, accepting the teaching he had offered her. She'd be a good pupil—she knew she had a great deal to learn. As they worked and lived together as man and wife, he'd grow accustomed to the presence of a woman painter. She would make herself indispensable to him, for he'd need assistance while he built his reputation. When she proposed again to join him in his workshop, the idea would no longer seem so strange. It would seem, instead, a natural transition.

Yes. That's what I'll do.

She would have to be patient. She would have to keep secrets. She felt a pang—she'd thought she would be done with those once she was out of Santa Marta. But it wouldn't be forever. And in the end she would succeed. He was star-sent. He was her heart's desire. It was impossible that he should refuse her what she wanted so much.

She closed her fingers around the talisman. *In a week, maybe two, I'll be gone,* she thought. *Beyond the walls of Santa Marta, out in the world. Married.*

It was only then, with a shock that turned her icy cold under the stuffy covers, that she realized something: Ormanno had never actually mentioned marriage.

Part IV

Heart's Desire

❖❖❖❖❖❖

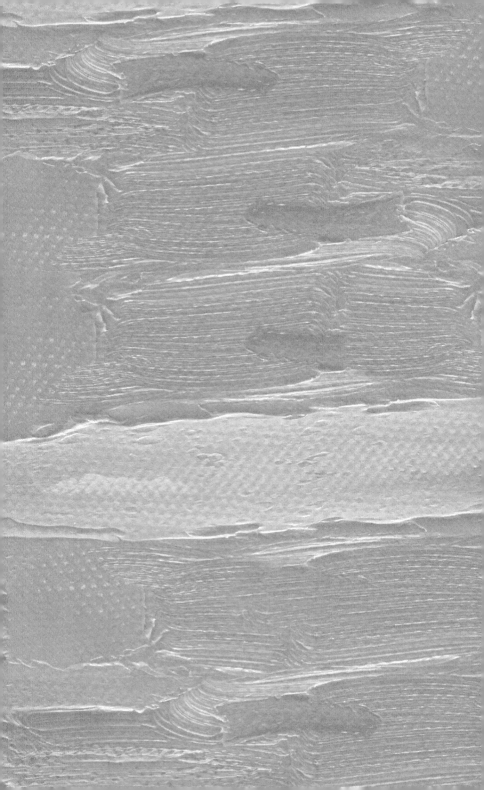

CHAPTER 19

✥ Madonna and Child ✥

In the middle of the next afternoon, just after the bell for None, Paola, the youngest novice, came to the workshop door.

"Giulia," she called. "Giulia!"

Giulia turned from the supply shelves, where she was taking down a box of cinnabar. "What is it, Paola?"

"You've got a visitor. In the parlor."

"A visitor? For me? Who is it?"

"Dunno. I'm s'posed to tell you to come right away." Paola turned and trotted off.

Giulia put back the cinnabar and began to untie her apron. It could only be Ormanno. But why would he come to the parlor? Had something gone wrong? She'd had a bad few moments last night, until she remembered that Anasurymboriel was bound to bring her her heart's desire—and that meant a husband, not a lover. Ormanno *would* ask her to marry him; the talisman assured it.

But now the icy dread gripped her again. *Has the enchantment failed? Has he come to tell me he's changed his mind?*

"Who do you think it is?" Angela, also at the shelves, was selecting pigments. They were for herself; Giulia had volunteered to do Angela's share of that afternoon's work so the young nun could have some uninterrupted time to spend on her practice painting. "You haven't any family here, have you?"

"No." Giulia hung her apron on its peg, forcing herself not to rush. "I . . . I have a cousin, though, from Milan. He travels sometimes."

"Really? You never mentioned him."

Giulia left the workshop and hurried down the main hall of the convent's north wing. The choir nuns were all in church singing None; she saw no one but a pair of *conversae*, raking gravel in one of the courtyards.

She passed the mouth of the short corridor that led to the chapter room, where the choir nuns met monthly to discuss and vote on the affairs of the community. Giulia had never been inside the chapter room, but she'd walked by it several times with Angela, on their way to the parlor when Angela's brother, Alberto, came to visit. Candles in niches lit the main hall, but side passages like this one, whose rooms were not in use, were dark.

A flicker of motion caught her eye. Then there

were running footsteps, and she understood what was about to happen an instant before the hands fell on her. Her captors yanked her into the corridor, then ran her down its length and slammed her against the chapter room door. She managed to turn her face aside just in time. Pain burst across her cheek.

"That's for yesterday," Alessia hissed from behind her. "For blabbing to Suor Margarita."

Giulia tried to struggle, but there were three of them, and they had her held fast. In the dimness over her shoulder she could see Alessia's fury-twisted features, and also the pale face of Nelia. The third captor, she guessed, was Elisabetta. Costanza, who'd botched the attempted humiliation of Lisa, would be out of favor just now.

"You don't belong here," whispered Alessia. "A nobleman's bastard with a commoner mother, a *conversa* who thinks she's as good as a choir nun. I've known it from the day you arrived."

Giulia held her breath, refusing to let them see her fear.

"You'll never take vows at Santa Marta. Never, do you hear me?" Alessia set the point of her elbow between Giulia's shoulder blades. "I'm going to see that you're thrown out of here with nothing more than the clothes you stand up in. And it will happen sooner than you think."

She ground her elbow viciously into Giulia's spine. Giulia could not help herself; she gasped.

"And if you *ever* interfere with me again, or with any of my friends, I'll make you sorry. I swear it. Do you understand me, tattletale? Well, do you?"

"Yes," Giulia whispered.

"I didn't hear you."

"Yes!"

Alessia leaned in harder; it felt as if her elbow would go right through Giulia's back. Then she stepped away.

"All right. Let her go."

The prisoning hands fell away. Giulia's knees buckled and she sank to the floor. She stayed there, huddled against the chapter room door, as the girls' footsteps receded, as silence returned and her heartbeat began to slow.

She could still feel the imprint of Alessia's elbow between her shoulder blades, a knot of pain lingering like an echo. *Stupid,* she thought, in time with the throbbing in her cheek. *Stupid, stupid, stupid.* She'd known Alessia would retaliate. The oddness of the summons, brought during a time when the convent corridors were mostly empty, should have made her suspicious.

You'll never take vows at Santa Marta. Giulia shivered at the memory of that vicious whisper. The joke was on Alessia, though. In a week, maybe two, Giulia would indeed be gone—but by her own choice, not Alessia's.

Giulia pushed herself to her feet, smoothed her dress, and straightened her kerchief. She touched her cheek. It was swollen—there would probably be a bruise. She'd have to make up some kind of explanation.

At least Ormanno didn't come. At least nothing's gone wrong.

When Giulia arrived back at the workshop, Domenica, Perpetua, and Humilità were intent on the San Giustina commission. Benedicta sat at her lectern, and Angela was immersed in her practice painting. Lucida, at the drafting table working on one of her miniatures, was the only one who glanced up as Giulia entered.

"Saints' mercy, Giulia! What happened to your face?"

Giulia cupped her hand over her swollen cheek. "I tripped and banged my face on the floor."

"Let me take a look." Lucida put down her brush and came to Giulia's side. "Oh! I can already see a bruise! You must go to the infirmary and get a poultice."

The others left what they were doing and crowded around, exclaiming. Giulia, embarrassed by their concern, told them that she didn't need a poultice, just to sit down for a little while.

"Very well," Humilità said, "but you must have something for that cheek. Angela, fetch a bowl of water and a cloth."

Angela obeyed. The other artists dispersed back to their work. Giulia brought a stool over to Angela's lectern and waited as Angela returned with the bowl, balancing it carefully against the dip and halt of her limp.

"Who was your visitor?" Angela sat down and began cleaning paint from the brush she'd been using. "Was it your cousin, as you thought?"

Giulia wrung out the cloth and held it to her cheek, feeling the relief of the cool wetness. She'd intended to say the summons was a mistake and she'd arrived in the parlor to find no one there. Instead, she found herself telling the truth.

"It was a trick. Alessia and her friends were waiting for me. They wanted revenge for yesterday."

"Oh, that awful girl!" Angela dropped the brush and the cleaning rag on the little table that held her jars of pigment and other tools. She knew all about Alessia's bullying, and Giulia had told her about the incident with Lisa. "So you didn't fall? She did that to you?"

"Her and Nelia and Elisabetta. At least I think it was Elisabetta. I couldn't see."

Angela reached to place a paint-stained hand on Giulia's arm. "I know you asked me not to speak to Madre Damiana about those girls and the way they torment you. But I could talk to the Maestra. Something needs to be done. You haven't been yourself these past few weeks. You've been trying to hide it, but I can tell."

"No, Angela." Giulia couldn't meet the young nun's eyes. Was she really doing such a bad job of pretending? "Don't say anything."

"But they'll just keep making you miserable," Angela said, distressed. "And once Alessia takes her vows, she can do much worse. Speak against you in chapter meetings, even."

"Please, Angela. It would only make her angrier."

Angela sighed. "Very well. But if you change your mind, you must tell me."

"I will."

Angela took up her brush again. Then she paused, her face brightening.

"I know what will make you feel better. How would you like to work on my painting?"

"I'm not supposed to be painting yet."

"Yes, but I know how much you've been wanting to. The Maestra's in another world right now. . . ." Angela glanced toward the scaffold, where Humilità was intent upon the central panel. "She won't notice, and if she does . . . well, if she does, I'll just tell her that *I* think you're ready. After all, I've been training you as much as she has, and . . . oh, Giulia, I meant to wait till a better time to tell you this, but your horoscope came true! The Maestra told me this morning that she's going to let me paint the angel in the second thief panel, and if I do a good job she'll declare me a journeyman."

"Angela, that's wonderful."

"My first commission!" Angela's eyes were shining. "So you see, I'm as qualified as anyone to say you're ready to paint."

Giulia doubted that Humilità would agree. But her fingers were burning with desire, hotter than her bruised cheek. "Are you sure? I don't want to ruin it."

"You won't ruin it. It's just the grass, anyway. I can always paint over it if you make a mistake. Here. Sit on my stool. I'll watch over your shoulder, but I won't say anything unless you ask."

Giulia put down the bowl. The girls switched places. From the little table, Giulia took up Angela's palette and the brush Angela had cleaned, curling her fingers around the smooth wooden shaft of the brush, slipping her thumb through the hole in the palette. The tools felt both strange and known—known because she had often practiced holding them this way; strange because she had never before held them in preparation to paint.

Angela's painting was propped at an angle on the surface of the lectern. It was oil, not tempera, and the figures of Madonna and Child were already complete, lacking only the gold leaf for their haloes. Angela was filling in the background, a forest clearing with spring trees just leafing out and grass starred with white violets. Over the underpainted monochrome of highlights and shadows, she'd laid the first layer of color—yellow ochre for the grass, bone black for the leaves of the violets, and lead white for their blossoms. The greens and browns and lavenders of the final color layer were mixed and ready on the palette.

Giulia dipped the brush in the lightest shade of green, turning the handle so that the bristles spun to a point. Angela had not told her which color to choose—but she'd watched the painters so many times, listened so carefully to old Benedicta's wisdom. She knew instinctively that this exact hue, laid thinly over the black, would produce the depth and darkness of living leaves.

She held her breath. She set the brush to the panel, working tentatively at first, then with growing assurance—choosing paints, changing brushes, combining pigments when one of the mixed shades did not seem quite right. As she did, the workshop began to vanish. She forgot the pain in her cheek and back, forgot Angela beside her, forgot everything but the panel and the color blooming under her brush. She hadn't fully understood how different painting would be from drawing. Drawing caught the edges of things, the lines and the angles that separated one thing from another, but with painting there was no separation—only color blending into color, form laid upon form, light shading into shadow and back again. Yet what she was doing did not feel new. It was as if she were rediscovering something that her conscious mind had lost, even as her hands and heart and soul retained the memory. Beneath her brush, a world was born—grass and flowers, leaves and earth—as if, like God Himself, she possessed the power of creation.

She had to stop at last, for she had run out of green. She sat back on the stool, realizing as she did how cramped her arms and shoulders felt.

"Well, Angela." Humilità's voice came from behind. "It seems you have taken some authority upon yourself."

Giulia felt as if the bowl of water she'd been holding earlier had been poured over her head. She twisted around. Humilità was standing a little distance away, her arms folded across her paint-stained apron. Her wide mouth was a straight line and her black eyes were narrow, but she did not look angry, exactly.

"I'm sorry, Maestra," Angela said softly. "Her cheek was hurting, and I wanted to help her forget it. I didn't think there'd be any harm, just for a little while."

"Hm." Humilità stepped closer, leaning in to look. Giulia turned toward the painting again. For the first time she saw, really saw, what she had done. It wasn't perfect, not by any means. The grass looked stiff rather than soft, especially where she'd begun, and some of the finer details seemed amateurish. But the violet blossoms—she'd gotten them just right. And the rosette of their leaves, pale color smoothed over dark to create a hue that was more than just the sum of black and green . . . that was perfect.

"Hm," said Humilità again. Her expression was unreadable. She straightened and stepped back. "It appears you're feeling well enough to get back to work, Giulia, so that is what I suggest you do. You too, Angela. You've had quite enough time on your own today."

"Well, she didn't reprimand us," Angela said, as Humilità disappeared into her study. "That's a good sign, I think."

Giulia began to clear away the painting things. She was aware of the pain in her back and cheek again, but the thrill of the past half hour was still with her—though it stung that Humilità had made no comment on her work.

"Angela, I know I made a muddle of your painting, but it was wonderful. More wonderful than I ever imagined. Thank you."

"You didn't make a muddle. I'll have to do some overpainting, but not very much." Angela hesitated. "What you did was amazing, Giulia."

"I've been watching and learning."

Angela shook her head. "It's more than that. I had years more learning than you the first time I ever held a brush, and you should have seen the muddle *I* made. I got better. Perhaps even good. But I am just a painter. You . . ." She drew in her breath. "You will be Maestra one day."

"Angela—"

"You will be, I know it. If you asked the stars with

one of your horoscopes, that is what they would say."

In Angela's words Giulia heard the echo of Humilità's, that day in the market: *Perhaps you, Giulia.* Once again, her mind leaped toward that possible future, but this time with the memory of brush and palette burning in her hands. . . .

No. She shook her head, pushing the vision away. *That's not what I want. I want Ormanno. I want to go with him over the wall.*

And all at once Giulia understood, truly understood, that she was leaving Santa Marta. That today had been one of the last days she would spend in the workshop, grinding pigments, preparing paint, watching master artists at their craft. That this was one of the last times she and Angela would work side by side, talking about anything and everything that came into their heads. That soon she would never attend another of Lucida's supper parties, or take another lesson from Humilità, or talk to old Benedicta about color lore, or be scolded by Domenica. That when the San Giustina altarpiece was completed, she would not be there to see it. For she would be with Ormanno, and they would be far away from Padua.

Last night, that had thrilled her. But right now, this moment, it brought her not one bit of joy.

Could it be . . . could it be that she was sorry to be leaving?

Alessia's cruelty had not made her cry. But now, suddenly, she felt like bursting into tears.

"Giulia?" Angela was looking at her, anxious. "Are you feeling pain again?"

"No." Giulia scooped up some of the pigment pots.

"I'll just put these back on the shelves."

They worked together for the rest of the afternoon, grinding pigments and purifying walnut oil. Angela tried to chat, but Giulia replied with monosyllables, and after a while the other girl left her alone. Giulia knew Angela thought she was in pain, and she couldn't meet the young nun's sympathetic glances. It was a relief when the Vespers bell finally called her away.

Anasurymboriel came into Giulia's dream that night, the tame flame that allowed her to caress it, that danced willingly on her palm. But when she closed her hands around it, the soft thrumming suddenly changed. It battered against her hold like a moth frantic to be free. She woke gasping, with a nightmarish feeling of constriction, as if she were the one being held against her will.

It was the first dream of the little spirit that had not been pleasant. She couldn't guess what it might mean, or if it meant anything. She did not sleep again, lying open-eyed until the bell for Prime shattered the predawn silence.

CHAPTER 20

❖ The Altarpiece of San Giustina ❖

By Friday night, when Giulia stole out to meet Ormanno in the orchard, her cheek was a vivid shade of purple.

"My poor girl!" he exclaimed, when she told him what Alessia had done. He opened his arms and she went into them, turning the uninjured side of her face against his shoulder, trying to lose herself in the familiar feel and smell of him.

"I've made the arrangements," he said. "Next Friday night I'll come for you, and we'll shake the dust of Padua off our feet for good."

"Friday? No sooner?"

"It's not so long, my love."

"No, I suppose not."

But it *was* long. It was an eternity. Giulia wanted to be gone, she wanted the guilt and the regret to be behind her. She wanted to stop avoiding people's eyes, fearing they would read deception on her face. She wanted to stop lying. She wanted to confess her sins and do penance, and finally be able to pray again. She wanted to start anew, to take the first steps into the life she had dreamed of since she was a little girl.

She felt the lump of the talisman, pushed hard against her chest by the pressure of Ormanno's embrace. For the first time, she realized that she wanted to be free of it too.

"Are you happy, my orchard girl?"

"I will be, once we're on our way."

"There's not much in Padua that I'll miss. Though I do have one regret."

"What is it?" She leaned against him. The September night held the chill of autumn, and his warmth was welcome.

"I wish I could have seen your Maestra's altarpiece. The frame is done, and I don't think it has an equal anywhere in the city. But I'm sure it's nothing compared to the painting it will hold."

"Yes. It will be a masterpiece."

"You could show it to me, you know."

"What do you mean?"

"The altarpiece. We could go see it."

"Yes, and we could also grow wings and fly over the walls."

"Didn't you say the workshop is on the north side

of the convent, away from where everyone sleeps? And the nuns don't have to rise for prayers, so there's no one in the halls at night anyway? You've been coming to me for weeks with no one the wiser. Don't you think it would be fun?"

She pulled back so she could look at him. "You're serious."

He returned her gaze. "Why not?"

"*Why not?*" She pushed away from him, out of the circle of his arms. "Are you insane? Me sneaking out on my own is one thing, but you and I—if we were caught—"

"We'd be careful."

"But what if we weren't careful enough? You're the one who told me about the penalties for men who corrupt nuns. Besides, the workshop door is locked at night. Even if there were no living soul in the whole of Santa Marta, we couldn't get in."

He let out his breath. "You're right. Of course you're right. I'm sorry, Giulia. It was a bad idea."

"How could you ask me that, Ormanno? How could you even think of such a thing?"

"Don't be angry. I only thought it would be an adventure. I'm sorry I mentioned it."

They stood looking at each other. Somehow, their separation had increased; if Giulia stretched out her arm now, she would not be able to touch him. There was a pressure in her chest; something seemed to be rising between them, something that frightened her.

Ormanno's expression changed. He raised his head and looked beyond her, toward the orchard.

"What—" she began, but he held up his hand.

Quick and silent, he approached the trees. For a moment he stood listening, his body tense. Then he turned and came back to her.

"I thought I heard something," he said.

"What?"

"I don't know. Twigs snapping. Maybe I imagined it."

"Alessia." Giulia felt cold.

"The girl who hurt your face? You think she followed you?"

Giulia hesitated, remembering Alessia's malevolent whisper: *I'm going to see you're thrown out. . . . It will happen sooner than you think.* But she'd been so careful. Besides, she was under Anasurymboriel's protection.

"No. It must have been something else."

"Well, even so, it's probably best if I go," Ormanno said. "Giulia—I'll be two hours later than usual on Friday. There are some things I have to do before we leave. Come at one o'clock. No earlier—I don't want you sitting by yourself in the dark. One o'clock. Promise me?"

"I promise."

He took her hands. "Do you believe I love you?"

"Yes," she said, surprised.

"Good."

He pulled her toward him and kissed her lightly on the lips. Then he turned and scrambled over the breached wall. She heard the creak of the boat, the splash of the oars. Then silence.

She did not return to the dormitory right away. Instead, she sat down at the base of one of the fruit trees, amid the long grass that had gone dry and brittle with summer's end. She pulled up her legs and wrapped her arms around them, resting her chin on her knees, as she had done— so long ago, it seemed—in Palazzo Borromeo, when she went up to the attic to be alone. Clouds had closed over the face of the moon; the wall in front of her was a formless blur against the lighter expanse of the sky.

She could not shake off the pressure of the dark feeling that had risen in her as she and Ormanno stood looking at each other. She was still angry at him. His proposal—so strange, so outrageously unexpected— troubled her in a way that went beyond the thoughtless- ness or the danger of it. The idea of him intruding into Humilità's little kingdom of women made her queasy. He should not have asked. He never should have asked.

He'd been so inquisitive about the workshop. He'd asked so many questions, seemed so fascinated by everything she had told him. The natural curiosity of one artist about another, she'd assured herself— but she had never forgotten what he'd said about Humilità: *Your Maestra is a marvel not just for the paint- ings she makes, but that she makes them at all.* An excep- tion to the rule that women could not paint. Was that the real reason for his interest—the fascination with something that should not be?

She thought of how he'd instantly rejected her pro- posal to join him in his workshop. When she begged him to think about it, he had promised he would— but there had been a pause before he answered. She remembered that now. A distinct pause, as if he'd said it just to soothe her. As if . . . as if he'd lied.

She had told herself she could change his mind. But what if she couldn't? What if she went with him, over the wall and out into the world, and he never let her paint?

She closed her eyes, remembering how it had felt to work on Angela's Madonna and Child—to immerse herself in form and color, to weave magic with her brush. To think she might not have that, to think it might not be part of her life, was like something in her being torn apart.

She was shivering now. She didn't want these thoughts. She didn't want these questions. But she could not shut them out—and anyway, they were not really new, were they? They had come to her before. The other times, she'd banished them by force of will, or found some way to tell herself they did not mean what she thought they did.

This time, it was different. This time, she could not make them go away.

When she finally returned to the dormitory and climbed into bed—she could hear Alessia snoring, four beds down—she could not sleep. Miserably, she lay thinking and wondering, until, just before dawn, she remembered the astrolabe. She didn't have to torture herself with questions. She could make a horary chart. She could get answers.

The clouds had departed during the night and the morning was clear and bright. Pretending to have an errand, she left the workshop just after the bell for Terce, when she knew the corridors and courtyards would be nearly empty. The astrolabe, some paper, and a stick of charcoal were hidden in her sleeve. Her heart raced, and she thought of Maestro's warning. Was she ready for an answer she did not want? But how, not knowing, could she follow Ormanno over the wall?

Her mother's voice seemed to whisper in her ear: *The only person you can rely on is yourself.*

It was a long time since Giulia had thought of that. A long time, she realized, since she'd thought of her mother at all.

"I'm sorry, Mama," she whispered.

In one of the deserted courtyards, she raised the astrolabe to the sun and murmured her question: "Will I be a painter in Ormanno's workshop?" She took a sighting, then crouched down to transcribe the measurements, working quickly, trying not to think about what she was writing. Finished, she rolled up the paper, concealed it and the astrolabe again, and returned to the workshop.

There was a lot to be done that day, and she wasn't able to snatch any free time until the evening, when Angela, Lucida, Domenica, and Benedicta departed to sing Vespers, leaving the *conversae* alone. She carried a candle over to the bench where she and Angela had their drawing lessons, and pulled the paper from her sleeve. For a moment she sat looking at it, bracing herself. Then she unrolled it.

She'd tried to close her mind to interpretation as she transcribed the symbols, but what she saw now was no surprise. The signs in the first house, the house of the questioner, were malign, as clear a "no" as she had ever seen. The signs in the fifth house, the house of the question, were also negative—and they suggested not just that she would never be part of Ormanno's workshop, but that there might never be a workshop at all. This had not occurred to her—that Ormanno might not get what he wanted either.

She felt a sinking at her core, as if she'd just learned she had a fatal illness.

She got to her feet, crumpling the horoscope in her fist, and crossed to the San Giustina commission. The altarpiece was not illuminated tonight—Humilità and Perpetua were in Humilità's study, working on accounts. But the blue twilight of the court, and the candles and lamps burning elsewhere in the room, were enough to see by.

Over the weeks of August and early September Humilità had completed the scene at the foot of the Cross, and had nearly finished the thief at Christ's right hand. The thief's body was corded with agony, his mouth open in a cry of anguish. An angel hovered above his shoulder, with glorious wings of Passion blue. Passion blue shone around the Cross as well, in the cloak of the Virgin, the gown of Mary Magdalen, the garments of the crowd. Raised above them all on the Cross, Jesus was a monochrome of light and shadow, awaiting the moment when Humilità's brush would layer His body and His tormented limbs with color, bringing to life a suffering so real that all who looked on it would share, for just a moment, a shadow of that holy pain.

It was a masterpiece. In the time to come, Giulia thought, it would touch the minds and hearts of those who saw it, and they would wonder at it, and they would remember. The painting would become part of them; it would speak to them in Humilità's voice. In her painting she would live on, down the years and perhaps even the centuries, speaking the beautiful truth of her art to all who listened.

This is what I want. Giulia knew it, with utter clarity. This power. This passion. Could she tie her life to Ormanno's, knowing that if she went with him, she might never have it?

In the autumn twilight, she felt as cold as winter. Ormanno was the gift of the talisman. He was her heart's desire—the love, the home, the family she had dreamed of since she was a little girl. How could she think of turning away from that? From him? And what was the alternative—Santa Marta? The life Humilità had offered her? The life of an artist—maybe even of a Maestra—but still the life of a nun, the barren, loveless, childless, nameless life predicted by her horoscope.

But I would be painting.

And all at once, by some strange turn of memory or perception, she stood in the sorcerer's house again, the zodiac underfoot and the constellations overhead and the candles burning with flames that were not natural, and she heard the sorcerer say what he had told her as he placed the talisman in her hands: *Be very sure you know what your heart's desire is, or you may find yourself surprised by what you receive.*

She felt everything inside her go still. She thought of the horary chart she'd cast that hot afternoon in the workshop, the one that told her she already had her heart's desire. She thought of her first dream of Anasurymboriel, which had come on the night Humilità made her an apprentice. She thought of how the dreams had changed after she visited Matteo Moretti's workshop—she'd met Ormanno on the balcony that day, but it had also been the day Humilità spoke to her of finding a vocation in her art. Of how the dreams had changed again, becoming nightmares, after Ormanno asked her to leave with him.

She'd heard the spirit in her dreams. She'd sought the counsel of the stars. Had she completely mistaken what they were telling her?

The workshop's door creaked. Uneven footsteps advanced across the room.

"Giulia?" It was Angela, returning from Vespers to accompany Giulia to supper, as she often did. "Oh. There you are." She came round the scaffold, then stopped short. "Giulia, what's wrong?"

"What do you want more than anything in the world, Angela?" Giulia heard her own voice, as if from a great distance.

"To give glory to God through my painting. You know that."

"What if you found out that your heart's desire was really something else? And that getting it meant giving up what you always thought you wanted most, and settling for something you never wanted at all?

But you weren't sure you were right, and if you made a mistake, if you made the wrong choice, you'd never get another chance?"

"Giulia, what are you talking about?" Angela limped toward Giulia, her delicate brows knotted with concern. "I don't understand. What do you mean?"

"I don't know what to do," Giulia said, but it wasn't true. The talisman dragged at her neck, a cruel weight. Humilità spoke inside her mind: *For you, there is only here, with me.*

A tide of grief rose up in her. The tears spilled over, and she bowed her face onto Angela's shoulder and wept as if she would never stop.

CHAPTER 21

✤ The Breached Wall ✤

A hundred times, in the days that followed, Giulia fought the same battle of decision. She was still not sure she was right about the talisman. She still could not bear to think what it meant for her to stay at Santa Marta. But the truth was settling into her, like mineral pigment settling to the bottom of a beaker of water. No matter which path she chose, there must be sacrifice. She didn't know if she were strong enough to endure losing Ormanno and the life she had always dreamed of—but she did know, with absolute certainty, that she could not give up painting.

She was aware also that something strange was happening to her thoughts. More and more, she found herself remembering not Ormanno's arms or his mouth or his icy-bright eyes, but how appalled he'd seemed by the idea of a woman in his workshop, and how he had lied (she was almost sure of it) when he said he would consider her plan. How he'd asked her to leave with him, but not to marry him. The thoughtless, ridiculously risky thing he had proposed the last time they were together.

It was as if a door had cracked open; a door she had not been able to look behind before. A door she hadn't even realized she was holding closed.

Friday arrived at last, a chilly day with pouring rain. As the girls lined up for the refectory it was clear that Alessia and Elisabetta were unwell. When the food came out, Alessia closed her eyes.

"Suor Margarita, may I be excused?"

"Indeed you may not, Alessia, as I told you the first time you asked. Exert your will, and your belly will obey."

Alessia began to reply, but then her eyes widened. She shot up from the bench and bolted from the room. Elisabetta ran after her, hands clapped over her mouth.

"May the saints grant me patience." Suor Margarita rose. "Nelia, you are in charge till I get back."

Down at the end of the table, Giulia noticed, Lisa was smiling.

The meal ended, and Giulia set out for the workshop. She'd gone only a little distance when she heard Lisa's thick voice behind her, calling her name. She stopped and waited as the crippled girl caught up.

"I fixed her for you," Lisa said softly, or as softly as her garbled speech allowed.

"What do you mean?"

"Alessia. I got purgative powder from the infirmary and put it in those nuts she's always eating. She must've shared them with Elisabetta."

Giulia stared at Lisa, shocked. "You made her sick?"

"Yes. Because I hate her." Lisa's blue eyes burned in her lopsided face—pretty eyes, Giulia noticed for the first time, with long blond lashes. "And for you. She was going to tell Suor Margarita you sneak out of the dormitory at night."

Giulia opened her mouth, and found she could not speak.

"I heard her talking to Nelia. She said you go out to your lover, like a whore. She said she followed you and saw. She said the next time she was going to fetch Suor Margarita so you'd be caught and thrown out of Santa Marta. And you were nice to me. So I fixed her."

It really was Alessia the other night, Giulia thought. How could she not have noticed she was being followed?

"Don't worry, Giulia. I won't betray you. I'll keep your secret even if they beat me."

"There won't be a secret after tonight."

"Are you running away with him?" Lisa's lovely eyes opened wide. "With your lover?"

"He's not my lover. And I'm not going to run away."

Not until this moment, she realized, had she been completely sure.

A pair of choir nuns came around the corner, turning

identical disapproving glances on the two girls. Lisa waited until they were past, then leaned close.

"I'm glad, Giulia. I'm glad you'll still be here."

Giulia had no idea, later, how she got through the day. It took all her concentration to behave normally. Perhaps she wasn't doing a very good job, for she could feel Angela's eyes on her as they worked. Fortunately Humilità, immersed in painting, was too distracted to notice anything amiss.

At supper, Alessia and Elisabetta were missing, confined to bed by order of the infirmarian. Giulia could not bring herself to feel any sympathy for them. She endured the meal, then the recreation hour. When at last the candles were blown out, she lay staring at the ceiling, waiting as the distant city bells tolled ten o'clock, then eleven.

How was she going to explain her decision to Ormanno? She wasn't cruel enough to tell him the truth about the horoscope, but she did not want to lie. *Will he be angry? What will I do if he pleads with me?* Of course, she could avoid the problem simply by staying away—by leaving him, tonight of all their nights, to wait alone by the broken wall. But that was the coward's path. She owed him at least some explanation.

At last she could not bear it a moment longer. Ormanno had told her not to come until one o'clock, but what difference would it make if she was early?

She climbed out the window, as she had so many times before—though this time was different, for it was the last. The rain had stopped and the full moon peered down through tattered clouds. Her footsteps seemed to beat a refrain: *Last time, last time.* The last time she'd slip through nightbound corridors. The last time she'd plunge into the darkness of Lucida's courtyard.

When she reached the orchard she halted to tie on her sandals, her teeth chattering with chill and nerves. Then she began to make her way between the trees, holding her skirts above her knees to keep them out of the wet grass. Moonlight came and went as clouds scudded across the sky, and everywhere was the winey scent of windfall apples.

A light flickered up ahead. Good—Ormanno had come early too. *We can get it over with sooner.* Giulia quickened her pace. The light seemed brighter than usual—had he brought a lantern?

A strange noise broke the stillness, a metallic clanking. Giulia stopped short. Had she imagined it? Just as she was sure she had, there came a different noise: a heavy *thunk*. Then another, and another, accompanied by a splintering sound.

What on earth . . . ?

Now she heard voices—something spoken, a response, too low to make out the words. One of the voices was Ormanno's, she was sure of it. But whose was the other?

Why has he brought someone with him?

She ran toward the light. At the last moment common sense, or some other instinct, made her slow. She crept between the trees and halted behind a twisted trunk.

She'd been right about the lantern. It sat on the ground by the breached wall. By its light she saw Ormanno, kneeling in the rain-damp grass. He wore boots and a leather jerkin, and a large wallet was slung over his shoulder. His features, illuminated from beneath, were tense. Another man knelt nearby, his back turned so Giulia could not see his face.

"There's no *time* for this," Ormanno was saying, his voice tight. "We're already later than we should be because you couldn't stick to the plan."

"I just want to look at it," said the other man. "Hard to believe it's worth what you say. Hard to believe anyone would care so much about some bloody paint recipe."

"We can talk about this later, Didoni. You need to leave."

"All right, all right. I'm going."

The man got to his feet, turning as he did—a large man, Giulia saw, with fair hair and features flattened as if he had been in too many fights. She also saw the book he held in his hands.

A big book, with leather binding and a brass clasp.

Humilità's book of secrets.

Giulia felt as if someone had seized her by the throat. There was a roaring in her ears.

"Take the box too." Ormanno was on his feet now also.

"Why? It's no use now I've broken it."

"I want you to get rid of it. I don't want her to see it."

"Who, your doxy?"

"Don't call her that."

"Well, well. Got tender feelings for the little convent girl, have we?"

"Christ's wounds! Why can't you just do as I say? By God, if I hadn't needed you to pick the locks I'd never have used you."

Giulia clutched the wet bark of the tree that sheltered her, as if she hung over the edge of the world and would fall forever if she let go. Understanding tore through her. Ormanno's interest in the workshop. The things he had gotten her to tell him, under the guise of ordinary conversation, about how it functioned, where it was located. Watching her cross Lucida's courtyard at the end of their meetings, so he would know his way into the convent building. What he'd asked her to do last Friday night. . . . And if she had agreed. If she had agreed, what would have happened?

Hard to believe anyone would care so much about some bloody paint recipe.

He hadn't wanted her. He'd never wanted her. He had wanted Humilità's book. He had wanted Passion blue.

"*Used* me?" Didoni's voice had gone flat.

"You know what I mean."

"Do I? I remember the oaths we swore as boys, when all the world was against us. I'm starting to wonder if you do."

"You know damned well I do. Didoni, we cannot be at odds now. We must hold fast, or neither of us will get anything."

"Bloody hell," Didoni said. "Take the cursed book, then, and put it in the cursed box yourself. You can put it in the boat too. I've got my hands full with the rest."

He handed Ormanno the book, then dragged a bulging sack out of the shadows. Giulia realized where the clanking noise she'd heard earlier had come from.

"You always were a greedy sod," Ormanno said,

kneeling again to place the book in the box and prop the lid, which had been shattered off its hinges, on top. "We will get hundreds for this book, but still you had to have the candlesticks."

"That's paper and ink," said Didoni. "This is silver. I know what silver's worth."

Ormanno sighed. He rose, the box in his arms. "So. The three o'clock bell, you know where. I'll meet you in the street, and we'll go to the client together."

"Yes, *Maestro*." Didoni's tone was mocking. "You've only told me a hundred times."

He picked up the lantern. They were leaving, with Humilità's book. That could not happen. Giulia had no plan; she had no idea how to stop them, knew it was mad even to think that she might try. But there was no time to run for help. There was no one to call on. No one but herself.

She stepped from behind the tree, into the light of the lantern. "Stop." It was a whisper. She tried again. "Stop!"

As one, the two men sprang around, Didoni's hand going to the knife at his belt. There was an instant of frozen silence. Then Didoni dropped his hand and smiled an ugly smile.

"Well, well. Your doxy's early, Manno."

"Giulia." Ormanno moved toward her. "Why are you here? I told you one o'clock."

"Yes, because you wanted to be sure you'd be gone before I arrived." Giulia was shocked, and she was terrified. But she was also angry—a high clear rage that built in her as she spoke.

"No. No, I was going to take you with me. I *am* going to take you with me."

"Oh, really? And I was never to know that you're a liar? That you never stopped being a thief? That you used me to get inside Santa Marta so you could steal my Maestra's secrets? So you could break into her workshop and take her book?"

"Giulia, I swear I was going to tell you. Just later on, when we were away from here."

"When it was too late for me to do anything about it, you mean. This was your plan all along, wasn't it? *This* was why you came up to the balcony that day. *This* was why you climbed over the wall all those nights. Oh, you were so clever, getting me to tell you so many things, and I was such a fool. I believed everything you said."

"Giulia . . ." There was something like distress in Ormanno's face, but she knew it was false, like everything else about him.

"The joke's on you, Ormanno. Passion blue is in cipher."

"What?"

"That's right. All the important recipes are. Only the Maestra can read them. You took the book for nothing."

"Manno." Didoni set down the lantern and the sack. "What's she saying?"

"It's a lie. She's lying."

"I'm not. It's the truth."

"Speak to me, Manno." Didoni stepped forward, laid a heavy hand on Ormanno's shoulder. "Is she lying or not?"

"Maybe. I don't know." Ormanno shook his head. "It doesn't matter. As long as Passion blue is in the book, the client gets what he wants. It's not our fault if he can't read it."

"He'll say we cheated him. Maybe cut our fee."

"How is it a cheat? He wanted the book, we got him the book. Yes. This can still work. We won't wait— we'll go to him now. We'll give him the book. We'll say nothing about a cipher. We'll get our money and be out of Padua before dawn."

"You can't do this," Giulia said, in a voice she hardly recognized as her own. "I won't let you."

Didoni laughed. "And how do you plan to stop us, little girl?"

Giulia charged at Ormanno. He staggered, surprised, and lost his grip on the box. It fell, the broken lid spinning off, the book flying out. Giulia threw herself after it, scrabbling for it. Her hands closed on its heavy leather. Then she was up, clutching the book to her chest, tripping over the hem of her gown, staggering toward the trees, one step, another step, another—

Hands seized the long braid of her hair, yanking her backward. Her head snapped on her neck and she fell hard on the ground. Didoni kicked her onto her back, then stooped and tore the book—which despite everything she had not dropped—from her arms.

"You bastard," Ormanno said. "You've no call to be so rough."

"Should I have stood there and let her get away? By the saints, Manno—"

"All right, all right. Come, Giulia." Ormanno knelt

beside her. "No more of this. We have to leave."

He tried to slip his arms around her, to pull her up, but she hit him with her fists, shoved herself away across the wet grass.

"Get away from me." Her scalp burned; the muscles of her neck sang with pain. "Don't touch me."

"Giulia—"

"Get away, you liar, you thief! How could you think I'd go anywhere with you?"

"Enough." Didoni tossed the book aside. He caught hold of Giulia and wrenched her upright. She tried to struggle, but he clamped one arm across her breasts and one across her throat and lifted her off her feet, squeezing her so tight she could barely breathe.

"Your bitch is a problem, Manno. She knows everything and she can't be left here to blab. Either she comes with us right now, or she goes nowhere ever again, and I don't care which. Your choice."

"Put her down. Christ's wounds, Didoni! Let her go so I can talk to her!"

A pause. Then Didoni dropped her. She fell to her knees, gasping for breath. Blue sparks danced at the edges of her vision.

"Giulia, listen to me." Ormanno crouched beside her. "I want you to come with me. That has nothing to do with this. But Didoni's right. You know who we are, you know what we've done, and we can't leave you here. I'd rather you come willingly, but you *are* coming, one way or another, and I'll tie you up if I have to. Do you understand me?"

She looked at him, at his face shadowed in the lantern light—his pale eyes, his mobile mouth, his long light hair. It seemed she should see him differently, for this was not the Ormanno she knew, or thought she had known. This was the real Ormanno, Ormanno the thief. He had always been there, behind the mask he'd worn. The mask she herself, mistaking him for her heart's desire, had given him.

It's all my fault. This is all my fault.

"Yes," she whispered.

"Will you be sensible, then, and come quietly?"

"Yes," she whispered again.

"Never known you to want an unwilling woman, Manno," said Didoni from above. "You must really like this one."

"She'll come round, once I've had a chance to explain properly."

"It's your funeral."

Ormanno rose. From the wallet at his shoulder he pulled a wad of cloth, which he tossed at Giulia. "Here's a gown for you to wear. Leave your novice habit on the grass. Didoni, go over the wall now. Give her some privacy."

Didoni laughed, not pleasantly, but did as Ormanno said, slinging the sack of silver over first.

"Turn your back," Giulia said.

"You know I can't do that."

So she turned hers, and dragged the coarse gray habit over her head, wincing at the soreness of her neck. She was aware of Ormanno's eyes on her; a week ago, she would have felt a mixture of embarrassment and excitement to have him looking at her so, but now she just felt revulsion.

The gown was of some heavy fabric that showed red when the lantern light caught it. She pulled it on over her chemise; the laces at the back hung loose, as did the sleeve-ties at the shoulders, but it fit her well enough. Its bodice was cut low. She was glad for once of the chemise's high neck.

"I had it made for you specially," Ormanno said, when she turned to face him. "Do you like it?"

She stared at him, silent. He shrugged.

There was nothing left for her to do but hike up her skirts and climb over the wall. Didoni, standing on the ledge that ran at its base on the canal side, offered his hand to help her, but she ignored it. Ormanno followed, with the pieces of the broken box and the lantern. He had stuffed Humilità's book into his wallet.

They arranged themselves on the boat's wood plank seats, Giulia and Ormanno together in the prow, Didoni at the stern with the oars, the sack of silver and the lantern between them in the inch or two of filthy canal water that sloshed at the bottom. The boat rocked as Didoni pushed off. The wall of Santa Marta receded. The canal was narrower than Giulia had imagined, closed in by other walls and the backs of buildings. If she shouted for help, would anyone wake? The moon shone through gaps in the clouds, making a path on the water, and the only sound was the dip and splash of the oars—the same sound Giulia had heard from the wall's other side as she waited for Ormanno to arrive or listened to him leave.

Her anger and defiance were gone. She was cold,

trembling with shock. But what filled her mind, what made her bite her lips in order not to scream, was not Ormanno's betrayal or her own folly or even the danger she was in, but the other horoscope—the one she had cast in July, the one that said she would soon escape from Santa Marta. Since she'd decided not to leave, she'd assumed she must have misinterpreted it. And she had, just as she'd misinterpreted everything else.

Yet it had told the truth after all.

CHAPTER 22

❖ The Master Thief ❖

They pulled in at a narrow dock built out from the canal side. Bells tolled one o'clock as Didoni stowed the oars. Giulia could hardly believe so little time had passed. It felt like an eternity since she had left her bed.

Ormanno handed the sack and the lantern up to Didoni, then pushed Giulia onto the dock and into Didoni's hands. The big man held her roughly as Ormanno tossed the box and its broken lid into the water and watched them sink.

They climbed a narrow flight of stairs to the rain-wet street. Ormanno led the way, holding Giulia tight against him. To the casual glance, they would seem a pair of affectionate lovers, his left arm around her waist, his right hand gripping hers—but there was no one to see them, for the streets were empty. The heavy skirts of the red dress were too long; the hem was soon soaked, and Giulia stumbled as it tangled around her legs.

She did her best to memorize their route. She had no plan except to hope for some chance she could exploit. All her attention, all her concentration, was focused on that. She was truly alone now; Anasurymboriel, clearly, had deserted her—if indeed the little spirit had ever protected her at all. It seemed entirely possible that all those nights when she thought she felt its magic had been nothing more than her imagination, fueled by her belief in Ormanno's lies.

They turned at last into an avenue that seemed familiar, though it was only when they stopped that Giulia realized where they were.

"What's this?" Didoni demanded in a whisper. "I thought we were going to the client, not to your home."

"The client is here."

Giulia could not help herself; she gasped.

"Yes," said Ormanno. "I knew you'd figure it out."

"Oho!" Didoni laughed. "So your master hired you to steal his own daughter's secrets? Now there's a neat betrayal."

It made perfect, horrible sense. Who else wanted Passion blue so much? Giulia thought of Matteo Moretti, sitting across the table on the day she and Humilità had visited. The plan had already been in motion then. Even as he spoke with Humilità about her work, even as he pressed her about Passion blue, he had been preparing to rob her of her secrets.

He was the one who said I should sit on the balcony. Where Ormanno could find me alone.

She had not thought things could get worse.

Ormanno produced a key. He let them into the house, then locked the door behind them and urged Giulia along the hallway. The kitchen was pitch black, the windows shuttered and the stove fires banked for the night. Didoni held up the lantern while Ormanno unbarred the door. Then they were in the courtyard, the rain-damp flagstones gleaming under the moon. The workshop was dark. No light showed in any of the house's windows.

"I'll go up," Ormanno whispered. "You stay with her."

"Oh no." Didoni was smiling his unpleasant smile. "You won't do this without me."

"I'm not going to betray you, you fool!"

"I'm not a gambler, Manno. Never have been."

"I don't want you with me. He doesn't . . . he thinks I did this on my own."

"That's not my problem. I'm going with you, and she'll have to come too. Got to take precautions, though."

Didoni set his sack on the cobbles and untied a rag from around his neck. Quickly, before Giulia could react, he forced the rag between her teeth and knotted it behind her head. It tasted foul.

"Do you have to do that?" Ormanno asked.

"If you want her to keep quiet."

"Christ's wounds." Ormanno turned away. "This isn't how I planned things. Come on, then."

He led them up the stairs to the second floor. Here at last was light—a line of it under Matteo Moretti's study door.

Ormanno knocked. A pause, then footsteps, then the sound of the lock. The door opened. Matteo stood backlit against the candles burning on the table behind him. He wore a nightshirt, and over it a wide-sleeved brocade robe. The candlelight made a halo of his mane of gray curls.

"You're early," he said. He looked past Ormanno to Didoni, his brows drawing down. "Who's this? Why are you not alone?" His eyes came to rest on Giulia. "And what in the name of all the saints is *she* doing here?"

"She's coming away with me," Ormanno said. "When I go."

"Have you lost your mind, boy? A kidnapped novice—my daughter's prize pupil—there will be a hue and cry! I told you to beguile her, not to elope with her! How could you be so stupid?"

"Not so stupid." Giulia heard the tightness in Ormanno's voice. "Since I had her drop her novice clothes on the ground beside the wall. They'll think she was the one who stole the book."

"Well, perhaps. But did you have to bring her here? How much does she know?"

"What difference does it make? I told you, I'm taking her with me. You won't hear from either of us again after tonight."

"It looks to me as if she may not be entirely willing."

"That's my business."

Matteo regarded Giulia with the dark eyes that

were so much like his daughter's. "Well. The thing is done now. Where's the book?"

Ormanno pulled it from his wallet and placed it in his master's hands. Matteo stepped back, gesturing them into the room. They crowded inside, Didoni shoving Giulia forward with a hand at the small of her back.

Matteo closed the door and locked it, then brought the book close to the candles. He ran his hand over the leather of the cover, caressingly, like a man smoothing a lover's cheek. His face in the candlelight was controlled, but Giulia could read his eagerness in the tension of his stance. Drawing in a breath—she saw the deep rise of his chest—he opened the cover. He turned a page, then another, his fingers lingering on the paper, his eyes moving on what was written there.

"It's what I asked for."

"Of course it is," Ormanno said. "We're quits now, you and I. Pay us and we'll be on our way."

Matteo turned to face them, where they stood in the shadows. "I will pay *you*." He nodded toward Didoni. "You'll have to settle up with your accomplice."

"It's all arranged."

"And we are not quits yet. Not until I'm sure the recipe I want is here."

"Our agreement was for the book, not what's in it."

Standing just behind Ormanno, Giulia could not see his face, but the tautness of his body spoke his strain. Matteo's eyes narrowed.

"Is there something you are not telling me, boy?"

"You wanted the book. I got you the book. Now I

want to be gone. We must leave the city before dawn. Before the hue and cry."

"I wanted the book *so long as the recipe was in it*. It's useless to me otherwise." Matteo stepped forward. Giulia had forgotten how big he was: more than a head taller than Ormanno and nearly twice as wide. The candles were behind him again; his face was like a thundercloud, broad and shadowed, rimmed in light. "Is that what you are trying to hide? That the recipe is not in the book?" His voice dropped. His black eyes glinted. "Don't think to cheat me. Don't think it, Ormanno."

Ormanno let out his breath, surrendering. "Passion blue is in the book. But it may be in cipher."

"*May* be?"

"Giulia says it is."

"Get that gag off her." Matteo pointed at Didoni. "You. Do it."

Such was the power of his command that Didoni obeyed at once.

"Tell me, girl." Matteo's harsh gaze was trained on Giulia now. "Is it so? Passion blue is in cipher?"

"My Maestra—" Giulia's mouth was dry as dust. She coughed, cleared her throat. "My Maestra puts all her most precious recipes in cipher."

"Including Passion blue?"

"Yes."

"Show me." When Giulia did not move, he seized her and dragged her over to the table. "Show me."

Giulia turned the pages. It felt like a betrayal of Humilità—but he would find it anyway, so what was the difference?

"There," she said. Matteo pushed her aside and bent over the page. The candles were enough to read by, but by no means bright; even so, the little square of Passion blue glowed with color, like the flash at the heart of a sapphire.

"Ah, Violetta, Violetta," he said softly. "Ever you defy me."

He straightened. His eyes were like two stones. "What do you know about this cipher, girl?"

"Nothing." Giulia spoke with a defiance she did not feel.

"Nothing?"

"Nothing. None of us do."

"The recipe, then. You are her prize pupil, her favorite. You must have seen her make it."

"Never. And I wouldn't tell you if I had."

It was a mistake. She knew it as soon as the words were out, by the small smile that raised the corners of his mouth.

"You want to protect your teacher. As any pupil should. I understand that."

"I swear I don't know anything!"

He ignored her. "Ormanno, I fear you will have to delay your departure. I'm not convinced this young lady is telling the truth, so I will keep her with me for a while. If I am able to unlock the cipher, you'll get your money and the girl. If I cannot solve it, you may have the girl, but I will not pay you."

"That wasn't our agreement." The tremor in Ormanno's voice belied his defiant words. "You've no right to change the terms."

"And yet I am changing them. You are free to leave this moment if you don't like it."

"Haven't I served you well over the years?" Ormanno's body was rigid, his fists clenched. "I don't deserve this."

"You have been useful, as I knew you would be when I took you in. But you are a thief, Ormanno. You were a thief when I found you, and you are a thief today. You know well what you deserve."

"Sir, this isn't right." Didoni had stepped forward to stand at Ormanno's side. "You hired him to do a job and he did it, and now he's owed his money. Fair's fair. I'm sure you wouldn't want word getting out about this night."

The air around Matteo seemed to change. He did not appear to move, but suddenly he was standing only inches from Didoni.

"Do you think to extort me, you verminous cur?" His voice was soft. "I am chairman of the *Fraglia*. I am a wealthy and respected citizen of Padua, and I eat supper once a month with the chief of the city watch. I need only speak, and you will vanish, and all your *words* with you. Do we understand each other?"

Didoni snarled and reached for his knife. But Matteo was quicker. He caught Didoni's arm and twisted it. Didoni cried out. The knife clattered to the floor. Matteo kicked it into the shadows.

"Remove this creature from my house," he told Ormanno. "As for you, you may stay or go, I care not which."

They glared at each other. In Ormanno's face Giulia saw rage and defeat, and in Matteo's, contempt and power. And she understood that Ormanno was a liar and a cheat, but Matteo . . . Matteo was monstrous.

"What will you do with her?" Ormanno looked past his master to where Giulia stood by the table. She turned her face away before he could catch her eyes.

"She will be perfectly safe and comfortable. Now get out."

They obeyed. Matteo watched them go. Then he returned to the table and gripped Giulia by the arm.

"Come, girl. I know just the place for you."

CHAPTER 23

❖ Attic Prisoner ❖

Matteo brought Giulia up a narrow flight of stairs and pushed her into the room at the top. She caught the door as he began to pull it closed.

"How could you betray her so? Your own daughter?"

She had no real thought that he would answer, but to her surprise he paused, looking at her over the flame of the candle he had brought from downstairs.

"You think it betrayal? What of the training I gave her, female though she was? The place I secured for her? The fame those things bought her? And the one thing I asked in return, she would not give."

"But you have everything now. Her book. All her recipes."

"I'll see she gets her book back, once I have what I want. I've no interest in her book, apart from Passion blue."

He began to close the door again.

"How long will you keep me here?"

This time he did not reply. She heard the sound of the lock, his footsteps on the stairs. Then silence.

There was no light at all. From the hot, still air and the smells, she guessed she was in the attic, but in the muffling dark, with no idea of what surrounded her, she felt as if she had been severed from the world. She sank down on the floor, the heavy skirts of the red dress pooling around her. She was trembling. Her heart thumped hard and fast inside her chest. She could feel every bruise and hurt the night had given her.

She curled her fingers around the talisman, concealed beneath the fabric of her chemise. "Anasurymboriel," she whispered. "If you ever helped me, please help me now."

The words felt like ash in her mouth. Why should Anasurymboriel help her? Its task was done. It was not the spirit's fault she'd been too blind to see its true gift to her. Nothing that had happened between herself and Ormanno, from the first time she visited him in the refectory to this moment, had anything to do with the talisman at all. She knew it now for certain.

She clasped her hands beneath her chin. She hadn't prayed since she put the talisman on, but now, suddenly, she craved the comfort of prayer, craved it more than she feared the judgment of a God Whose will she had attempted to defy.

"God," she whispered, "please forgive me for turning from You for so long. Forgive me for trying to escape Your will. Forgive me for the mistakes I've made. I never meant to betray my Maestra. I never meant for any of this to happen. But it did happen, and I know it is my fault. Please punish me as I deserve, but if You can, please give me some way to make things right."

Her prayer brought no comfort, only a deeper awareness of her own hypocrisy—willing to sin as long as she believed she was getting what she wanted, repenting only after things went wrong.

She leaned her head against the door. It would have been a relief to cry. But no tears would come.

She woke to light, curled in an awkward huddle on the floor.

She sat up, her body aching, and pushed back her disheveled hair, feeling the soreness of her scalp where Didoni had yanked her braid. As she'd thought, she was in the attic; she could see barrels, sacks, furniture, and other items covered by dustcloths and tarpaulins. The light came through small grated windows set at floor level. She crawled over to one and peered out. It looked down into the courtyard; she could see the men at their carpentry and the boys at the washtub.

She thought of Santa Marta, where they would already have discovered her absence and the theft of the book. She remembered what Ormanno had said last night—that they would find her novice gown in the orchard and assume she was the thief. Soon, or possibly right now, Humilità would believe that Giulia had betrayed her.

Which I did. Though not in the way she will believe.

She couldn't bear to think of that, so she got to her feet and began to explore. All she accomplished was to fill the air with dust and worsen her thirst. There were no exits other than the door she had come in by. The door itself was thick and solid in its frame; when she tried to shake it, it didn't budge. Some of the window grates were loose, but even if they had not been impossibly high, they were too small for her to wriggle through.

No escape, then. She'd have to hope there would be a chance later on, when Matteo took her out of the attic. *If* he took her out.

What will he do with me? She was here because he thought she knew something—but she didn't know anything. What if he didn't believe her? How long would he keep her? And if he did believe her . . . or if he didn't believe her and managed to unlock the cipher . . . either way, she knew too much. Could he afford to let her go—even with Ormanno, even if she swore to leave Padua forever?

Her heart was pounding again. She felt sick. She sat down by one of the windows and closed her eyes and breathed deeply, trying to calm herself.

A little while later, she heard the rattle of the lock. The door opened partway. Someone set down a tray and pushed it into the room with their foot. She caught a glimpse of red underskirt.

"Lorenza." It came out as a croak. "Please help me."

There was no response. The door closed again. The lock turned.

She crawled to the tray. There was a cup of watered wine, a hunk of bread, some cheese, and a pear. Ravenous, she ate and drank everything. Then she went back to the window overlooking the courtyard. Ormanno must be down there in the workshop, as if nothing had happened. She felt a surge of loathing—for him, but also for herself. He was false, false to his fingertips. Why had she never seen through his pretense?

Because I wanted so much for him to be what I thought he was. Because I saw sorcery where it didn't exist. Because I didn't know my heart's desire, and didn't see the magic where it really was.

She wished she had something to wear other than the red dress he had given her. She hated its feel against her skin.

Lorenza returned as the light began to fade. Giulia started speaking as soon as the door began to open.

"Lorenza, please let me out. Please, you could come back tonight when everyone's asleep. No one would know."

The tray slid inside. The door started to close.

"Lorenza, please! For my Maestra—for Violetta's sake! Don't let him keep me here!"

The door stilled. Giulia held her breath.

"I'm sorry, child," Lorenza whispered.

The door closed quietly. Giulia heard the lock.

Giulia ate and drank—not because she was hungry, but because she knew she needed to keep up her strength. She used the pottery bowl she'd designated as a chamber pot. Then she curled up on an improvised bed of dustcloths and waited as night descended and darkness filled the attic. She tried to tell herself that it was a good sign that Lorenza had answered her. She tried very hard to believe that over the days to come (how many days? How many pitch black nights?) she would be able to persuade the old woman to set her free.

Since there was nothing else to do, she closed her eyes and slept.

A noise jolted her awake. It was still night. She heard a shuffling, then a scraping.

The lock! Lorenza came back!

Giulia sat up, her heart racing. The door opened, admitting a soft wash of candlelight. But the person who entered was not Lorenza.

"Giulia!" Ormanno strode over to her and knelt, setting down the candle and the keys he carried. He had on the same clothing he had worn the other night. A bundle was bound to his back. "Are you well? Did he do anything to you?"

"Why are you here? How did you get in?"

"Lorenza lent me these." He gestured to the keys. "She isn't any happier about you being here than I am."

So her plea had worked, after a fashion.

"Come, we must go. I want to be out of Padua before dawn."

"Did Matteo change his mind about paying you? Or—" Giulia felt cold. "Did he break the cipher?"

"No. And he hasn't paid me. He'll never pay me,

the cipher is just an excuse. Didoni has sworn to slit my throat if he doesn't get his share, so I'm cutting my losses and leaving, and I'm taking you with me."

"I'm not going anywhere with you."

"Giulia, I know you're angry—"

"Angry? *Angry?* After all the lies you told me? After you used me? After you betrayed my trust? How did it work, Ormanno? Was it you who made the plan, or was it your master?"

His eyes shifted away from hers. "It was his idea. He had me spying on your Maestra while I was working on her fresco. I told him about meeting you, and he remembered that when he learned she was bringing you with her. He said he had a job for me, told me what he wanted me to do. He offered me . . . a lot of money. You know I need money."

"And you thought I'd be easy to seduce," Giulia said bitterly.

"You can't exactly blame me. You practically threw yourself at me, that day on the scaffold."

Giulia felt her cheeks grow hot, for it was true. "How many *jobs* have you done for him?"

"A few." He shrugged. "He's found it useful to have a thief in his employ."

"That's why he took you in, isn't it? Not for kindness or mercy. Because you were a thief."

"I don't *want* to be a thief, Giulia. I haven't wanted it since I was twelve or thirteen and realized I truly had a talent."

"Then why have you never stopped?"

"How could I stop? You've seen how he is. He has . . .

evidence of the things I've done. He could have me locked away. He could make me disappear. This job, the job with you—it was going to be the last. It was going to cancel my debt to him, so long as I left Padua and never came back. You were just a girl, a pretty girl. What did I care if I broke your heart?" He reached out and captured her hands. She tried to pull away, but he gripped her tight. "But I didn't know you then. Now I do, and I want you to come with me. What does it matter if the way we started was false? We know everything about each other now. I know you love me. Don't pretend you don't."

He leaned toward her as he spoke, looking into her eyes, for all the world as if he really meant what he was saying. And perhaps he did. Perhaps he really had come to care for her. But it no longer made a difference.

"I *did* love you," she said. "I wanted the life I thought we could have together." How strange it was to be speaking to him like this. In spite of everything, the familiarity of him, the feel of him, still called to her body. But he was already gone from her heart. "I know now you'd never have given it to me. You'd never have married me. You'd never have let me paint."

"*Paint?* Is that what this is about—you painting in my workshop? I told you I'd think about it. And I would have married you. Of course I would have."

"*Would have*, Ormanno? Why not *will?*"

"Giulia—"

"It isn't just me, anyway. I'm not the only one you've betrayed. My Maestra has been hurt as well."

"But that's their business, my master's and hers.

Their old rivalry and struggle that we got caught between. We're done with it now. It doesn't concern us."

"That's not true." Giulia succeeded at last in pulling her hands free. "I want you to let me out of this attic. But I won't leave Padua with you."

"Giulia." He sounded exasperated now. "Be reasonable. You haven't many choices."

"This isn't something I've just decided, Ormanno. I was never going with you. That's the only reason I came to the orchard last night—to tell you."

"What, that you were going to stay at Santa Marta? After all you said about never becoming a nun? I don't believe you."

"It's true."

He shook his head. "But why?"

"Because," she said, putting all her force, all her passion behind the words, *"I could paint."*

He stared at her, his icy eyes glinting in the candle-light. She could not tell what was happening behind the mask of his face. But then, she never had been able to.

He sighed at last and sat back. In the sound, in the way his body changed, she saw that he had accepted her refusal. A tender place inside her felt the sting of that, of how easily he had let her go. But it also told her that she had made the right decision.

"What will you do?" he asked. "Santa Marta will never take you back now."

She looked away from those words, down at the flickering candle flame and Lorenza's keys.

"I want you to go, Ormanno. And I want you to leave me the key to your master's study."

"Surely you don't think you can get back your Maestra's book."

"You've no reason to care one way or the other."

"True enough, though I'd enjoy knowing he got cheated in his turn." Ormanno shook his head. "But you can't do it. Even if you could get into his rooms without waking him, the book is probably hidden."

"I have to try," she said.

"If he catches you . . . Giulia, I don't know what he'd do."

"Give me the key, Ormanno. You owe me that much."

Reluctantly he picked up the ring and sorted through the keys until he found the right one. He snapped open the ring and handed her the key.

"And don't think to wait for me outside so you can steal the book again and try to sell it to someone else," she said.

"What an opinion you have of me." He looked pained. "No. I am finished here. Finished with my master and his schemes, finished with thieving, finished with Padua, finished with my past." He smiled, with a flash of his old sly humor. "From now on, I'm a new man."

He got to his feet.

"Give me a head start," he said. "An hour to get well on my way, in case things go wrong for you."

She nodded.

"I never meant for this to happen, you know." He gestured, indicating the attic.

"Good-bye, Ormanno."

He hesitated, as if he wanted to do or say something more. "Well . . . good luck, then."

He turned away. Pain stabbed her briefly as she watched him leave, piercing the part of herself that had thrilled to his touch all those nights under the summer stars.

He did not look back. And then he was gone.

CHAPTER 24

❖ A Flash of Blue ❖

After Ormanno's footsteps on the stairs had faded, Giulia huddled in her nest of dustcloths and began counting, just as she had on the nights she stole out to meet him. In the airless attic, the candle burned with a steady flame, though it could only push the darkness back a little way. She watched it as she counted, her knees drawn up to her chest, her arms wrapped tight around them. She tried not to be afraid.

When she had finished her third count of a thousand, she untied her sandals, her fingers clumsy with nerves. She knotted the laces and hung them around her neck, then got to her feet, the key clutched in one hand, the candle in the other. She tiptoed to the door, which Ormanno had left open, and began to descend the stairs, placing her bare feet carefully, praying the boards would not creak. Around her, the house was wrapped in a profound silence. She might have been the only living creature in it.

The stairs led down to an open porch that ran across the rear of the house, with a view of the workshop and the deserted moon-bright courtyard. There was enough light here that she could see her way, so she blew out the candle and left it on the floor. She turned to the left, passing closed doors: one, two, a third. At the fourth, she stopped. This was Matteo's.

With utmost care, she fitted the key into the lock and turned it. The click as the lock disengaged seemed as loud as a cannon shot. She paused, holding her breath, but the quiet did not break.

She eased the door open, just wide enough that she could slip through. The unshuttered windows flooded Matteo's cluttered study with moonlight, creating a monochrome landscape of silver highlights and impenetrable shadows, like a panel waiting for the painter's brush. To the left, the door to the bedroom stood ajar.

In memory, Giulia heard Humilità's voice: *He keeps his recipe book hidden under a loose floorboard under the window. He thinks no one knows. . . .*

But Humilità knew. And because she knew, so did Giulia.

She had to go in there now, into the room where Matteo lay sleeping, and, under his nose and within reach of his hands, locate his hiding place and rescue Humilità's book. For a moment she could not move, paralyzed by the enormity of what she was about to do. At last, with an effort of will, she forced herself forward. *Slowly, slowly,* she thought, as if instructing someone else. *Put your feet down softly. Don't brush against the table. Watch out for that stool. There's the door—careful, don't touch it. Don't make a sound. Not . . . one . . . sound.*

The shutters were open in the bedroom too, but there was only one window and the room was much darker. Giulia could make out the bulk of a big bed to her left, from which came the sound of snoring. Between the bed and the window, the moon plated the wide planks of the floor with silver.

There. Somewhere in that pool of ghostly light was the board that hid Matteo's secrets.

Bunching up the heavy skirts of the red dress, she lowered herself onto her hands and knees. Soundlessly she crawled to the window. She started her search closest to the wall, pressing the boards to see if any were loose, running her fingers along the ends and edges in case there were any notches or catches. Bathed in moonlight, she felt horribly exposed—all Matteo had to do was lift his head and open his eyes, and he would see her.

It seemed an eternity before she found what she was looking for—a plank that gave a little when she pressed it. Feeling along its edges, she discovered a notch cut into its end. She fitted her finger to the hole and pulled, gently at first but then, when the board didn't budge, with more force. The board came up with a pop, so suddenly that she almost pitched backward. She froze, breath held, but Matteo's steady snoring did not pause.

She laid the plank carefully aside. The moonlight

couldn't reach into the space beneath, and as she thrust her hand into the blackness she had a brief vision of rats or other vermin waiting to sink their teeth into her flesh. Of course there was nothing of the sort—only a cavity about a hand-length deep between two joists. Her fingers touched the rough lath that supported the plaster ceiling of the room below, then the leather cover of a book.

It was Matteo's book, not Humilità's. She knew that the moment she lifted it, for it was too light and had no brass catch. She set it next to the board and reached under the floor again.

The cavity was empty.

No. It can't be. She thrust her arm into the space, sweeping her hand back and forth, reaching as far as she could—but there was nothing, only grit and dust and splintery lath.

She sat back on her heels, trying to ignore the pounding of her heart. The book had to be here. Surely Matteo wouldn't have hidden it outside his rooms. But if it wasn't under the floor, where was it?

His study. Maybe he was working on it and didn't bother to hide it before he went to sleep.

Abruptly, Matteo's snoring ceased. Giulia heard him grunt, heard the sheets rustle as he moved. Her muscles locked. She crouched where she was, helpless, waiting for discovery. But after a moment he began to snore again, rasping and regular.

Giulia let out her breath. With shaking hands she returned his book to its hiding place and fitted the board back into the gap. The board would not quite go all the way down, but she left it, not wanting to risk any more noise than she had to. If she were lucky, Matteo would assume the carelessness had been his.

She crept away from the window. The relief of passing back into darkness was intense. In the study once more, she began to search, inspecting the small table where she and he and Humilità had eaten lunch that day, then the big worktable, careful to replace everything just as she had found it. She opened the cabinets and the chests; she felt along all the shelves. She checked the window seat. She even lifted the canvas that shrouded the unfinished paintings. When she had looked everywhere she could look, she looked again, fighting a growing sense of desperation.

At last she paused in the middle of the room. The book was not in the study. It was not under the floor. But there was still somewhere she hadn't searched—or at least, had not searched fully. The rest of Matteo's bedroom.

Her skin prickled with dread. More than anything, she didn't want to go back in there . . . but she had no choice. This was the chance she had prayed for, the only chance she would ever have to atone for what she'd done. She could not leave without trying everything.

Far away in the city, bells tolled five o'clock. She didn't have much time.

She curled her fingers around the talisman, as she'd done so often for comfort and courage during her months at Santa Marta. Once again she crossed the study and entered the bedroom. Just inside the doorway she paused, letting her eyes adjust to the deeper dark. She'd barely glanced around the room before; now she saw there were chests here too, and a shadowy mass against the wall that must be a cabinet. And of course the wide expanse of the bed, the quilt humped by Matteo's body, the pillows and sheets gleaming white below the headboard.

And there by the pillows, for just an instant, Giulia thought she saw something—a flash of blue. It was gone almost as she glimpsed it, and when she looked again she couldn't find it. But something *was* there, pale against the pale sheets, partly hidden by the covers.

Could it be . . . ?

On silent feet she stole forward. Before she reached the bed, she knew she'd found it—Humilità's book, lying amid the tumble of linens, open to the page for Passion blue. Even with so little illumination, she could not mistake that block of writing, the blank space beneath, the swatch of color at the top—though in the dimness it did not show as color, only a featureless dark square. Somehow, when she looked toward it from the doorway, it must have caught what small amount of light there was.

Matteo lay on his back, the mane of his hair spread across the pillow, his arms flung out. She crouched so that her eyes were level with the mattress. Holding her breath, she reached for the book. With infinite care she began to draw it toward her, listening all the while for any change in Matteo's breathing.

Something came with the book: a sheet of paper. She set the book gently on the floor and tilted the paper toward the window and the moonlight. On it she saw writing, in what she presumed was Matteo's hand.

A copy. Matteo had copied the recipe for Passion blue.

She laid the paper in the open book, then closed the cover. Clutching the book to her chest with one hand, she twisted up her skirts with the other and crept away from the bed. The ten steps it took to reach the door were the worst of the night. Each second, she expected Matteo to wake and come roaring after her.

She quickened her pace once she reached the study. She'd left the key in the door; outside on the porch, she pulled the door soundlessly closed and locked it again. Let Matteo wonder, when he woke to find the book had vanished, what spirit had passed through his walls in the night.

Then she was on the stairs to the courtyard. She flew across the chilly flagstones. It wasn't until she put her hand on the latch of the kitchen door that she remembered that it had been barred on the inside when she and Ormanno and Didoni had passed through it the other night.

She lifted the latch. The door, not barred after all, swung easily open. She saw light—the glow of a small oil lamp, burning on the big table in the middle of the kitchen. Beside it, Lorenza sat on a stool.

Giulia froze. For a moment they looked at each other. Then Lorenza got to her feet.

"Come in," she whispered, and beckoned.

There was nowhere else to go. Giulia stepped into the kitchen, tightening her arms around the book. Lorenza came forward and closed the door, then held out her hand. "The key."

Wondering, Giulia placed Matteo's key on the old woman's palm. Lorenza tucked it into her belt. She returned to the table and took up the lamp.

"Come," she whispered again.

She led the way along the hall. In the anteroom at the front of the house, she unbarred the outside door and pulled it open.

"Go," she said. "Give my girl back what belongs to her."

"I will," Giulia said. "Lorenza . . . thank you."

"This wasn't for you." The old woman's face was deeply weary in the yellow light of the lamp. "This was for Violetta."

Giulia stepped into the street. At her back, the door closed without a sound.

Giulia ran. The book clutched in her arms, her skirts tangling around her legs, she raced along the dark avenues of Padua as if she were being pursued by devils. She halted at last under an arcade, gasping, her heart pounding as if it might split her chest.

No one had followed her. Behind her, the street was empty.

I did it, she thought with dawning amazement. *I got the book. I escaped.*

She could not quite believe it.

Her breathing was calming now, her heart slowing. She pushed back her sweat-damp hair and looked around her. Dawn had broken as she fled; its gray light showed her the cobbles of the street, the arcaded buildings on both sides. She had no idea where she was—she'd run blindly, making turns at random. But if she could manage to find the market, she might be able to get back to Santa Marta on her own. She had no notion where the market was, though, or even in which direction to seek it.

I'll just have to ask, she thought. *I found my way to the sorcerer's house. I can do this too.*

She'd begun to shiver in her sweaty clothes. Her sandals still hung around her neck—she hadn't paused to put them on. She did that now, wincing as the leather touched her feet, filthy and bruised from pounding over the cobbles. Then she set out again.

The city was waking up—housewives throwing back shutters, tradesmen with their carts or barrows, laborers with their tools. Some ignored her when she asked for directions. Some gave her instructions that she could not follow in the labyrinth of streets. One man, a stout merchant with a covered wagon, leered and offered her a coin. She hurried away, her cheeks burning.

It was almost full daylight now. The strain of the long night was settling on her, like hands pressing her toward the ground. She was hungry, and terribly thirsty. Turning a corner into yet another arcade, she realized suddenly that she could not take another step. She sank down against a column, her arms still tight around the book.

Just for a moment. I'll just catch my breath, and then I'll move on.

She didn't know how long she crouched there, the noise of the city swirling around her. Something splashed her from a passing cart; someone kicked her, uttering a curse. In her dazed, exhausted state, it all felt distant and unreal. But at last she became aware of a voice, saying the same words over and over.

"Girl. Girl. Girl, wake up."

With enormous effort Giulia opened her eyes. Bending over her was a tall woman in a dark cloak, with a pale face and hair like spun gold, braided in a coronet around her head.

"Girl," the woman said again. "Have you lost your way?"

Giulia tried to answer, but her mouth was too dry. She nodded.

"Here." From her sleeve, the woman produced a flask. "Drink this."

The flask held cider, crisp and delicious. Giulia drank it all.

"Thank you." She offered the flask back to the woman. "I was . . . very thirsty."

The woman slipped the flask into her sleeve again. "Where is it you wish to go?"

"Might you be able to tell me the way to the market? Or possibly the convent of Santa Marta?"

"The convent." The woman smiled. "I know it well. It's not far from here, but the way is complicated. Better that I show you."

"I don't want to put you to the trouble—"

"No trouble." The woman's eyes fell for a moment to the book, still clutched to Giulia's chest, then shifted back to Giulia's face. "Rise now, girl, and follow me."

She waited as Giulia scrambled to her feet, then set off at a measured pace. Giulia limped after her. The cider had given her back some strength; she was still exhausted, but at least she could walk. After a little while she smelled the odor of the canal—and then suddenly they were in a street she knew. She could see the church of Santa Marta in the distance, and beyond it, the long red snake of the convent wall.

"Here we are." The woman turned, still smiling her enigmatic smile. She stood under the first sun of the new day, her golden hair gleaming like gossamer. Her eyes, Giulia saw, were the blue of summer skies.

"Thank you. I'm sorry to have taken you out of your way."

The woman inclined her head. Without another word she started back in the direction in which they'd come. As she walked by, her cloak parted for a moment and Giulia glimpsed her gown—blue like her eyes, but deeper, more lustrous. Then she was past, walking at that same steady pace. She entered the shadow of an arcade and vanished from Giulia's sight.

Slowly, Giulia made her way down the avenue and stopped before the wooden door that marked the entrance to Santa Marta. Beside it was the grate that covered the opening to the wheel, through which the nuns brought the things of the world into the convent without breaching their sacred space. How easy it would be to slip the book through that opening, where it would be discovered the next time the wheel was turned. Humilità would have her secrets back. Giulia would never have to face her, or admit what she had done.

But then Humilità would never know the full truth of what had happened. She'd see Matteo's copy of the cipher and guess he was responsible, but she would never realize how profoundly her father had betrayed her.

No matter what I do, the ending is the same, Giulia thought. She could put the book into the wheel and walk away. Or she could ring the bell and confess—and then, surely, be thrown out again. *Santa Marta is lost to me.*

Painting is lost to me.

She bowed her head over the book she held so tightly. For the first time since Ormanno had kidnapped her, she allowed herself to truly understand.

She raised her face at last and rubbed the tears from her cheeks with her sleeve. Only one thing was left: after so much lying, to tell Humilità the truth. She could never make things right. But she could at least tell the truth.

She crouched down and opened the book to the page for Passion blue. The square of color caught the light, impossibly brilliant, as if the sun were shining not on but through it.

I'll never see Passion blue again.

She removed Matteo's copy of the cipher and folded it, then unfastened the talisman and her horoscope fragment from around her neck and thrust them, with the paper, inside the bodice of the red dress. She closed the book and rose.

The bell rope hung by the door. For an instant, she was seized by a vivid memory: of herself, standing before the sorcerer's gate on the day everything began. It seemed a lifetime ago. She hardly recognized that girl, the girl she had been then—a girl who thought to bend the stars to her will, careless of the consequences. A girl who did not know her heart's desire, and so had lost it.

She stepped forward and rang the bell.

CHAPTER 25

❖ The Great and Beautiful Gift ❖

Once she realized who Giulia was, the doorkeeper fairly dragged Giulia inside. But it was not Humilità she summoned, as Giulia requested, but Suor Margarita.

"What have you done, you wicked girl?" The novice mistress had come running; her cheeks were flushed and she was breathing hard. "Where have you been?"

"I need to talk to Maestra Humilità," Giulia said.

"Oh no, my girl." Suor Margarita put her hands on her hips. "I'm the one you'll talk to. Confess this instant where you have been these last two nights."

"I . . . I was kidnapped."

"*Kidnapped?* Is that what you call it? Don't take me

for a fool, Giulia Borromeo. I know all about your midnight excursions. Alessia has told me everything."

Alessia. Giulia had forgotten her. "It isn't what you think."

"Is it not? Look at you, got up like a harlot! And now your young man has ruined you and abandoned you, and you think you can come back to us as if nothing had happened!" Her eyes fell on the book. "What is that you're holding? Give it to me at once!"

"It's for Maestra Humilità—"

"Do you dare defy me?" Suor Margarita stepped forward and slapped Giulia across the face, then wrenched the book from her grasp. Instinctively Giulia reached after it, but the gatekeeper seized her shoulders and held her back.

"Send for Suor Veronica," Suor Margarita instructed the gatekeeper. "Tell her I need her to open a discipline cell."

"Please." Giulia's face throbbed from the blow. "Just let me talk to Maestra Humilità—I can explain everything—"

"Oh, you'll explain. You will indeed." Suor Margarita tucked the book under her arm and took hold of Giulia's wrist. "Now come, and quietly, or I'll slap you until your ears ring."

Suor Veronica, the bursar, was already waiting when they reached the discipline cells. She selected a key from the ring she carried and unlocked one of the doors. Suor Margarita thrust Giulia through it.

"Are you ready yet to tell me the truth?"

"I *have* told the truth."

"Have it your way, then, stubborn girl. I shall

return tomorrow and ask again. Use the time to pray upon your sins."

"Give the book to Maestra Humilità!" Giulia cried, as the door began to close. "Please! She needs it back!"

The key scraped in the lock. Giulia heard the two nuns' footsteps, fading away.

She stood staring at the iron grate set into the heavy oak of the door, dazed. Ten minutes ago she had been free, standing in the street. Now she was a prisoner again. But Humilità would come to her, once Suor Margarita gave her the book.

Surely she'll come.

She turned. The discipline cell was tiny—perhaps twice the width of her outstretched arms, and only a few steps longer than the bed that was its only furnishing. A chamber pot stood in one corner. A crucifix hung below a grated clerestory window.

She was shivering. A blanket was folded at one end of the bed; she shook it out and pulled it around her, then lay down on the thin straw mattress. The sun reached through the window, casting a rectangle of light on the whitewashed wall opposite. She could hear her heartbeat in the silence, until sleep took her and she heard nothing at all.

The sound of the lock roused her. For a moment she did not know where she was, but then came the rush of memory. She sat up just as the door swung open.

It was Humilità.

The workshop mistress closed the door, then stood against it, her hands tucked into her sleeves, her expression unreadable. Giulia scrambled off the bed.

"Thank you for coming, Maestra," she said. She could not have been asleep for very long—the rectangle of sun had moved only a little way across the wall. She was acutely aware of the picture she made, in her dress of harlot red, its skirts filthy from her flight, her hair half-pulled out of its braid. Her blistered feet stung as if they were resting on coals.

"Margarita believes you ran away with your lover." Humilità's voice was remote and cold. "And that you have returned because he abandoned you. Is that true?"

"No, Maestra. It isn't true."

"But you did steal my book. Why did you bring it back?"

"I didn't steal it, Maestra."

"Do not lie to me, Giulia. The truth is what I want, however terrible it may be."

"I didn't steal it," Giulia repeated. "But . . . it is my fault it was stolen."

She reached into her bodice and drew out the folded paper. Wordlessly, she held it toward Humilità.

A pause, then the workshop mistress stepped forward and took it. She unfolded it. Giulia, watching, saw how her face changed as she read, how the blood drained from her cheeks. She stood for a moment without moving, except for the slight trembling of the hand that held the paper. Then the strength seemed to go out of her all at once, and she sat down heavily on the bed.

"Tell me," she said, in a voice Giulia hardly recognized. "Tell me how you came by this."

And Giulia did. She told Humilità how she had

planned to escape, how she had met Ormanno, how he had deceived her and how she had embraced his deception, how her change of heart had led her to discover his true intentions. When she spoke of what had happened in Matteo's study, Humilità's face went tight and her mouth turned down—but other than that she betrayed no emotion, and she did not interrupt, even to ask a question. It was harder than Giulia could have imagined to speak into that silence.

"I know you have no reason to believe me," she said at last. She hadn't confessed the talisman, for she did not want to be accused of sorcery. But that was the only thing she had held back. She'd admitted every one of her lies. She'd spared herself no condemnation. "I can't prove I didn't know what Ormanno planned, or that he kidnapped me against my will. But I swear before God that all I've said is true. I . . . I know I betrayed you even so, because I lied to you, I lied to everyone, even though I never meant for anything to come of it except me leaving Santa Marta. I know that everything that happened is my fault. I'm sorry. I'm so sorry."

She had run out of words. At some point during her story she'd sat down again, to spare her burning feet.

"I know my father," Humilità said softly. Her face was still dreadfully pale. Her eyes were fixed on the paper in her hand. "I know the man he is. Even so, I never imagined—" She broke off. "And yet . . . and yet, I cannot honestly say I am surprised."

Giulia had tried to prepare herself for Humilità's reaction. Fury, disbelief, grief, or all three—those she had expected, but not this quiet, immediate acceptance. It made her feel, if possible, even worse.

"But to use you against me, my pupil, of whom I had such hopes. . . And Ormanno! So competent and charming he seemed when he was here, though I understand better now the source of his curiosity about me. I suppose I cannot fault you completely for allowing yourself to be deceived by him, since I was taken in as well. I wonder . . ." Again Humilità paused. "I wonder if he lied to you about more than you think. Perhaps the scheme was his and he tempted my father to it, not the other way around."

Giulia swallowed, her throat dry from so much talking. "I think he told the truth."

"Can you ever know which is which, from a liar?"

"No," Giulia admitted.

"Well. It hardly matters. This." Humilità held up the paper. "This is what matters." Her dark eyes, so like her father's—not just in their shape and color but in their power—bored into Giulia's. "Did you really love that boy, Giulia?"

"I thought I did. But I think I mostly loved what I thought he could give me. I've always wanted to . . . belong somewhere. And then I learned I wanted painting. I thought I could have all of it, with him."

"You were deceiving yourself," Humilità said harshly. "You would have been a rival. No man can bear that from a woman."

"I should have understood sooner. I know that, Maestra. I know I was stupid. I know I was selfish. But I didn't know what I wanted when I came here. I didn't know what it was *possible* to want."

"I told you what was possible, in the market, the day we went to my father's house." The anger was there now, hot and bitter. "Perhaps I expected too much. I saw your unwillingness to be among us, but I thought I could speak to your talent. I thought that even if your mind did not fully comprehend, your talent, the great and beautiful gift God gave you, would understand."

"It did," Giulia said miserably. "I did."

"But too late."

The words were like stones. Giulia had known—of course she had known. That did not lessen the pain.

Humilità got to her feet. She still held her father's copy of the cipher, crumpled in her fist.

"One more question. Why did you come back?"

"I had to bring you the book and the copy. I had to tell you what your father did."

Humilità shook her head. "You could have placed them in the wheel. I would have guessed the truth, or close enough, when I saw my father's writing. I want to know why you knocked on the door and asked for me. Did you think, by returning to me what is mine, you could convince me to take you back into the workshop?"

"No. I know . . ." For a moment Giulia lost her voice. "I know there's no chance of that. I just needed to tell you the truth. All the truth, about everything."

And suddenly Humilità's coldness was gone, and Giulia saw in the workshop mistress's face a pain to match her own. An unbearable surge of guilt and remorse rose up in her. Until that exact moment, she had not understood that she had come to love her proud, demanding teacher—the woman who had offered her

her heart's desire, but only on her own terms. The woman who had offered her the freedom of her art, but only if she remained a prisoner. The woman whose forgiveness she wanted more than anything.

"Oh, Maestra," she said, as the tears spilled over.

Humilità turned away. "I'll see you're brought something to eat and drink."

"Will you tell Angela I'm sorry? And the others, too. Will you please tell them I'm so very sorry?"

Humilità did not reply. She opened the door and passed through it, locking it again behind her, leaving Giulia alone with the knowledge of everything she had lost.

A *conversa* brought penitent's food: a jug of water, thin soup, stale bread. Giulia ate and drank, then pulled her hair from its snarled braid and finger-combed the tangles out. She used what was left of the water to wash her face and neck. The talisman, still thrust down inside her bodice, made a chafing lump; she pushed it to a more comfortable position.

I should break it, the way the sorcerer told me, and set Anasurymboriel free. The spirit had finished its task—its true task—long ago. *After I'm banished. I'll do it then.*

She curled up under the blanket and fell asleep.

She woke again to the turning of the lock. She'd slept the clock around—the rectangle of sun had returned to the place it had been when she first entered the cell.

It was not the *conversa*, as Giulia expected, but Suor Margarita.

"Get up." The novice mistress's voice was colder

than January. "Madre Damiana will see you now."

Suor Margarita led Giulia through the convent like a prisoner being taken for execution. Two choir nuns accompanied them, one leading the way, the other walking behind, reminding Giulia of the day she and Angela had passed Ormanno in the hall. Choir nuns and *conversae* paused to stare as the little procession went by, making Giulia even more conscious of her gown, so very red amid the sea of white and black and gray.

Madre Damiana sat at her desk, as she had the first time Giulia had ever seen her, her abbess's staff leaning against the wall behind her. Humilità was there also, standing before the window with her back to the room, her stocky figure dark against the light. She did not turn as Giulia and Suor Margarita entered.

"Leave us, Margarita," Madre Damiana said.

The novice mistress obeyed. The silence that followed seemed to last forever. Giulia waited, her eyes lowered, her hands fisted in her red skirts. She'd begun to tremble; she had to clench her teeth to stop them from chattering.

"Humilità has told me all you told her," Madre Damiana said, in her strong, slow voice. "You are not the first novice to break her vows, or to dally with a paramour. Not by any means. But to bring a man inside our walls—to assist him in defiling our sacred space—to facilitate the theft of something so precious to us . . ." Madre Damiana paused. "Never has such a thing occurred, not in the three hundred years since Santa Marta's founding."

"I'm sorry." Giulia forced the words past the tightness in her throat. "I'm truly sorry for my actions, and for . . . for the trouble I brought to the Maestra and to Santa Marta."

"Did you allow him to become your lover?" Madre Damiana's voice was like a whip. "Before God, girl, tell the truth."

"No. He was never my lover, I swear it."

"So you are not ruined. That's a little comfort, at least." The abbess clasped her ringed hands on her desk. "You should know that I do not trust your expressions of contrition. When Humilità came to me, I had already determined not to readmit you to our community, regardless of the offense it would doubtless cause the Borromeo family."

Giulia had tried to prepare herself for those words. They still went through her like knives.

"Humilità, however, believes your remorse is genuine. She points out that though you were responsible for the theft of her book, you are also responsible for its return, and for preserving the secret of Passion blue."

She spoke for me. Surprised, Giulia glanced at Humilità, who still stood unmoving.

"She has suggested that, rather than expelling you, we allow you to atone for your wrongs in the place where you committed them, among the people you hurt. I am by no means convinced she is correct. I fear also that she is guilty of the sin of covetousness, for I suspect it is principally your talent she pleads for. But she believes she can quell your rebellious nature, and in my affection for her, I have agreed that she may try. Accordingly, Giulia Borromeo, you will not be banished. You will remain at

Santa Marta, and you will continue as Humilità's pupil."

Giulia gasped.

"Do not imagine that this is a light reprieve." Madre Damiana's face was as implacable as a carved saint's. "Every morning and every evening, for the duration of your novitiate, you will spend an hour on your knees, praying for forgiveness. Because of your facility for deception, you will live apart from your fellow novices. You will make no more horoscopes, but accept that God's will is and should remain a mystery. And if you ever flout our rules again—if you lie about so much as a crumb of bread filched from the refectory table—you will be immediately expelled, and there will be no second chance. Is that clear?"

Giulia felt as if she were dreaming. She nodded.

"In thirteen months, when your novitiate ends, you may choose to take solemn vows and your penance will be deemed fulfilled. If you choose to leave us, however, your dowry will be forfeit, to pay in some measure for your keep and for the silver that was stolen from us."

"Yes, Madre Damiana," Giulia whispered.

"One more thing. Your . . . absence . . . could not be hidden. But the violation of Santa Marta by this band of thieves is a shame and a disgrace that would, if it became known, provide certain men of the Church with an excuse to rob us of the freedoms we enjoy here. That I will not tolerate. Accordingly, I have told the community only of your failed elopement. The chapel has been closed until the silver can be replaced, and only Humilità, myself, and the other artists know of the theft of the book. Margarita does not understand what it was she brought to me yesterday." The abbess leaned forward. "You must never speak of this, Giulia Borromeo. Not even to your confessor. I require you to swear before God."

"I swear. Before God, I swear."

"For the next two weeks, you will remain in confinement in the discipline cell, to meditate on your sins and to cultivate repentance."

"Yes, Madre Damiana."

"Have you anything to say before you begin your penance?"

"Thank you, Madre Damiana." Giulia's voice shook; she tried to steady it. "For your mercy. Thank you, Maestra, for giving me another chance. You won't regret it. I swear you won't."

Humilità stood like a stone, like someone in a room all by herself. She gave no sign that she had heard.

"You may go," said Madre Damiana. "And tell Margarita to fetch you novice garb, by my order." Distaste flickered across her face. "We must get rid of that gown as soon as possible."

Locked into the discipline cell once more, Giulia pulled off Ormanno's dress and put on again the shapeless gray habit and kerchief of a novice, which she'd never imagined she would be glad to wear. Then she sat down on the bed.

In Madre Damiana's study, she had felt she was dreaming. Now she felt she had woken from a dream, delivered from the worst nightmare in the world.

I will paint.

She closed her eyes. Less than an hour ago, she'd

believed she had lost everything. Now, incredibly, what she wanted most had been given back.

I will paint.

It wouldn't be easy. More than a year of prayer and penances. More than a year of living apart like a pariah under Suor Margarita's angry eye. No matter how fully she managed to atone, no one at Santa Marta would ever forget what she had done—she would always be remembered as the girl who went over the wall with her lover and returned in disgrace. She would forever be the subject of whispered stories, like the one old Benedicta had told.

But I will paint.

Could she atone? Would the other artists ever forgive her for deceiving them? Could they learn to overlook the harm she had done? Would she and Angela be friends again?

And Humilità. Humilità had believed her. Humilità had interceded for her. Yet in Madre Damiana's study, the workshop mistress had turned away as if Giulia did not exist. As if she could not even bear to look at her.

I'll make it right. Somehow, I'll find a way to make things right again.

She knew where she had to start.

She drew the talisman out from beneath her pillow, where she'd slipped it when she put on her new garments. The tray with her evening meal had not yet been removed; she took the iron spoon from the soup bowl and knelt on the floor, placing the talisman on the tiles in front of her.

It was time to set Anasurymboriel free.

She ran her finger over the face of the pendant,

over the graceful copper inlay and the deep azure of the lapis lazuli, thinking of the flash of blue she'd glimpsed in Matteo's bedroom, remembering the woman in the blue dress who had led her back to Santa Marta. The little spirit, faithful to the end, had been with her even when she believed it gone. But she would not miss it. She would not miss the weight of the talisman around her neck, or the weight of the secrets that came with it.

"Thank you, Anasurymboriel," she whispered. "For giving me my heart's desire in spite of myself."

She gripped the spoon. She drew a deep breath and brought the handle down, hard.

And again.

And once more.

It was done. The talisman had split into three pieces, held together still by the lattice of the inlay.

She'd wondered if she might feel something, or see something, as the spirit was released. But there was nothing. Just the crack of impact and the force of the blow shuddering up her arm.

She tore a piece of fabric from the bottom of her chemise and rolled the broken talisman into it, along with the silver chain that had held it. She tucked the little package under her kerchief, wedging it into the coil of her braid. She'd think of a way to dispose of it later.

On impulse, she pulled the pouch that held her horoscope fragment from beneath her chemise and removed the scrap of paper inside. The paper had yellowed over the years, but the uncompromising words of the prediction were as clear as ever:

> . . . *major affliction by Saturn, and*
> *the Moon and Sun in barren signs, there*
> *is thus no testimony of marriage, or of chil-*
> *dren. She shall not take another's name,*
> *nor shall she bear her own at the end of life,*
> *but shall . . .*

She'd battled against those words for most of her life. In doing so, perhaps, she had only made it more certain that they would come true. To stay at Santa Marta was to embrace the fate she had fought so hard—to be husbandless and childless, to be rechristened with a name not her own—even though that fate, in the end, was nothing like the lonely servant life she'd feared so much. Even though that fate included painting.

Madre Damiana's stern prohibition returned to her. *You will not seek again to find your future in the stars, but accept that God's will is and should remain a mystery.* What would it be like to do that? Not to constantly struggle against her destiny, but simply to allow it to unfold?

She didn't know. Perhaps, in the time to come, she would find out.

She replaced the paper in the pouch and hid the pouch under her gown again. Then, still on her knees, she folded her hands together and closed her eyes.

"Merciful God," she whispered, "please forgive me my sins. Forgive me my pride and selfishness. I promise I will do better."

The silence swallowed her words. She'd have to

learn to pray again, after so long. But it was a start.

That night, she dreamed of Anasurymboriel. The spirit was not small this time, not fixed in form, but huge and infinitely changeable—now a sheet of fire, now a storm of sparks, now a roil of flame. Only the color was the same—cobalt, indigo, lapis, sapphire, cerulean, azure, blue. Passion blue, the most celestial blue there was, the hue of heaven brought down to Earth.

It had been confined; now it was released. It had been held; now it was free. Those were simply the conditions of its being. Human categories like anger, or joy or gratitude had no meaning for it. Giulia sensed its power, fully manifest for the first time—the same eternal power that moved the spheres, so vast and strange it could only be felt, never comprehended.

It did not communicate in any way she recognized. Yet she understood that it had stayed for her, that it had remained in the paltry human world long enough for her to fall asleep and dream. And as she realized this, the blueness gathered itself and fell on her, sank into her, cool and sweet, into her mouth and eyes and skin, into her muscles and bones and blood. Briefly, with the blue inside her, she was inside the blue, felt it blazing from her body as if she herself had become a star.

Then she was herself again, just herself. For a moment longer Anasurymboriel remained, raging, coruscating, changing. Then it surged toward the heavens, arrowing toward its home. And Giulia heard the chiming of the spheres as it passed through them, the music of the cosmos.

CHAPTER 26

❖ Coming Home ❖

The bell rang for Prime, waking Giulia from uneasy sleep. She opened her eyes on the predawn darkness, remembering: Today she would return to the workshop.

She'd been moved the night before to a new cell, in the corridor that housed the poorer choir nuns. It was as bare as the disciplinary cell, though quite a bit bigger. Like the disciplinary cell, the door had a grate, so that anyone could look in at any time and see what she was doing.

The two weeks of her initial punishment had not been as bad as she'd feared. She'd spent a good deal of the time sleeping, and the rest of it thinking, recalling the color lore she'd memorized, imagining the drawings and paintings she would make when she had paper and implements again. Suor Margarita came twice a day to make sure she performed her morning and evening penances. Lisa came also, sneaking away when she was supposed to be working. The crippled girl pushed two small sweet apples and a slice of good bread through the bars of the grate, then lingered to describe Alessia's fury on discovering that Giulia was not to be banished after all. Lisa giggled as she spoke of it, and Giulia found herself laughing too. She couldn't remember the last time she had laughed.

Lisa, she thought, might become a friend. Small comfort, though, for the loss of Angela.

She got up, shivering in the early morning chill, and lit her candle. She put on her habit and bound up her hair, then knelt before the crucifix on the wall, wadding up her skirt to spare her knees, though she imagined Madre Damiana would not approve. She did pray during these sessions, and hoped that God was listening. But she also drifted, thinking whatever thoughts occurred to her.

She rose from her knees when the *conversa* came with her breakfast. She'd barely had time to finish it before the lock rattled again—Humilità, come in person to fetch her.

Giulia had not seen the workshop mistress since the day Madre Damiana announced her punishment. Humilità did not speak, but simply waited in the doorway, her face composed within its frame of wimple and veil. Her expression held no welcome, but as far as Giulia could tell, no condemnation either. Giulia chose to interpret that as a hopeful sign.

She blew out the candle and they left the cell. Humilità led the way at her usual brisk pace. Giulia kept her eyes properly downcast, but she was still able to see how the nuns they passed looked at her, when normally a novice would be beneath their notice. It would be this way, she knew, for a long time to come.

When they reached the workshop door, Humilità paused.

"The others know about the book," she said. "But I have not told them . . . who it was who wanted it. They believe you never knew the person to whom Ormanno intended to sell it. I must trust you never to say otherwise."

"I never will, Maestra, I promise."

"You will have to earn their trust again. It will not be easily done."

"I will earn it, Maestra, I swear. And your trust too. I swear that also."

Humilità's hard dark gaze acknowledged nothing. "Know, Giulia, that Damiana was correct. It was not for your sake I begged mercy, but for the sake of your great gift, the waste of which would be a worse affront to God than any sin you are capable of. That is why you are still part of my workshop. That is why I am able to bear your presence, in spite of what you have done."

The coldness in her voice took Giulia's breath away. "Will you ever forgive me?" she said. "I brought you back the book. I brought you back Passion blue."

"Yes. And there is a part of me that wishes you had not."

And for the first time, Giulia understood the true root of Humilità's anger: not what Giulia had done, but what she knew. Or rather, at what she had forced Humilità to know. She remembered Humilità's joy in returning to her home. Even though the workshop mistress must always leave again, she'd known she could come back. Now she never could.

How can I ever make up for that?

Humilità's face softened a little. She reached out and touched Giulia's shoulder.

"We will find our way," she said. "Day by day, we will find our way, together."

"Yes, Maestra," Giulia whispered.

Humilità opened the door. The smell of the workshop came flooding out, oil and pigment and glue and dust and a hundred other things, familiar in a way beyond recognition, beyond thought or memory or desire.

Home, Giulia thought, the word coming to her like an indrawn breath.

All the artists were there: Angela at the shelves, Domenica and Benedicta at the San Giustina commission, Perpetua at the long table with ink and paper, even tardy Lucida, laying out the materials to paint one of her miniatures. As one, they stopped what they were doing and looked up. In their faces Giulia saw the same caution, the same distance, that had been in Humilità's.

Stepping over the threshold was one of the hardest things she had ever done.

She crossed to the shelves where Angela stood, feeling the others watching. *It won't always be like this,* she told herself. *It will get easier.* She reached for her apron.

"I'll fill the washtub, shall I?"

Angela nodded, her face averted.

Giulia dragged the heavy tub into the courtyard and began filling buckets at the fountain. The sky was overcast; the weather had turned during her confinement, and the autumn air held the promise of winter. Across the way, the closed door of the little chapel reproached her.

Back and forth she went, fitting herself to the familiar routine, until the tub was full. She tipped the last half-bucket down the drain, then set the bucket on the flagstones and put up her hands as if to adjust her kerchief. Instead, above the knot, her fingers found the little lump of the shattered talisman, tucked into her braid.

She'd carried it there every day, waiting for this moment. The drain was the perfect place to dispose of it. It would never be found.

She glanced around. The artists had gone back to their work; no one was watching. She pulled the little package free. It was just a broken pendant now, a few bits of stone and a twist of copper wire wrapped in a scrap of linen. Even so, she held it in her palm a moment before reaching again for the bucket. Pretending to empty it, she dropped the talisman through the grating of the drain, into the darkness below.

She thought she might hear it fall. But there was no sound.

She set the bucket aside. As she did, the sun emerged from behind the clouds, flooding the court-yard with light, spilling warmth like a benediction across her head and shoulders. She turned toward the workshop. The sun lit up the great half-finished altar-piece—the crowd at the foot of the Cross, the agonized thief, the half-finished form of Jesus. The jewel colors shone with impossible brilliance, impossible inten-sity, as if the painted figures were on the verge of stir-ring into life. In the gown of Mary Magdalen and the cloak of the Virgin, in the wings of the angels, in the caparisons of the horses and the clothing of the crowd, Passion blue—the secret she had saved—blazed like cool fire, seeming not simply to absorb the sunlight into itself, but to emit its own mysterious radiance, like the breath of paradise.

And inside Giulia's head, suddenly, words, as if someone had bent and whispered them into her ear:

Heart's desire.

She knew, with a certainty that flared in her like the sun, that all would be well.

The clouds were closing in again. The light dimmed. The painted figures flattened into stillness, and the colors were just colors once more.

Giulia knelt a moment longer. Shadows swam before her eyes, as if she'd stared directly into the sun. At last she got to her feet and put away the bucket. She returned to the workshop, to the familiar sounds and smells, the familiar presence of the other artists—the place where, in spite of everything, she belonged. Humilità ignored her as she passed. Domenica paused to glare. Lucida fixed her attention on her miniature, and Perpetua turned her face away. But Angela, at the preparation table, looked up as Giulia approached, and the corners of her mouth lifted a little before she lowered her eyes again. When Giulia took her place beside her, she did not move away.

The sky was completely overcast now. But Giulia could still feel a little of the warmth that had touched her in the courtyard.

Yes. All will be well. ❖

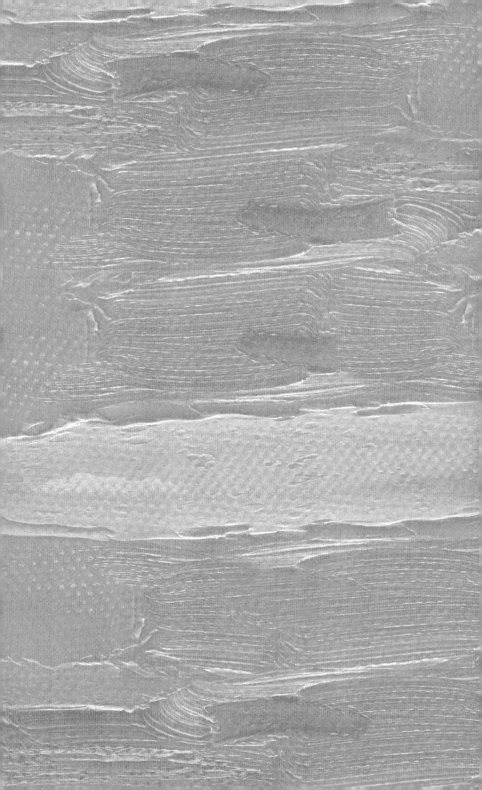

AND NOW A SNEAK PEEK FROM

COLOR SONG

COMPANION TO *PASSION BLUE*,

COMING IN FALL 2014 FROM SKYSCAPE

Part I

The First Song

❖❖❖❖❖❖

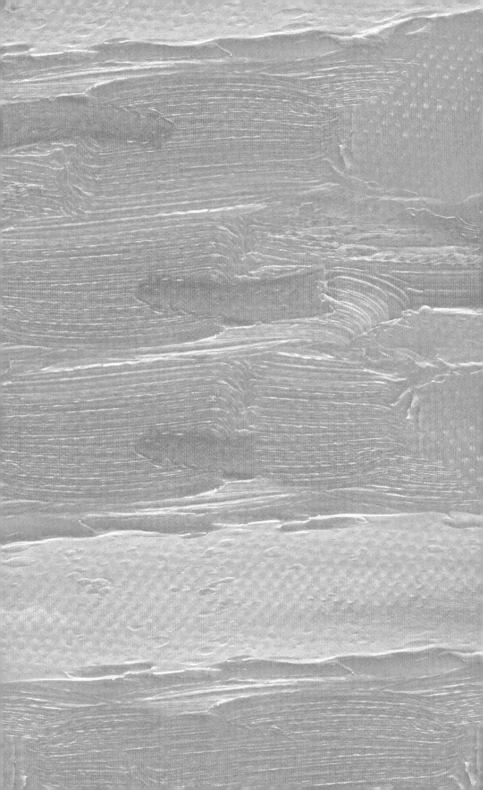

CHAPTER 1

✣ TRANSFORMATION ✣

Painting workshop of Maestra Humilità Moretti

Convent of Santa Marta, Padua, Italy

November, Anno Domini 1487

On the day the colors first sang to her, Giulia woke with a restless sense of anticipation, a breathless certainty that something was about to change—although within the high brick walls of the Convent of Santa Marta, change was rarer than roses in November.

The weather was raw and blustery, the sky thick with clouds. Midway through the morning, Giulia's teacher, master painter Humilità Moretti, set up her easel in the courtyard and summoned Giulia from her duties in the workshop to assist.

From among the pots of paint that crowded the small table at her side, Humilità selected one whose tight-corked throat was sealed with wax. Only a single paint was ever closed this way. Without meaning to, Giulia drew in her breath. Humilità glanced at her, and for a moment their eyes held: an acknowledgment of secrets, of a shared and painful memory.

With a knife, Humilità broke the wax and levered out the cork. The wind snatched the cork as it popped free, whirling it to the ground and tumbling it across the flagstones, the vivid gleam of the paint it had protected flashing as it rolled: the color known as Passion blue—bluer than sapphires, bluer than oceans, the most precious of all the workshop's paints. Giulia chased after it, catching it before it could fall into the drain at the courtyard's center. As she picked it up, she thought she heard the sound of bells.

Returning to Humilità's side, she watched her teacher measure Passion blue onto her palette. It glowed like a sun-struck jewel amid the duller smears of umber and bone black and verdigris, though there was no sun in the clouded sky to make it shine—a mysterious illusion of inner light that no other painter could duplicate, though many had tried. The formula for its making was known to Humilità alone, a secret she had guarded for more than twenty years.

Normally Giulia could lose herself in watching her teacher work, imagining herself into Humilità's hand and Humilità's eyes until it almost seemed it was she who held the brush. But today she was distracted by

the malicious wind, the penetrating cold, the rest-
lessness that prickled through her body and made it
impossible to stand still. And the bells. She could still
hear them, an insistent, chilly chiming that made her
feel even colder, for it reminded her of ice, of sunlight
shimmering on snow. She'd never heard such a sound
at Santa Marta. Where could it be coming from?

At last Humilità set aside her brush and carried
her painting indoors, leaving Giulia to clear the worktable. Humilità had taken the pot of Passion blue as
well, to lock up in her study; but a residue of the shimmering paint remained on the palette, seeming to
draw to itself all the light of the cloudy day. Beneath
the hissing of the wind the bells chimed on—fainter
now, Giulia thought, as if whoever was ringing them
had moved farther away.

In the warmth of the workshop, she returned the
paint pots to their places. Still the bells teased at her
ears, sounding exactly as they had in the courtyard,
and it struck her suddenly that this should not be.
Inside, surely, they should be fainter, or clearer—but
not the same.

The chiming followed her as she set Humilità's
used brushes in a jar of turpentine to soak, then carried the palette over to a table to clean it. Pausing,
she closed her eyes, concentrating on the slippery fall
of notes. She hadn't realized quite how lovely they
were—and, somehow, less like bells than she'd first
thought, almost unearthly in their silvery cadences.
They sound like . . . She groped for comparisons. *A cas-
cade of stars. A rain of crystal.*

She opened her eyes. On the palette, the smear of

Passion blue gleamed, as if the candles burning on the table favored it above the other colors. It drew Giulia's gaze like a tether. She let her vision blur, let her eyes fill up with blue, with swirling azure currents and glinting sapphire radiance. The bell-music deepened, reaching into her, resonating inside her head.

It's the paint that's singing. The thought rolled up from indigo depths. *It's the voice of Passion blue.*

Something flashed through Giulia's body, a bolt of cobalt light. The palette snapped back into focus. The blue was just a smear of paint again. But she could still hear the bells, chiming, chiming; and her heart, suddenly, was pounding with dread—at the absurd, no, the *mad* thought that had felt utterly true in the instant it came to her. *True* in a way impossible things should never be.

She snatched up a scraper and dragged it hard across the palette's wooden surface. The soft oil paints came up easily, the colors smearing into mud. Even the jewel essence of Passion blue could not survive such mingling. Again and again she scraped, until the palette was clean.

The bells were silent now. She could hear only the ordinary noise of the artists at their labor. But around her, the familiar landscape of the workshop had grown strange, as if she were looking through someone else's eyes. She was cold, as cold as she'd been in the wind-chilled courtyard.

Am I going mad? She put her hand to her throat, thinking of the talisman she'd worn all summer and then destroyed, of the celestial spirit that had been imprisoned inside it. *Am I being punished for the sin of putting my trust in magic?*

No. They were just bells. Real bells, rung by real hands.
I'll never hear them again.

But within herself, she knew differently. And the next morning, when Humilità uncorked the pot of Passion blue and the crystal chiming rose, Giulia understood that something inside her had irrevocably changed. She would never be the same.

❖ Author's Note ❖

I fell in love with the Italian Renaissance when I was a child. My family traveled widely while I was growing up, and we made several trips to Italy. I can still remember the thrill of seeing Botticelli's *Primavera* for the first time, of walking through the echoing spaces of Milan's vast cathedral, of exploring the narrow alleys and magnificent palazzos of Venice. I loved the landscapes and the architecture and the history—but best of all I loved the art, and the colorful, turbulent lives of the artists who created it.

It wasn't until I began studying art history in college, though, that I realized that not all of those artists were men. In a time when women weren't educated and had almost no rights, a handful of female painters managed to establish and maintain careers, including Sofonisba Anguissola, who became a painter at the Spanish court, and Artemesia Gentileschi, the first female painter to be accepted as a member of the Academy of Fine Arts in Florence. I became fascinated by these women, whose lives and art were nearly forgotten in the centuries after their deaths. How did they manage to defy convention and follow their passion? What obstacles did they have to overcome, what social pressures were they forced to cope with?

Passion Blue grew out of those questions, as well as my interest in the techniques of the Renaissance painters, so different from those in use today. It's been wonderful to write a book that lets me invite readers into the painters' world, at least for a little while.

A few of the locations in the book are real—the Duomo and the *porte* of Milan, the Palazzo della Ragione and the fruit and vegetable market in Padua. Palazzo Borromeo and Santa Marta are my own invention, however.

All the characters are fictional as well, though Maestra Humilità Moretti is based on a real painter nun, Suor Plautilla Nelli, who was the mistress of a painting workshop at the Dominican convent of Santa Catarina di Siena in Florence in the middle of the sixteenth century. Plautilla is one of the earliest recognized female Renaissance artists.

We don't know many facts about her life. She was born in 1523 to a noble family; her father, Piero di Luca Nelli, was also a painter, and may have helped to train her. She entered Santa Catarina in 1537, when she was just fourteen. Santa Catarina had a long artistic tradition and the convent was known throughout Italy for its artist nuns. Plautilla taught other nuns to paint, and her studio eventually became famous beyond the convent walls, with its work in demand for altarpieces and private commissions.

Accounts of the time suggest that Plautilla produced a large body of work, but only a few of her paintings and drawings have been authenticated, including the beautiful fresco of the *Last Supper* that she painted for Santa Catarina's refectory. The fresco (which, sadly, is badly in need of restoration) now hangs in the refectory of Santa Maria Novella in Florence.

Plautilla was elected abbess several times. She died in 1588.

❖ Acknowledgments ❖

No writer brings a book into the world alone. Thanks are due to many people.

My wonderful agent, Jessica Regel, who saw the manuscript through several incarnations before finally finding it a home.

Jean Naggar, Tara Hart, and the rest of the crew at the Jean V. Naggar Literary Agency, who work so hard on their clients' behalf.

My amazing and meticulous editor, Melanie Kroupa, who looked deep into the book and saw how to make it the best it could be.

Everyone at Marshall Cavendish, for turning a work of imagination into a reality.

Ann Crispin, trusted beta reader, and Michael Capobianco, fellow publishing wonk, who were there at a really important moment. There's no one I would have wanted to share it with more.

Alisha Niehaus, whose suggestion about what I should write next planted the seed that grew into *Passion Blue*.

Meredith Charpentier, who gave me my first chance.

My mother, whose sharp editorial eye has guided me through all my books.

And last and most, my husband, Rob, plot consultant extraordinaire, whose love and support make it all possible.

Victoria Strauss is the author of fiction for both adults and young adults, including *Worldstone* and *Guardian of the Hills*, which a starred *Booklist* review praised, saying, "mysterious dreams, suspense-filled legends...and the fine characterizations weave together beautifully to make this adventure fantasy a winner." She is also the co-founder of Writer Beware, a unique anti-fraud resource that provides warnings about literary schemes and scams. She lives in Amherst, Massachusetts. Visit her at www.victoriastrauss.com.

Made in the USA
Middletown, DE
27 October 2021